THE GONE-AWAY MAN

Lisa is on her way to the remote Australian outback to find her grandfather—her only living relative. But before reaching Pardalote, the cattle station of which she is now part-owner, she first has to pass through Finch's Creek. Here, at the lonely bush hospital on the edge of the outback, she helps the nurses to entertain the patients. And here she comes to know Jim Ransome.

Jim Ransome owns the cattle station next door to Pardalote, but he and Lisa's grandfather are sworn enemies and Lisa's hopes are dashed when she sees the attention Jim pays the beautiful, sophisticated Imelda. But how can Lisa forget this rugged, impossible man—the man whose smile makes him unforgettable. . . .

THE
GONE-AWAY
MAN

Lucy Walker

BEAGLE BOOKS • NEW YORK
An Intext Publisher

BEAGLE BOOKS, INC.
101 Fifth Avenue, New York, NY 10003

The matron of the Inland River Hospital looked at Lisa with some consternation. Her expression said—'Now, what do I do about this one?'

The girl was pretty with her wealth of short dark hair, her deep sea-blue eyes, moist red mouth and the absolute stillness of her face. She might have been a portrait instead of a person except for the occasional blink of the very dark-fringed eyelids. She stood so still too. She was not tall, but not small either: just medium. And she was quite silent. She had obviously guessed she was a problem.

The matron had the half irritated feeling that the girl was taking *her* in too. This, of course, would not do at all.

Lisa was thinking how young the matron was. Twenty-four or five, perhaps. Out here—running this bungalow of a hospital—alone in the Never Never!

Lisa was awed at the youthfulness, yet the authority of the matron, but her still face told nothing of these thoughts. She'd been through too much to show feelings about anything at all.

'It's really too bad,' the matron said at last, and pushed a wisp of hair out of sight under her snow-white cap. 'I'm sorry for the plight you are in, my dear. But how on earth did you come out here so far on such a wild goose chase? Why have you let the truck-driver go on without you? He will eventually get as far as Darwin, you know.'

The matron's expression changed as she looked over the girl's shoulder to the distant dust-cloud made by the mail-truck's hastening departure.

'The mail man told me he would bring me out from Goldstone.' Lisa's soft voice was perplexed. 'He told me that this was the jumping off place for Pardalote. I couldn't get to Pardalote any other way—'

'Nobody can get to Pardalote this way, or any other way, unless old Mr. Lindsay allows it. And he doesn't allow it. If you are his granddaughter, as you say you are, you ought to know that, surely?'

'But this is the nearest town. At least it reads like a town on the map. Heavy black letters—*Finch's Creek* . . .'

'A hospital and an air-field! That, dear girl, does not make a town.'

Lisa looked away from the matron, at the sprawling timber-and-iron out-houses of the hospital, then down at the timbered veranda floor on which they both stood. A flight of red-winged parrots flew overhead, screaming as they went, to arrive in the branches of a ghost-gum standing near the windmill. For quite one minute they were busy settling, then finally giving themselves up to taking in the visitor. Each turned its head showing one unblinking caustic eye, the better to see the newcomer.

Lisa was embarrassed, but did not *quite* show it.

'I'm sorry,' she said at last, looking back at the matron with her sombre sea-dark eyes and her still face and mouth that showed how very vulnerable she really was. She bent down to pick up her travelling bag as if to move on, then realised only too truly there was nowhere to move on to. Nowhere to go.

'Exactly,' said the matron, reading the actions for what they meant. 'You cannot go back and you cannot go on. We'll just have to take you in, won't we?'

Lisa watched the other, saying nothing. Showing nothing of her thoughts.

A still portrait of a face, the matron thought again. *So very pretty. No, that's the wrong word. Beautiful really, if she wasn't dusty and dressed in that very short dress. In another place and time she could be on a gallery wall somewhere in Europe.*

'Well come in,' she said aloud. 'I'll get one of the girls to show you a room. I daresay you'd like a shower and something to eat. After that we'll think about what to do with you.'

'Thank you,' Lisa said. She stood aside for the matron to go through the screen door. This was a gesture to her hostess's importance.

The matron, irritated by the fact she was at a loss what next to do about this, her latest visitor, was touched by the girl's good manners.

'Oh well,' she said resignedly. 'We're always dreadfully short-staffed. We can find you something to do until we come to some conclusion as to how you can be got to Pardalote. We can broadcast messages on the transceiver radio. It's just barely possible someone might eventuate out of that remote and quite mysterious valley. I don't think they have a transceiver!'

They had entered a short vestibule. From a passage on the right a young nurse in a pale blue uniform came scurrying along.

'Oh Matron—' she began. Then she broke off as she took in Lisa, travelling bag and all. Her expression said —*Not another*! Then catching the matron's eyes she buttoned up her lips as if to keep words from tumbling out too freely. Lisa decided the nurse was probably about her own age—eighteen or nineteen.

'Yes Nurse Dean?' the matron asked.

'It's that Mr. Ransome again. He's so restless, and he *will* try to get out of bed. We keep telling him he's got to stay quiet. With an eye operation it's imperative he lies still. It's too early for his next needle isn't it?'

The matron looked at Lisa with a sudden interest.

'At least we have a job for this young lady,' she said, a hint of relief in her voice. 'We'll give Mr. Ransome to *her*.'

'Another visitor waiting for a flight to Rocky Creek or Mount Hesitant, Matron?'

'I wish she were. No, Nurse Dean. I'm afraid Miss Tonkin is waiting for some kind of transport to *Pardalote*. Probably a camel-train, or a team of wild donkeys. I can't think of anything else likely to go out there.'

She caught the listening look on Lisa's face again, and was sorry for her words. She didn't like being inhospitable but really, it was hard enough running a hospital in this outback place, without the constant stream of visitors deposited in it. Mostly they came to wait for feeder-line aircraft to carry them to any one of the distant stations stretching north and south. Or east to the Territory border for that matter. Ever since the hospital had been built down at the cross-tracks by Finch's Creek it had become a four-way house for travellers.

'Come with me, Miss—er—Miss Tonkin,' the young nurse said politely. 'It's quite a nice room really. Small, you know. Its last occupant was the Bishop. He'd been up to

7

Stray's Find to dedicate a new church. A little bush church, of course. But still—'

She chattered on as she ushered Lisa down a short timbered passage, then along a covered way to a neat row of wooden rooms. There was a gap between the top of the walls and the suspended lid-like roof. This was for the free flow of air in the worst of the heat.

All the doors stood wide open, except for their wire screens. They were indeed little rooms. Each contained a neatly covered bed, a chair and a dressing-table. That was all.

Nurse Dean stood aside for the visitor to enter her room. 'My name's Marjory,' she said brightly. 'Actually I'm awfully glad to see you. Anyone to keep an eye on that Ransome man! As a matter of fact, he's a pet, but the Flying Doctor only operated on his eyes yesterday: and he simply must *lie still*.'

'I'm glad I can help. I don't feel quite so much of a nuisance. My name is Lisa.'

'Funny, but you look just like your name. Don't ask me why, but you do.' Marjory Dean followed Lisa into the cubicle of a room. 'Actually we adore visitors. The bush is so empty. Matron adores them too really, as long as they're not sort-of lost. You know—the kind that land here and haven't any arrangements made about *how* they move on. Are you one of the "lost" kind?'

She folded her hands inside her apron bib, then looked contrite. 'I'm sorry—' she said. 'I mean—well, you do know where you're going don't you?'

Lisa put her travelling bag on the floor and sat on the edge of the bed.

'Yes,' she said simply.

'But the *how-of-it*? Nobody ever got to Pardalote, you know. *Wait!* I have a brilliant idea!'

She sat on the bed beside Lisa.

'Mr. Ransome himself! That is, when his eyes are better. He runs cattle out that way. Next door, or something. Of course out there in the Great Unknown "next door" could mean a hundred miles away, or something—'

Lisa smiled, and Marjory Dean opened her mouth, almost in envy. Lisa had the most glorious set of shining white

8

teeth. The smile changed the stillness of her face to something very gentle and quite lovely.

'My mother,' Marjory went on judicially— 'used to say "Everyone loves a smiler". You shouldn't look so serious Lisa. Maybe it's because—'

'I'm lost? Not really Marjory. Something will turn up, won't it? Like your patient Mr. Ransome. He's even given me something to do while I wait. I did send transceiver messages all-over, so that my grandfather would know I was coming. I can't believe he doesn't have a transceiver.'

'I've heard of one or two rare cattle stations that haven't. But I've never heard of anyone contacting Pardalote, I'm afraid. It's not even on the map, you know. All the stations are *supposed* to be on the map, but that one just *isn't*.

'Maybe my grandfather is something of a recluse.'

'Don't you even know him?'

'No. My mother hardly ever spoke of him. I wish I'd asked her more. It's too late now. She died three months ago.'

Lisa's face was very still again : portrait-like.

'Oh, I'm so sorry.'

The myriad of red, yellow and green-winged parrots outside had had enough of resting on the ghost-gum. In a sudden whirr, then with a chorus of parrot talk, they took off. Lisa, sitting on the bed in the 'guest room', could hear and feel them winging overhead circling the sprawling bungalow building and its outhouses, then taking off into the bush. For a moment she closed her eyes.

Ah, if they could only take me with them, she thought.

'Well,' said Marjory Dean, jumping up and straightening first her apron then the small white peaked cap she wore perched on the crown of her wispy fair hair, 'if I don't hop it I'll have matron after my skin. I'll send Gertie along with some tea. The shower house is in the little annex on the veranda outside the passage door. Having the end room does have some advantages. You're nearest to the bathroom. Also you're the only visitor just at the moment.'

'Thank you,' Lisa said. 'Then will I come and find you? Or the matron? I mean—about looking after Mr. Ransome. Is he an elderly man?'

9

Marjory Dean laughed and her brown eyes were like polished bronze, full of lights.

'Oh quite!' she quipped. 'About thirty, and a bit more. Actually rather gorgeous, if you go for that station-owning outback type. Except of course his eyes are bandaged. All you'll mostly see is a long lean frame. The whole lot of him is almost as brown as his face.'

'You mean?'

'You can sponge him down if you like. Or if Matron says. It's like trying to hold down a wild buffalo.'

'Oh no!' Lisa said alarmed. 'That is, I wouldn't be competent. I was a Kindergarten assistant, not a nurse.'

Marjory was at the door. She slipped into the passage, then put her head back into the room, her eyes more mischievous than ever.

'Good. That's just about what he needs. He's real "Kindergarten type" when it comes to resisting discipline. I'll tell Matron. She'll be thrilled.'

She was gone and the only echo of those last few words was the sound of her soft-soled shoes whispering down the timbered way to the main building.

What a day, Lisa thought, as she sat irresolute on her bed. The guest room was far enough away from the main body of the bungalow hospital to mute all sounds that came from there. Outside the sun blazed in the heat-white sky. The trees stood still and the bush lay still as if in a long waiting silence. There was a sort-of timelessness about its waiting. It had to be that it listened and waited for eternity.

Only the engine, in its iron-roofed out-house, thrummed.

Gertie, the nursing-aide, with huge black velvet eyes and a half-moon of a smile, brought in some tea and fresh-made scones after Lisa had had her shower. She had changed one dusty short dress for another of cream-coloured linen. The material might be a bit hotter than pure cotton, but at least it was the nearest to white that she had. Also she liked it. With its hint of shaping it helped to keep up her morale.

Matron was busy elsewhere when Lisa entered the main ward of the hospital. Marjory Dean was not about, but

10

another nurse, this one a plump middle-aged woman with a good-natured face, came quickly to greet the newcomer.

'You're Miss Tonkin, aren't you?' she asked with a welcoming smile. 'Marjory said we may call you "Lisa". You don't mind do you? I'm so very much older. My name is Ann Davitt. Married. I'm the senior nurse under Matron Small. Sometimes I'm called Assistant Matron.'

'How do you do?' Lisa said politely. 'Matron said something about a patient I could *mind*—'

Mrs. Davitt's eyebrows went up but her eyes and her smile were more amused than anything else.

'That sounds almost like child-minding,' she said. 'Marjory told us you had worked in a Kindergarten. I'm afraid she has already broken the news to Mr. Ransome. He was *not* amused.' Her smile was quite broad as she said this last.

'Oh dear!'

'Don't worry, child. He's really very nice but I fear no one has ever held him down on a bed before. We've told him it was either a Kindergarten assistant or a strait-jacket. He didn't have much choice did he?'

'Will he mind that much?'

'Of course he won't. We told him you were a beautiful girl from the city with a soft and endearing voice.'

'Goodness!' said Lisa. 'That's not me is it? What did he say? That he hates all women, whatever kind of a voice they have?'

'No. Do you really want me to tell you? He's quite a man of *will*, is our patient Ransome. Of course he's a very big gun in the world of station-owners. But a patient is always a patient, no more nor less than any other sick person.'

'Perhaps I'd better not know.'

'You might as well, then you'll know what you're in for. He said—'

Mrs. Davitt paused and looked at Lisa with arched eyebrows and a quizzical smile, wondering how this girl would take Patient Ransome's remarks. 'He said—"Then put her in the next bed to me tonight. That's when any man most needs minding. I can't sleep on this damn hospital bed anyway."'

Lisa laughed. Mrs. Davitt, like Marjory Dean before

11

her, was surprised and quite enchanted by the sudden light and charm in the girl's face.

Yes, she thought, as she led Lisa down the ward then through a covered way to the next ward—a one-patient room—her face is really beautiful, like a wall-picture!

On the far side of the room—all shutters up, and therefore almost outdoor—was a bed where a man, dressed in tan-coloured tropical pyjamas, was lying on the sheet. He was blindfolded by a thick swathe of gauze bandage. He was long enough for his feet to touch the rail-end of the bed.

He would be very tall standing up, Lisa thought.

The fan on a bracket nearby was flickering ripples into the discarded top sheet which was lying at the end of the bed. The man was breaking a match into tiny little pieces between the long brown fingers of his right hand.

'Hallo,' he said, not turning his head, as he heard the footsteps coming towards him. 'Who goes there this time? Tiger Matron or Saucy Dean?'

'Neither,' said Mrs. Davitt in a warm, patently consoling voice. 'I've brought a visitor to have a chat with you.'

'Oh!' he said. 'Mother Davitt, is it? So now you've brought me the school teacher! I warn you that next time anything threatens, mothers, cajoles, or attempts to bribe me I'll get up from this raking bed and walk home, blind-folded and all. The whole damn hundred and seventy-eight point nine miles of it.'

Lisa looked down at her patient. Yes, he was very tall! His mouth was good and the little hint of white teeth as he spoke looked good too. He had a strong chin and a firm throat. Everything about him was powerful. And sun-browned.

Anyone so full of sound, and so furious in appearance, could really carry out his threat and walk off, she thought.

It was almost as if he heard her speaking aloud.

'You wonder why I don't do it, Miss What's-your-name-Teacher?' he asked. 'Well, any minute now—'

'I'm not a teacher and my name is Lisa. I was just an

12

assistant in a Kindergarten. Rather like Gertie being a nursing-aide—'

He groaned.

'Nursing-aide!' he said exasperated. 'I hate the word *aid*. Till that raking shot-gun went off and I collected the blast dust in my eyes I've never needed *aid* in my life.'

'No, of course not,' Mrs. Davitt agreed soothingly. 'We all know you are a station-owner, Mr. Ransome. And that you handle big mobs of wild cattle and do all your own staff-aiding out at Nangardee. Now it's your turn to have a little—'

'Dear Heaven!' the patient implored. 'Am I being mothered all over again? Sister Davitt, would you please treat me as grown, six feet one inch high, thirty-two years of age: and as one who owns a cattle run. Likewise operates prospecting leases, miner's rights and all—. The lot covers several hundred miles of wild country. I'm capable of running the whole blasted State if asked—'

'Yes, Mr. Ransome,' Sister Davitt said, not quite so soothingly. 'We all know you are very important. *When you have your eyesight, of course.*'

Her strike went home for he stopped twirling the pieces of broken matchstick between his fingers and suddenly lay still.

'When I have my eyesight?' he queried. Suddenly Lisa was sorry for him. The lion was brought down and was wounded. What use to roar now? And he wasn't sure about how bad or not his eyesight might be.

'I'll leave you with our visitor for the time being,' Mrs. Davitt said complacently, having reduced the non-hero to stillness again. 'Lisa, don't let him move his head, if possible. One of the lead pellets Dr. Anderson had to remove was very near the pupil of his left eye. Some shot-dust was near enough to endanger his right eye too. The only hope for complete healing is absolute stillness. Keep your voice low and see that he is not excited, please. Otherwise we'll have to give him another needle.'

'Yes, of course,' Lisa agreed quietly.

'Talk about something interesting, if you can. But nothing controversial,' the nurse said. 'Nothing that might make him turn his head suddenly. His post-operative treatment is the same as for cataract removal. *No sudden movement at all!'*

'She understands like she understands children in a Kindergarten,' the patient said savagely. 'Don't tell any shock stories about earthquakes or floods. Only about dobs of do-gooding: and about birds, bees, and fairies at the bottom of the garden!'

Mrs. Davitt shook her head knowingly at Lisa and went away.

Lisa, awed by the need not to startle, slipped on to the chair by the bed.

There was quite a minute's silence, then the patient spoke. His voice was unexpectedly quiet this time.

'Are you there, Lisa? Are you still there, Lisa-whatever-the-rest-of-your-name-is?'

Lisa's heart softened in an unexpected way. She felt almost sad for this proud difficult man. There had been a genuine pleading note in his voice. As if he *needed* her to be there.

'Lisa Tonkin is my name,' she said helpfully. 'I'm still here. I shan't go away.'

'Lisa Tonkin!' His lips moved as if he were repeating this. There was quite a silence.

'Perhaps you don't like my name?' Lisa suggested gently.

'Like it? Oh yes. Quite!' He had been frowning thoughtfully under the bandages, but now his mouth smiled, just that shade wickedly. 'Tonky for short?' he asked. 'It conjures up wicked visions of city life. Honky Tonky! Lisa, do you know what a Honky Tonky is?'

'Well . . .'

'Of course you don't. Your voice is the voice of a nice quiet girl. Gently brought up. Fit and passed all correct to be teaching other people's precious little children—'

He was being sarcastic again. Lisa did not answer.

'Are you still there, Tonky?' he asked. The pleading note was back again.

'I think you are a very spoilt man, Mr. Ransome,' Lisa said quietly, but meaning it. 'When you know I'm here, you are rude. When you think I might have gone away you act like a small boy.'

'Like the ones you teach?'

14

'I *don't* teach, Mr. Ransome. I just help.'

'How?'

'I look after the equipment. The toys too. Building blocks and picture-books. That sort of thing. I keep them clean, and mend the books. Sometimes I join in with the games. I play the piano for the children to dance—'

'Piano? Good Heavens! Do they still have those things? I thought it was all Beatles and guitars these days.'

Lisa did not answer, and there was quite a silence again.

'Tonky, are you still there?'

'Yes. I'm here. I won't go away without telling you. You see, in spite of the things you say, I know you really want me here—even if I *have* worked in a Kindergarten.'

His mouth smiled and it was quite a smile.

Lisa's heart stirred again. There was something poignant about a tall strong man lying helpless on a bed. It touched her, somewhere deep inside her.

'Why are you here at Finch's Creek, Tonky?'

'Please call me Lisa. I like it better.'

'Okay. My name's Magool. James Magool Ransome. Call me Jim for short.'

'Magool?' Lisa asked, wondering.

'That's it. Aboriginal for "Head". The Boss-cocky. Eldest son of the eldest son of the eldest son—and all that. The natives named the first Ransome who came out west across the Territory Border, and that's what it's been ever since. I advise you to cut it short to Jim to make things easy.'

Lisa laughed. Her quiet still face broke up into real loveliness but Magool *alias Jim* Ransome could not see that. He sensed it in her laugh though.

'How old are you Lisa? How tall, how fat, and what colour are your eyes?'

'I'm not a bit fat,' she said indignantly. 'In fact I'm quite slim—*I hope*.'

She decided to do a little tricking too. She would draw a fantasy picture of herself—just for fun. 'I'm nineteen and I'm tall, like a daffodil is tall. I have piles of beautiful golden blonde curls on my head, and my eyes are hazel—like light shining on honey. I wear nice expensive clothes —' She quite enjoyed this fibbing. In a minute she'd turn herself out as a raving beauty.

'Then what in the name of fortune are you doing out

in the bush at Finch's Creek? That's a long way for a gorgeous well-dressed beauty like you to come for a job. The sun will burn your peaches-and-cream skin to a frizzle.'

'I haven't come for a job if that is what you think,' Lisa said firmly. 'I'm a visitor. I'm waiting for my grandfather to send for me. He's a great big station-owner like you. Maybe he will even come himself. Only, of course, he's very busy. Mustering and all that—'

'Strange kind of *big station-owning* man if he's mustering when he has a visitor waiting to be collected. What's wrong with his overseer? And the stockmen?'

'Well,' said Lisa, still gently, but not at all at a loss. 'Maybe his overseer is mustering too. Probably he's also doing whatever other things have to be done on stations just now. He probably manages things a little differently at Pardalote from the usual—'

'*Pardalote!*'

Lisa leaned forward and caught his head as he lifted it. The word 'Pardalote' had come out like the flick of a stock-whip. Lisa had caught his head between the palms of her hands before he turned it, and she now held firmly.

'You mustn't!' she said. 'You mustn't move like that. Because of your operation I mean—' She broke off. Then asked anxiously: 'You didn't open your eyes, or anything?'

'I can't open my eyes. My lids are sealed to my cheek bones with sheets of galvanised iron. The nurses are pleased to call it *sticking plaster*—the understatement of the year!'

'What a relief! I mean—that you didn't open your eyes.'

Her hands were on either side of his cheeks, holding his head to the pillow as if afraid there was still some spirit for head-turning breaking loose inside him. He lifted his hands and held hers imprisoned to his face.

'Cool hands! Just keep them there Lisa. I don't mind your being tall, fair, beautiful and expensively dressed if you hold my head for me. It aches like thunder-on-the-range, but those do-gooding nurses won't give me an aspirin—not even *one*. They say it might argue the point with the needle they jab in me every four hours. Lisa— Beautiful blonde Lisa—did you say *Pardalote?*'

16

Lisa remembered now that the nurses had said Mr. Ransome's station was somewhere out near Pardalote. She blushed a deep red at the thought of her boastful speech about her grandfather. Mr. Ransome—that is this *Magool* Ransome—might know him. Lisa knew little about Pardalote except that her mother had once lived there, had run away from home to marry a jackeroo from next door —someone of whom her father had violently disapproved. He had died when Lisa was a child. Grandfather Lindsay had never written to Lisa's mother since. Maybe he didn't even know that Lisa's mother was dead? Then there'd been the mystery of her mother leaving her a third share in the station. Then the lawyers saying there was no such place. The Pastoral Lease map didn't show the station. The Crown Land Department officer had said there was no such specific *grazing lease*.

Lisa had come north to find out. Also she had come to find her grandfather because she had neither brother nor sister, father nor mother. Only such a person could know how lonely it is when one is nineteen, and alone in the world.

She held Magool Ransome's head between her hands while her blush died slowly away. She wondered at the strength of his two hands holding hers to the sides of his face. She'd never felt a man's face before. She'd never felt a man's hands on hers like this either.

Slowly he released her, and Lisa sank back on to the chair.

'Don't do that again, will you?' she pleaded. 'I mean jerk up your head. Not about holding my hands, of course—'

'So you like holding hands do you, Tonky? Not just small children in a Kindergarten either? With all those blonde curls and the honey-coloured eyes there'd be lots of men about I daresay. Of course with a name like Tonky—'

'Don't-say-what-you-were-going-to-say-about a Honky Tonky, Mr. Ransome,' Lisa said all in one breath. 'I can guess your next words in advance.'

'Call me Jim for short.'

'You mean to be funny, but I happen to know what a Honky Tonky is.' Lisa was getting quite indignant.

'A place where wild men from the outback have a cool supper with a more than pretty cool girl—'

'You're still being funny Mr.—'

'Jim for short. Of course you could begin with Magool and come by slow and patient steps to plain Jim.'

'You don't mind the double name? The "plain" as well as the "Jim"?'

'Score!' Magool Ransome's mouth smiled and this was quite wonderful. It was a flashing and really kind sort of smile. Very misleading probably.

2

Soft-soled feet came in from the covered way and across the room. Sister Davitt was bearing down on them carrying a white enamelled tray covered with a linen towel.

'Well, well!' she declared as if speaking down to small children, but meaning it all kindly. 'Our patient is lying quiet and docile it seems! It must have been a good angel that drove you in on that freight truck, Lisa. Time for Mr. Ransome's needle now, I'm afraid. This will really put him to sleep and keep him quiet.'

'So you lot can all go out and play two-up with peace-of-mind?' the patient snorted. 'Don't you have any other sick people in this hospital, Mother Davitt?'

The nurse had placed the small tray on the table and was already busy swabbing Magool Ransome's arm with methylated spirits.

Lisa looked away. She didn't want to see the needle go in that long strong brown arm. This dismay wasn't as if he was a child. It was just that it must be humiliating for so tall and strong a man to be lying there blindfolded while strange women jabbed him with needles.

Lisa had a heartfelt care, all of a sudden, for Magool's masculine dignity.

'There you are,' Sister Davitt said soothingly when the job was done. This was the voice of one accustomed gently to deal with difficult adolescents. Lisa, watching the patient's face, could see his mouth twist—not in any pain

18

from the needle, but from the sheer rejection of being 'mothered'.

'I think I'd just smack him,' Lisa said unexpectedly. 'With words, if not with blows. I think he understands that sort of treatment better.'

Sister Davitt went on gently rubbing the arm to start the injection circulating.

'Well, you see Lisa, my dear, I'm a nurse,' she explained. 'I'm used to all kinds of people. Oh yes, Mr. Ransome, you might be high and mighty out there in the bush wherever your station is, but right here you're merely one more patient. One of hundreds over the year—'

'I'd sooner sleep on the back of a crocodile than in a hospital bed,' the patient said with no pretence at good manners at all. 'Lisa—'

He stopped because getting the word 'Lisa' out was difficult.

Sister Davitt looked at the girl with raised eyebrows. 'You see?' she said. 'He's going off already. He'll be out like a light in two minutes. Then we can all have some peace. There's tea in the staff-room, dear. And Gertie's made you some more sandwiches. You'll be tired of them, but dinner's not far off. We have it early here so the night nurse can come on by seven o'clock.'

'Doesn't he—Mr. Ransome—have any dinner?'

'Oh yes. The night nurse gives it to him about nine o'clock. Then we let him stay awake till after midnight. Another needle then to keep him quiet right through till morning, and also while the other patients are being sponged down.'

Magool Ransome's arms lay nearly inert beside him. Sister Davitt tucked two small pillows on either side of his head to keep it from moving. She passed two long wide bandages under the pillows then across his chest. Finally she tied these, one on each side of the bed. From the top side of the bed she brought down two more sling bandages and slipped them under his arms, and in turn tied these to a cross-belt.

'That's very clever,' Lisa said slowly.

'It's a godsend really,' Sister Davitt said. 'A sort of strait-jacket for his upper half. It will keep him from turning in his sleep.'

19

From under the arms upward, Magool Ransome, the impatient patient, was literally tied down.

'Don't be sorry for him, my dear. He's out-to-it like the sun gone down. After all, he is still in the post-operative stage and we do have to save his sight. You understand? The treatment is necessary.'

'Yes, I know.'

Lisa stood looking down at the man. Her face was still again, as if no expression ever passed across it. Her heart was a little sorry, not for a man being cared for back to the point of good health, but for Magool Ransome himself —a tall strong sarcastic man: king of his own roost, miles out somewhere in the bush, now reduced to a mere inert figure on a bed. Being stared at by strangers, too. How he would hate it!

Just another tree fallen in the forest—like hundreds of others!

Lisa blinked. What funny thoughts went through her head. First a lion brought down, and now—a fallen tree!

She was suddenly aware that Mrs. Davitt was watching her with faintly arched eyebrows.

'My dear,' she said. 'You'd never make a nurse would you? Moreover, the first advice given to recruit nurses is *Never feel love for your patient*. It is really no more than *pity* in disguise. Besides, the patient invariably has a sweetheart or wife somewhere else. Sick people always turn out to be quite different once they're upright and well again.'

Lisa helped the nurse to put the tray in order, then fold the top sheet over the sleeping patient.

'Yes,' she said after a short silence. 'I suppose he would be married. Have children too. It's just that he's not exactly like a family man, is he? I mean—too intolerant. After all, he must *want* to have his eyesight back.'

'Well, you'd think so. He's listed as "single" in the register. Though I must say the young lady who brought him in along with some sort of geologist visitor was very proprietorial about him. She kissed him good-bye and all that. He didn't seem to object either. Well—would he now? She was a very striking person. Very intelligent and knowledgable too about his accident. Nurse Dean called her a *knock-out*—'

They were soft-walking across the room again, out into

the glaring heat, then under the covered-way leading to the main hospital.

'But she—this intelligent striking person—didn't wait while he had his operation?' Lisa asked thoughtfully.

'Well no, she didn't. She had to go back with the other man, of course. He's looking for minerals somewhere out there in the Never. He'd lent his utility for Mr. Ransome to be brought in. Just as well she went, otherwise we might have had *two* visitors in the guest quarters. You and her.'

'All the same,' Lisa said, 'I think I would have waited if he belonged to me. I don't mean just Mr. Ransome. I mean anyone I cared for, and who was injured. I would wait till I knew the operation had been successful—'

'*You*, dear child, don't live permanently at Finch's Creek. There is nothing here but a hospital and an airfield. So boring for some.'

'But she could have stayed by him to stop him moving. The same as I do. That would have been something to do.'

'Not Miss Imelda Bannister, I fear. Well, not by the look of her anyway. She had her own important affairs to attend to, no doubt. Now here we are at the staff-room, my dear. You go right in and make yourself comfortable. Then you might like to have a look around. There's quite a nice walk down to the creek. I must run off on the rest of my jobs.'

Time passed, and Lisa had been four days and three nights as visitor-cum-general help at the Inland River Hospital, but still no word had come from her grandfather. Or from anyone else at Pardalote.

She had stopped mentioning the station because there had been too many raised eyebrows each time she had done so in the first two days. Some of the staff had said there was no such place. Others said it probably was no more than a camp on some creek in some valley; much haunted by parrots. After all the name *Pardalote* meant a kind of parrot. The night nurse hazarded a guess that, as Mr. Lindsay's name was known—specially by the aborigines coming in occasionally for treatment—he was probably a hermit, or an 'eccentric', living somewhere in a parroty valley in the unmapped areas farther out.

These remarks were made to Lisa in a gentle kindly

21

way, as if by telling her these things, they were letting her down lightly. If she ever found her way to Pardalote—and Patient Ransome could possibly help her to do that—she might get an awful shock. She would be prepared in advance. A *station* indeed!

On the other hand an old bush native in the main ward, suffering from a kind of paralysis, said he had once worked for Boss Lindsay.

'Old-fella Lindsay,' he said reminiscently, as Lisa fed him his evening meal as if he too were a child. 'Him okay as boss.'

The helplessness of sick people touched Lisa in a strange way. She thought of her mother's death. For the first time she was glad her mother had gone so suddenly—while watering the garden. She had been looking at the westering sun over the sand hills towards the sea. Then falling. Fallen. Gone. Just like that.

The shock had stunned Lisa. This was half the reason why she had come to the far north looking for her grandfather. It wasn't only the mystery of a share in an unknown mythical station. It was disbelief in the suddenness of death, and the awfulness of loneliness.

Now she was learning a new kind of mercy. The mercy of not being sick at all. Her own mother's going had been blessed, after all.

'Plenty-fella cattle. Horses too. Much grass all-along Pardalote,' the old aborigine was saying. 'Old-fella Lindsay got much money. Plenty fella acres.'

'How does he sell his cattle?' Lisa asked.

'Overseer drove 'im up big valley, all-along old drover's track back over north-west territory. Cattle go along Wyndham. Sometimes now they go all-same long new beef road.'

'He has a house? A real house, like this bungalow?'

'Big-fella house like his gran'father build long-time. My father go with him. My father stockman for *Old* Old-fella Lindsay. They bin out Pardalote a hundred years maybe. I bin buck-jumper one-time for Old-fella Lindsay.'

'I wouldn't take too much notice of Jimmy Come-up,' Matron advised Lisa later. 'He's a very old man. He's been buck-jumping all through the north for many years and he tends to forget which station has what name. And he has no idea of time. There are squatters in some of those valleys outback, it is true! They don't always have a lease. Not quite regular I understand.'

Yet there was something about the aborigine Jimmy Come-up that made Lisa believe him. This was not wishful thinking either. She had the evidence of the things her mother had told her. Things about the big mustering days Jimmy Come-up spoke of. How the homestead walls had been made of wattle and daub, then lined with hessian. And how stone by stone, brought in from the break-away, the walls had been given a solid outer mainstay that would last as long as a Lindsay could ride the hills. And the homestead looked like part of the hill itself. Lisa's mother had told her about the parrots, thousands and thousands of them. Of big grey emus coming in by the homestead trough at sundown to play around like children at a party. Of the steep rise to the west hill, all granite topped, iron red at sundown, where she used to go to meet the jackeroo from the next holding. That was the man who had become Lisa's father—and so soon, and young, to die.

The next holding. Could that be Magool Ransome's place? Lisa hoped not.

And yet—

Why had something stricken her heart as she kept watch by his side? Why had there been a quiet sort of *surprise* in her to see him, a tree-strong man, lying there so helpless with his eyes bound up so he couldn't see?

Her mother had never mentioned such a name as Ransome. But then her mother had left so much unsaid. Undone too. The bequest of a share in a *station that wasn't*, for instance!

On the seventh day of her stay at the hospital Lisa began really to wonder what next she should do. The hospital, like the radio service at Goldstone, had sent out transceiver messages far and wide. These had been relayed on from known station to known station but no radio answer had come back from Mr. Lindsay.

23

'Of course it's *quite* probable your grandfather does not have a transceiver,' Matron said, sorry for the still lostness in the girl's face. 'There are one or two squatters who just don't believe in modern gadgetry. Very conservative. We'll wait another day or two and if we don't get any signal we'll ask Mr. Ransome's advice. Don't look worried Lisa. We like having you here. It's all turned out quite happily for us. You've been such a help—reading the magazines and papers to the patients, specially to Mr. Ransome. You've been such a godsend where *he* is concerned. A difficult patient—'

'Anyone could have done that,' Lisa said, playing fair to Marjory Dean and Gertie, as well as the night nurse, who often did such things.

'Not with your kind of voice,' Matron remarked. Then added cryptically. 'That's why he always demands *you*. A very selfish man, I'm afraid.' She patted down her apron and became busy-looking again. 'That reminds me. Elston Station radioed this morning that their plane was going overhead at midday and would drop the latest papers from Goldstone. Read *"The Australian"* to Mr. Ransome *first*, won't you Lisa? He's so much better behaved when he's satisfied himself about the day's news.'

So Matron does a little indulging of the star patient too, Lisa thought!

What will his eyes be like? Lisa wondered sometimes. What colour? He would open them and discover she had short black hair instead of a pile of blonde curls and that she wasn't tall at all: nor beautiful. Her few dresses were very simple compared with the extravagant claims she gave to them as each day she described, for the benefit of his blind curiosity, just exactly what she didn't really wear at all.

She also wondered about Imelda Bannister—the girl who had come with him after his accident.

Imelda! What a wonderful name! Imelda herself had to match it, of course. Beautiful and probably arrogant! Oh well! Isn't that just what would suit Mr. Magool Ransome—Jim for short! He was really very like that himself. Insubordinate and arrogant. Except when he teased her. Then he was—well—*different*! Sometimes she thought he

24

was being 'difficult' on purpose, because other times he forgot and became kind, and even amusing.

The day after Matron's talk the Flying Doctor's plane came winging overhead.

There was hustling and bustling in the hospital because, besides the unbandaging of Mr. Ransome's eyes, two lots of tonsils had to come out of the throats of two timid aboriginal children. A stockman had been brought in with suspected appendicitis too.

Dr. Anderson would have a busy time, and the tiny operating theatre had to be scrubbed with antiseptics, and scrubbed again. *And again.*

After the scrubbing bouts Lisa did not stay around to help. She went for a long walk. She was going for that walk because she couldn't bear to be asked to stand around and hold bowls or trays while the bandages were unwound from Magool Ransome's eyes. She didn't want to see his eyes if it was found he couldn't see properly.

His sight blighted! It wouldn't just be a case of the tree brought down. It would be worse. The tree broken and useless. For ever.

Besides, she didn't want him to open his eyes, with perfect sight, and discover a medium-sized girl with straight black hair and no curls at all. She walked down to the creek and marvelled at the water lying shining still under the shade of the river trees. She could see by the mud banks how much the water level had sunk since the Wet had receded into distant time. Soon, maybe in a few weeks, the river bed would dry out altogether, except for a mud pool here and there and maybe the billabong near the hospital.

Everything was so hot and so still. *So waiting.* It was almost as if the creek and the billabong, the stiff still trees, and the pindan beyond, were like *her*—waiting for something to happen. Her grandfather to come? For Mr. Magool Ransome's eyes to open? The very stillness all around made Lisa feel that these living things had the patience of eternity in their make-up. If only she had that too!

After a long time she walked back to the hospital. The two sets of tonsils were out, and the stockman's appendix was half out. Magool Ransome's eyes were to come last in the order of things. He still wore bandages.

'Of course, silly!' Marjory Dean said. 'We have to have the shutters open in the daytime because of the heat. That lets the glare in too. Doctor Anderson is not going to remove Mr. Ransome's bandages until near or after sundown, when there's no glare.'

Lisa said— 'Oh!' and pretended she was not disappointed, only mildly interested.

'So,' Marjory went on. 'Be a sport and go and read the Reader's Digest to him. Dr. Anderson brought a whole swag of reading stuff with him on the plane. Patient Ransome is no longer *patient*—if he ever was. Any minute now he'll start scratching those bandages off for himself.'

'Yes, of course,' Lisa said quickly. 'I suppose the doctor didn't recommend his going back on the injection routine?'

'My dear girl *no*. That was only for the first forty-eight hours. Then, of course, you fell from heaven, and saved us all.'

'I'm glad I've been needed,' Lisa said doubtfully, hoping Marjory was right.

She couldn't think of anything else to say. Her face was very still again. So much that Marjory Dean wondered, not for the first time, what went on in the girl's head.

'By the way,' she said. 'That old aborigine, Jimmy Come-up, said there are two cars coming. One soon, and one "long-time maybe two baccas after sun-up to-morrow" —if you know what *that* means. How those bush people always know something is coming we never can tell. They always *do know*, and it's not always smoke signals either.'

'The didgeridoo,' Lisa said. 'My mother told me that. She said it's the sounds they make, and the sounds travel along air currents like homing pigeons—'

'As I don't believe in witchcraft it must be something like that,' Marjory conceded. 'Now, Petto, I'm off for an early meal. It's me for duty when Dr. Anderson finishes in the theatre. I guess I'll be around when they take off Mr. Ransome's bandages. Someone had better clear away all nearby throwable things from his bedside—*just in case*—'

For once Lisa did not volunteer. Neither did she read the 'Digest' to the star patient. She thought the safest

26

thing she could do, for her own peace of mind, was have an early meal with Sister Davitt, then go for another long walk. She salved her conscience by sponging down the two tonsil cases, dear little boys who were stoically good about the post-operative pain in their throats.

Mr. Magool Ransome could take a lesson—Lisa thought as she patted two troubled little black brows, and bestowed her rare shining smile in a way that made the children try smiling in return.

'I'll be in to see you before I go to bed,' she promised. She then departed quickly, for Dr. Anderson, swathed in white head-cap and coat was striding down the long ward en route to the covered-way and Mr. Ransome's bed. Matron, hastening along on one side of him, looked straight ahead, but Marjory Dean, also in attendance, flicked her eyebrows at Lisa and lifted one thumb. Like the smoke signals this was a sign. *D-hour for Mr. Magool Ransome*— Jim for short!

Lisa fled: fast!

The outside temperature was falling but the western sky was burning red. The bush trees stood silhouetted against it, utterly still, making a black frieze against a crimson background. Dark leaping figures flitted towards the windmill as the kangaroos came in for their nightly party. A flock of white cockatoos roosting on a ghost-gum raised their yellow combs as they eyed Lisa. She meant them no harm so they put their yellow top feathers to rest again and closed their all-seeing eyes.

Lisa walked and walked. She didn't know for how long. One hour? Or two? She meant it to be certain that Magool Ransome would not only have his bandages off, know the best or the worst, but have been put to sleep and silence by the time she returned. When she did come in she crept into the little guest room at the end of the passage intending to put herself to bed in her own silence and privacy, but in this she was frustrated. Marjory Dean was lying prone on her bed, almost asleep in spite of still being dressed in her duty uniform. She looked at Lisa through half-slitted eyes—hiding mischief—as the other girl came in.

'Well?' she asked. 'Don't you want to know the news?'

27

'My grandfather has sent a message?'

Marjory sat up with pretended exasperation: all semblance of dozing gone.

'Blow your grandfather! Don't tell me you don't want to know about Patient Ransome's eyes? And also about—'

'He can see?' Lisa asked hoping her voice was natural.

'Of course he can see. I know why you went away, Frighty-miss. You were scared he might be blind for life.'

'Weren't you all anxious?' Lisa parried. 'After all—he is *your* patient. Not mine. I'm only—'

'Only the girl who sat by his side and coddled him back to a state of reasonable behaviour.'

Lisa sat on her bed and looked at her hands.

'Funny,' she said. 'I didn't coddle him at all. That's what Sister Davitt did. You too, a little bit. I just answered him back the same way as he spoke to me.'

'And didn't he love it? You too!' Marjory looked at Lisa, mischief still in her eyes. She was waiting for the other to show some reaction, but Lisa did not look up. Her face had the picture-portrait look on it again.

'What colour are his eyes?' she asked quietly, carefully.

'Grey. Oh, very steely! There was nothing handy for him to throw at anyone, so no one got hurt. Not even Imelda—'

'*Imelda?*'

The dark fringes of Lisa's eyes flew up. She was off guard now.

'Yes. She came. One of those cars that Jimmy Come-up prophesied was on its way. Imelda, at least, had faith! Or calm certainty as becomes her type. Whichever! She came armed with Mr. Ransome's clothes, and had made sure that geologist fellow who came last time was left behind *this* time.'

'But he couldn't leave hospital yet awhile. I mean Magool Ransome couldn't—' Lisa wasn't hiding anything any more. She gazed at the other girl. Marjory read alarm as well as astonishment in Lisa's face.

'Poof! If all the pellets were out—and they were: if all the tiny little wounds had healed—and they had: why then not even Dr. Anderson or Matron was going to keep Mr. Impatient Ransome in bed: let alone in a hospital!'

'He's gone?'

Oh no! she thought in her heart.

'Sorry Lisa, he's gone,' Marjory said. 'They've both gone. The patient and the girl. Ransome and Imelda.'

Lisa's lips were moist. Her eyes, very dark, were wide but not now showing what she thought or felt. Her face was still and shadowless again.

Yet she was repeating to herself over and over—

He went without saying good-bye! Oh, how could he!

She waited, her face empty except for the natural simple loveliness of a young girl, of which she was so unconscious, but which God, in connivance with her parents, had blessed on her the day she was born.

For quite one minute Marjory too remained silent.

'Sorry, old girl!' she said at last, getting up from the bed, smoothing down her apron, then settling her cap once more in its usual precarious position. She tilted it a shade forward from the crown of her head. 'That's how the billabong burbles,' she added. 'You see it, but you never hear it. Water comes and water goes—then one day when the Dry is extra dry it's gone altogether. Even the crocodiles go too. And now Mr. Impatient Magool Ransome—'

Jim for short—Lisa nearly finished the other's sentence, but saved herself in time.

Marjory turned from the mirror to Lisa.

'They're all like that,' she said bluntly. 'Patients, I mean. They're one of the hazards of the nursing profession! They come, they fight you or eat out of your hand; and you hold them in the hollow of *your* hand. Then they're gone. Sometimes just *gone*, and that's all. Sometimes gone with one Imelda or another.' She sighed. 'They always seem to be good to look at too—those females who come to collect their boy friends from the hospital bed.'

Lisa said nothing as the other girl went to the door.

'Have to get back on duty, old thing,' Marjory said. 'See you in the morning.' She went out, but she shut the door carefully and gently behind her, as if not to disturb someone else's private grief.

He went without saying good-bye to me! Lisa thought again. *He didn't leave a message— Not even one about helping me to get to Pardalote! He just went!*

She felt as she had once felt as a child when her mother was ill, and no one had remembered her birthday. Not then, or even later.

The next morning Jimmy Come-up's second prophecy came true. Another car came, and it brought Lisa's not-so-mythical grandfather. He came to take her to that unknown hidden valley—Pardalote Station.

3

Matron, Lisa and nursing-aide Gertie stood under the shade of the hospital veranda and watched the dust ball bowling along through the trees beyond the side stretch of pindan. How right Jimmy Come-up's prophecy had been! Another car was coming.

Jimmy had had his first smoke after breakfast, and bang-on eleven o'clock he was taking his second. Minutes later he was telling Sister Davitt—'That car come plenty fast longa any time now. Old-fella Lindsay coming.'

Sister Davitt had hastened to Matron, and Matron had hastened to find Lisa where she was once again cajoling and amusing the two little tonsil cases.

'It ought to be uncanny,' Matron said briskly. 'But I've seen it happen a dozen times before. Jimmy Come-up says your grandfather—"Old-fella Lindsay"—is coming. Certainly *something* is coming because the parrots went screaming overhead from the east—quite the wrong direction for this hour of the morning. They always announce impending arrivals.'

Lisa unconsciously copied Marjory's mannerisms when in the presence of Matron. She smoothed down the skirt of her dress as if it was a duty apron.

'I couldn't bear it if he were *wrong*,' she said anxiously. Matron looked at the sea-dark eyes in the troubled face. She could have bitten her tongue for breaking such news in advance.

'Well, never mind, Lisa,' she said in a softer tone. 'Let's

go and see *who* is coming. We could hope couldn't we? Let us promise ourselves not to be disappointed. Yes?'

Marjory Dean was off-duty and asleep. So Gertie had come to complete the welcoming party. She kept guard on Lisa's left side as they stood on the veranda waiting.

They all three gazed out beyond the windmill, past the water trough to where a group of ghost-gums stood on the small rise that broke the monotony of the landscape in that direction.

What lovely trees, Lisa thought. *Their trunks so snow white and their leaves so green! Their twisted branches are like arms.*

She had to think of something rather than that that dust-ball, which was a car travelling in quite a sober circumspect way for the outback, was possibly her grandfather coming.

The car came round the curve of the rise by the ghost-gums, then proceeded up the track past the windmill. It actually came right past the hospital bungalow where the three waiting figures were standing on the veranda. Finally it came to a leisurely stop under a shade tree on the west side.

Lisa's eyes opened wider, and Gertie's eyes rounded. Matron straightened her already very straight cap. None of them spoke because all three were astonished. The man had driven right past them and had not even looked their way.

The car, in spite of its fine coat of red dust, was in magnificent condition. It was a huge omnibus of a car: a Dodge at least fifteen years out of date. Yet it was kept in prize condition as if brand new.

The man at the wheel was elderly, straight-faced and thin-lipped. He wore his broad-brimmed pastoralist's hat square on his head. It likewise was in perfect condition, as if straight out of a band-box. When he delivered himself up from the driver's seat, they could see he wore an out-of-date dark tailored suit, a stiff-necked collar, and a dark tie. Everything about him was in a carefully groomed state, but very old-fashioned.

He appeared quite unaware of the three figures on the veranda. Yet clearly he wasn't blind. He reached in the glove-box for a cloth, and methodically wiped and polished the windscreen. Next he walked at a leisurely pace round the car flicking away the dust. Finally he put the cloth back in its compartment, shut the car door quietly, and only then did he turn to come the twenty yards towards the veranda.

Lisa stared and stared.

Could this be her grandfather?

'Good morning, Matron,' he said raising his hat, then putting it back with slow care, square on his head. With some infallible instinct he had read authority stamped in the bearing of the figure in the centre of the trio, and correctly diagnosed her status. 'I am Henry Lindsay. I understand you have my granddaughter here as a guest?'

Matron was now as cool as marron in the hillside creeks.

'Good morning, Mr. Lindsay. Welcome to Finch's Creek. Yes, I do have your granddaughter here. A very charming and helpful guest.'

She was exactly matching her manner and speech to that of the newcomer.

'This young lady here on my right,' she continued with elaborate dignity, 'is your granddaughter, Lisa Tonkin. Am I correct?'

They stood above him on the veranda. Mr. Lindsay stood below the step level and so he had to look up at the girl.

'Good morning, Lisa,' he said showing no emotion whatever. 'You are very like your mother.'

Lisa's face crinkled.

Something doubled up and hurt her in her chest. It wasn't this distant, unaffectionate man. It was the knowledge that she looked as her mother must have looked as a girl. Her mother had not seen Henry Lindsay for more than twenty years.

'Good . . . morning . . .'

She was utterly at a loss.

'And the other young lady?' Mr. Lindsay enquired, looking to Matron's left.

'What me?' Gertie asked before Matron could speak. 'I'm just Gertie. Got no other name. Was brought in here as a kid and left in a spare bed down in the main ward. All to the good too, if you ask *me*.'

'Gertie,' Matron remonstrated gently. 'We could tell

32

our guest about that later, if necessary.' She turned to the newcomer. 'Will you come in, Mr. Lindsay?'

'Just long enough for my granddaughter to collect her clothes and any other possessions she may have. I will take a cup of tea thank you. A large cup, strong. No milk or sugar.'

Lisa stood fixed to the spot where she had been standing this last twenty minutes. Except for his first enquiry of Matron she, his granddaughter, might not have existed.

Once on the veranda Mr. Lindsay removed his hat again, showing grey-streaked brushed-down hair, and a deeply sunburned face and neck. That was all that Lisa could notice for, though he stood aside, with a grave but pedantic kind of courtesy, for Matron to precede him through the door, he took no further notice of his grand-daughter whatever.

He disappeared into the shade of the bungalow passage with Matron—stiff and formal in the only dark tailored suit seen in the tropical north for unaccountable years. His brown broad-brimmed cattleman's hat he held dangled low at his side. He carried his head up as a lord of the earth might have done. He was an awe-inspiring figure.

The two girls left on the veranda looked at each other in silence.

'My, what an apparition!' said Gertie. 'Right out of the past isn't he? Better yours than mine, Lisa. See what I mean when I say best-thing that ever happened to me was being left in a spare bed in the ward—aged one week! I've had a hundred mothers looking after me—come and go—but no grand-pops, thank goodness.'

Lisa moistened her dry lips.

'I suppose we'd better follow them in,' she said at last.

Lisa never after could remember the details of that day. She had moved about, talked a little, as if she had been stunned. All her actions came from some kind of self-hypnosis.

Shortly after midday she found herself in the great black car, sunk in one of its deep dark leather seats, moving steadily and noiselessly—for it had that kind of an engine —over the gravel track that led away from the hospital out into the real unknown. She hoped she had said good-bye and 'thank you' adequately to Matron. She would

33

write later and say it all over again, and make it as heartfelt as she really meant.

She had said good-bye to Jimmy Come-up—the only person to whom her grandfather had really talked at length, and to her two little tonsil patients. She had waved to the several others in the ward who had called cheery farewells to her.

She had said good-bye to Marjory Dean, and Gertie, and Mrs. Davitt. Also to the kitchen girls, the yardman, the water man and the engine-house man. But she had done it all in a daze, frightened of saying too much, and therefore saying too little. She had been bothered a little by the looks of anxious care in everyone's eyes. She hadn't known they had taken her so much to their hearts.

Then she was beside her grandfather in the car, and suddenly the hospital was miles behind them.

Mr. Lindsay did not speak to his grandaughter at all, so Lisa too remained silent.

She began to watch the way they were going. Her grandfather had turned into sheer trackless bush but after a while Lisa could see that if there were no real car ruts, or a made way, at least there *was* a way of sorts. It led over coarse grassland—spinifex—always directly towards a *space* between clumps of trees in the near distance. Once in amongst the trees again, she could see the way led between fallen trunks, broken tree-branches at the side. Then, much later, they drove between great granite outcrop boulders that could have been thrust up there a million years ago to point the track for Lisa and her grandfather to-day.

Mr. Lindsay never wavered in his direction. He knew exactly where he was going and he knew every bush, rock, tree and boulder which he needed to pass.

'Grandfather,' Lisa said, breaking into speech at last. 'Where is Pardalote?'

'You will see where it is when you get there.'

She ought to have been silenced but some new determination made her resist this state of affairs. Her mother had lived here, somewhere in this huge wasteland. Her mother had perhaps travelled this way. The occasional flights of cockatoos, disturbed in their noon-day roost, had perhaps seen and known her mother. People said this kind of white cockatoo with a bright yellow comb lived for at least a hundred years. *They* would have seen Lisa's mother —long ago.

The thought brought stinging to the back of Lisa's eyes. These white birds winging overhead looked down at her, Lisa, and perhaps *thought she was her mother*—if birds thought at all.

'Pardalote isn't on any of the maps,' she said. 'Not on the Pastoral map, or in the Lands Department. Most stations are mapped, aren't they?'

'Not with any good reason.'

An odd remark, Lisa thought. Her grandfather *meant* to be different from everyone else, except maybe Jimmy Come-up. Lisa softened as she remembered her grandfather talking easily and for a long time with the old paralysed aborigine. As an equal too. There was something human in him after all.

'Mother spoke of Goldstone so I knew it was up here somewhere. At Goldstone they told me the jump-off for Pardalote was *probably* Finch's Creek. Nobody was sure. The mail-freight man took me out to the hospital. I thought it was a town—'

'Rubbish,' her grandfather said, very staccato-like.

'You mean about Finch's Creek being a hospital and not a town?'

'I mean about people being busybodies concerning Pardalote. They talk through the tops of their hats.'

'Why isn't it on a map, grandfather?'

'Because I never put it on a map. Nor my father, nor his father before him. Nobody's business but a Lindsay's business. We don't suffer interference.'

Lisa was silent for a long time after that. Did people themselves mark their station leases on a map? It was all Crown Land.

Then she thought of Mr. Magool Ransome—who possibly lived somewhere near.

'Do you have any neighbours, Grandfather?' For the first time Mr. Lindsay swerved a little as if he had had a jolt to his arm.

'No. Not what you would call *neighbours*.'

'There was a patient in the hospital. His name was Magool Ransome—'

The car rattled sideways over new-grown bushes. It was quite a minute before her grandfather had it back on the grassland.

'Have nothing to do with the Ransome, unless or until *I* say,' he said. For the first time since they had left the hospital he turned his head and looked directly at his granddaughter. His eyes were a pale expressionless blue.

In spite of the exhausting heat, Lisa felt chilled.

Her father had died when she was a baby. Was it because of *him* that her grandfather would not regard the Ransomes as *neighbours*? They were the 'next door' people, surely? Her father had come from *there*? He had been a jackeroo which meant he was learning the station business as an apprentice on someone else's station. So he wouldn't have been a relation of the Ransomes. Lisa was relieved about that!

Mile by mile they drew nearer the highlands. Then, turning a rounded hill, they were in amongst trees again. These were mostly mulga-type trees, though here and there, alone or in twos or threes, stood the lovely graceful ghost-gums. They seemed so lonely—yet strong and serene in that loneliness. Lovely trees!

The car turned round another hill and they were between the low walls of a small gorge. They were running over the rounded pebbles and stones of some dead and long-lost, dry-out river-bed.

This river-bed was a perfect road for it led on through a small gorge, then deep into yet another, twisting and turning as only a water-course could go—even if it was in the long-ago time.

'It's like a track, isn't it,' said Lisa. 'Except it's natural. It's a dried-out, dead river, isn't it?'

Her grandfather did not answer.

No water had flowed here for many thousands of years. Weedy bushes sprouted between the rounded stones. Above, there was nothing but mesa of weather-worn rock, cracked into great square blocks by the heat. In places a brave twisted lone tree peered out of the granite face: fixed by roots held deep in crevices.

Old-fella Lindsay seemed to know which bush to round and which buttresses of fallen rock to avoid. Clearly this was a *way-in* from the known places of the south-east of Pardalote: but unmarked. Only those who knew it would find it!

The stream-bed narrowed even more, and the car climbed a 'bank'. Then they were on top of the highland. Below, in front of them, stretched a valley as verdant in its semi-tropical growth as anything Lisa had ever imagined.

In the near distance were groves of trees. Down the slopes—except on the west side—were the savanna-like grasslands, now yellowing in the heat of the Dry. The Wet had come and gone more than a month or two and the grasses were beginning to dry out. But up the rocky, partly wooded sides to the north and east of the valley, all was green. Water was there, her mother had told her. It came from seepage through the hills' sides.

As they drove from the south into the valley, the sun went down behind the western ridges.

Darkness came on as fast as a curtain falling.

The homestead, when they came to it at last, was just as her mother had told her, and just as Jimmy Come-up had described in his quaint pidgin English. Brown as the red-brown earth except where it was studded by built-in granite blocks. The walls were of red-brown pisé, compacted so hard it might have been brick or stone. The veranda floors were timbered by hand-hewn planks. Inside the house the light came from great kerosene lamps hanging from the raftered ceilings. From a large stove at the end of a long kitchen-living-room came firelight. Here and there stood hand-cut, hand-made furniture as old as the homestead must have been. In a corner stood a large jar from which protruded a bunch of tapers. These would be used to light the lamps.

Lisa was tired, stiff and hungry.

She was too dazed to notice the details of the homestead except it was like something out of a dream a hundred years old. What she did notice, because this surprised her, *was a woman*—stirring at something on the fire: then bustling about as if she too had some firm right to this old, old homestead. She was middle-aged, thin, austere, and not welcoming. On the contrary, Lisa knew at once, she herself was the one *not welcome*.

'Mrs. Watson!' her grandfather explained shortly. 'My housekeeper. She'll give you something to eat and show you a room.'

Lisa attempted to say 'How-do-you-do' but Mrs. Watson, after the first direct adding-up look, had turned away to the stove.

'That door there on your right,' she said, not turning round. 'Take a taper for the light. You can have a shower in the shower-house on the back veranda. It's through the middle door.'

This was the only welcome Lisa had as she came home to her mother's house.

Yet as she went to the door, she heard something that lifted her heart.

'That Mr. Ransome, for all his spell in the hospital, was up on the range to-day,' Mrs. Watson was saying. 'I can tell that roan horse of his. It's the one he rode in the Wyndham races last season. What is he doing up there the day after he comes home from Finch's Creek?'

Lisa, closing the wire door slowly behind her, heard her grandfather's blunt reply.

'He'll have been on his own side of the west hills if it was Jim Ransome. That's for certain. Time'll tell what he's doing up there. Till then we'll mind our own affairs.'

Jim Ransome!

From a far-away time Lisa heard the music of a memory—

Call me Jim for short, Lisa—

So the Ransome's station, Nangardee, really was the one next door to Pardalote! Magool Ransome—Jim for short—sometime rode the dividing line on top of the range too!

For Lisa, a door seemed to open into Heaven.

4

In the morning, unaccountably, Lisa felt better. Through her square, deep-set window she had seen her grandfather, dressed like a stockman, hat and all, going across a gravel yard. He walked right through a host of chicks and hens as if they didn't exist, and into a railed stockyard. Minutes later she saw him riding away, the straightest back she had ever seen, and on the most beautiful horse she had ever dreamed of seeing.

For all the world, through that window set in a wall eighteen inches thick, she might have been looking at a normal farmyard in more settled places. A creek ran at the bottom of the home paddock, and great cadjebut trees lifted mighty arms to the sky above the valley. Hedged in near the homestead was a vegetable garden. A cow was cropping in a paddock to the side. It was like a dream because Lisa knew this was the wild country. It was the Never Never. South, and over by the Territory border was the desert country. Yet here was a verdant kind of paradise.

Funny, but she wasn't frightened any more. Not exactly lonely either—in spite of the housekeeper's indifference. *There really was a neighbour.*

Besides, it might be exciting to explore this valley.

Magool Ransome lived over there on the west side. She was sure of it from what the house-keeper had said. She, Lisa, had a bone to pick with him if, one day exploring over those steep gorge sides, she came across him. She had petted him and cajoled him. She had lighted his cigarettes for him, and read to him; allowed herself to be teased by him, and generally made use-of.

Then for his part, he had simply gone away without saying good-bye. He had not left a message. He had *gone.*

Well . . . of course there had been Imelda!

Lisa found her way to the outside shower. She felt a little uneasy again, as she had to pass through the living-room. But it was empty and the only sign of life was a low fire crackling in the big stove. Back in her room later, she dressed in the plainest, most workmanlike clothes she possessed—a white shirt, light tan shorts with long tan socks, and brown leather shoes. She made her face up to protect it from the heat. She had a feeling that ' making-up' for *effect* would not appeal to Mrs. Watson.

Lisa wanted to be useful in the homestead, but mostly she wanted to go outside and inspect the exterior of this old colonial homestead, and the things immediately around it.

When she went back into the living-room it was to see a young man, with a bronzed face and burnt-fair tousled hair, sitting at the large wooden table in the centre of the room. He had not been seen last night. His legs, sprawled out under the table, were clad in tight-fitting khaki trousers. He too, like her grandfather, wore short-legged high-heeled stockman's boots. He was eating cereal out of a bowl, and reading a paper spread in front of him. On the far end of the table lay his large stockman's hat.

He looked up slowly as Lisa came in. For seconds she stood and he sat—each looking at the other. He did not smile, so neither did she. Then, almost reluctantly, he gathered in his legs, pushed back his chair and stood up. He leaned one hand on the back of the chair and the other on the table. It was a lazy-seeming way of standing, yet not ungraceful.

'Well!' he said.

He looked at her slowly, meditatively, as if assessing her positive, or nuisance value.

Lisa said nothing. The still listening-look was on her face again.

The man opened his eyes a little wider and began to show real interest.

She wasn't tall enough to be called beautiful. She was simply dressed and carried herself in a natural way.

He wondered—*Why does she look like this? As if waiting? For what?*

'So!' he said at last, 'interesting, after all! That is, if you can speak as well as just *look*.'

He was being deliberately outbackish, Lisa thought. He was not going to make any personal 'moves' until she, the stranger, showed her true form.

'Thank you,' Lisa said, not smiling. 'I pass muster? You were not expecting someone like me?'

'That's about it,' he said.

He pushed a chair out from under the table with the toe of his boot. 'Sit down,' he invited. 'Want something to eat? Cereal in that packet there. The tea's in the big pot on the side of the stove. It stays there all day. Nights too. You like stewed tea? That's the way we drink it here.'

Lisa moved cautiously to the table and sat down. The man sat down too.

Like almost everybody in the north, she noticed, he had blue eyes. They were pale like her grandfather's sun-faded eyes. They were thoughtful, even keen, yet were saying nothing.

For one moment Lisa thought he was about to say— 'Fetch yourself a bowl and spoon, or eat off the table'. He had that kind of manner. There was nothing in front of her but a brown earthenware sugar bowl, and a large packet of cereal. The worn but characterful stockman's hat sat in pride of place at the end of the table.

She was wrong. He kicked back his chair and stood up again. Then he walked with the faint rolling action of a horseman over to an enormous cupboard at the side of the range, and brought back a bowl, a spoon, and a small plate and knife. Also a cup and saucer. He put them in front of Lisa, almost *carefully*.

Was he making fun of her? She had no idea.

He walked round behind her, sat down again and passed her the cereal packet, then the sugar bowl.

'Bread rolls are under the cloth on the side hob,' he said. 'The tea pot's on the other side. If you want steak-and-eggs I guess you have to get up at five-thirty in the morning. That's breakfast time out here at Pardalote. It's snacks for now, I'm afraid.' He was neither sharp nor polite. Just stating facts.

'This is all I want, thank you,' Lisa said tipping some of the cereal into her bowl.

'Milk's in the—'

He changed his mind about telling her where she could find the milk for herself. Once again he eased himself up from his chair, walked out on to the back veranda and came back with a large jug. He planted it firmly on the

41

table beside her. Then cautiously, as it were, he went back to his seat and the newspaper. This was one of the bundle of papers brought from Finch's Creek by her grandfather last night.

Lisa ate in silence. She thought she understood what was going on in this man's head. He had been against her coming to Pardalote, but now that she had come, he had found her not too catastrophic.

Presently he turned a page of the paper. Lisa pushed back her chair and went to the stove to pour herself a cup of very black tea. She weakened this 'brew' with some hot water from the iron kettle simmering on the hob. She came back to the table and sat down again. He looked up, taking her in all over again. He was nearly smiling.

'My name's Lisa Tonkin,' she said.

'I know. I'm Tom Watson.'

'Well . . . now that we've broken the ice . . .'

'No ice out here, Lisa,' he said. 'Nothing but blistering heat. We don't have refrigerators and things like that at Pardalote. If you want soft living you'll have to go back from where you came, I guess.'

'I don't want soft living.'

Then she smiled at him. It was only just a smile, but it broke the barriers.

If Tom Watson ever looked at a garden flower he might have thought her face was like one now.

'You see—' she pointed out. 'I want to stay a little while on Pardalote, that's all. It was my mother's home—'

Tom Watson reached in his shirt pocket for the makings of a cigarette. He went slowly about the business of rolling a slim pencil of tobacco in a sliver of paper. He was 'thinking-slow', Lisa thought. Her mother had told her all outback men from the real Never country did this. They took their time.

'We'll see about that,' he said when finally he came to some conclusion. Lisa wondered who it was Tom Watson included in the 'we'.

'Are you Mrs. Watson's son?' she asked after two sips of tea.

'That's right.'

'I met her last night,' Lisa said. 'I was awfully tired, and

42

very dusty. I don't suppose I made a very good impression
—'

Silence.

'I mean, one never does after travelling all day—'

He lit his cigarette as slowly and methodically as he had rolled it. His eyes caught hers, then as if off guard for a split second, he smiled. It was just a glimmer, a glimpse of white teeth. It had come and gone before she really believed it.

'My mother's finishing-up in the dairy right now,' he said.

'Dairy?'

'That's right. No powdered milk on Pardalote. No frozen food. Everything fresh off the land.'

'Lovely!' Lisa smiled again.

Tom Watson showed a thoughtful reaction to this smile. It lit Lisa's face from within into something enchanting. It made dents—without her knowing it—in Tom's armour.

A minute later there came footsteps crossing the back veranda. Mrs. Watson came into the room. She carried a bucket of milk, and a jug of cream. She stood quite still and looked at the pair sitting at the solid, old, enduring table. Her expression was thoughtful, not so unwelcoming as last night.

'You shifted those horses in the home paddock, Tom?' she asked.

'A half hour gone,' Tom said, drawing on his cigarette again. 'Next job's rounding up the two bay geldings to send out for "Old-fella." McPhee'll be wanting them maybe.'

'Then you'd better make a start, hadn't you?'

'In good time,' he said, quietly. He went on smoking, looking at Lisa, and 'thinking-slow'. Mrs. Watson went to the stove, lifted a large shallow bowl from the top of the range to the stove, then poured into it the milk from the bucket.

Lisa had already pushed back her chair, and was standing up.

'I'm afraid I haven't said "Good morning" yet,' she said apologetically. 'I must have over-slept. At least—I didn't realise everyone rose so early at Pardalote.'

43

'Everyone who works for the land gets up early,' Mrs. Watson replied quietly, not turning her head.

'I hope I may help—' Lisa began, walking uneasily towards the stove. It was a very big living-room, so this exercise took quite a few steps.

'You can begin to-morrow, *perhaps*,' Mrs. Watson said, nodding. She put the bucket down while she eased the milk-laden bowl to the middle of the stove. Lisa, not knowing quite what to do, picked up the bucket.

'Perhaps I can take this out for you,' she offered. 'Does it go—?'

'It has to be scalded.' Mrs. Watson turned and looked at the girl thoughtfully. Was she appraising her willingness now?

'In the dairy?' Lisa asked. She was only too anxious to go to that same place and do all the scalding in the world. Anything to be useful—and to escape those 'considering' Watsons: mother and son.

She wished to please, if that was possible, but was uncertain how to go about it.

'What would you know about such places as a *dairy*?' Mrs. Watson asked, surprised.

'My mother told me how—' Lisa broke off. Something had flashed in Mrs. Watson's eyes.

'Your mother had no concern with Pardalote.' Mrs. Watson said firmly but judicially. 'She went away and was cut-off by her father—'

'My mother is dead,' Lisa said very quietly.

A shade, quickly veiled, crossed Mrs. Watson's face.

'That doesn't change things,' she said more gently. Her glance swung anxiously to her son, still sitting at the table. He did not look up.

'Tom,' his mother said, regaining her composure. 'Take Lisa to the dairy. I expect she would like to see it. You'd better show her where everything is kept. There's still scalding water in the boiler. Maybe, after all, she can lend a hand. It'll keep her occupied. Pardalote's a lonely place for a young girl.'

Some other message from mother to son followed along unseen wave-lengths. Tom seemed willing now to abandon the newspaper, and even take an interest in escorting the newcomer to the outside world.

'Come on, Lisa,' he said. 'This way.' His expression had, like his mother's, softened in a guarded way. He stood by the door to let her go through first. He took the bucket from her hand as she passed him. Lisa smiled at him gratefully, but not too freely in case he misunderstood. She wanted to be friendly, that was all.

When she went out on to the veranda, into the outside world, she immediately had a glorious feeling of space. Now she would be able to put to the test the pictures nurtured in her imagination by her mother. Over to the east was the 'sunrise land'. And over the west wall of the range was the 'sunset land'. That was where her father had come from. *That was where Magool Ransome lived!*

So near! Perhaps ...

Ah! But there was someone called Imelda. If Imelda could take him away, she could hold him too. And keep him.

Lisa could now see in detail that the homestead was indeed built against a hillside. The back of it was almost dug into the rock and was impacted by dried-out clay.

No wonder it is cool inside, she thought. The Lindsays, three generations ago, had built solidly and well.

From overhead the homestead was surely camouflaged. By accident or design? It stood low-roofed, brown-eyed like the country around: embraced by the hill. It was also surrounded by the tall eucalypts that shaded it. It was a red and green and gold world, overhung with a sky white with heat. There was colour everywhere like the pictures painted by the aborigines which she had seen in the galleries of the city down south.

Lisa passed that first day without too many bruises to her feelings, or too many spoken mishaps with Mrs. Watson. Fortunately there were no clashes with that strong-man out-backer, Tom Watson. There was a state of suspended judgment between them.

In fact, after a lunch of cold beef and beautiful salads, Tom's attitude visibly improved. He had been a long time shut in the little 'office', off the side veranda, in some sort of conference with his mother. While this was going on, Lisa had washed up the lunch dishes and put everything away —in its proper place—with anxious care. She felt that as far as Mrs. Watson was concerned, this little job might be a testing point.

To her disappointment her grandfather did not come home that night.

'I was expecting him in,' Mrs. Watson said somewhat uneasily.

'He's gone to the Number One out-camp,' Tom replied. 'He'll probably stay there a couple of days checking the stores. He'll be away longer if he goes on to Knob Hill. He has a new-come bunch of men working out there.'

'He's not all that well these days,' his mother said.

'He's a law to himself. Always was.' Tom was stating a simple fact, and in that kind of voice.

Lisa tried not to be hurt that her grandfather, having brought her to the homestead, had then simply gone out to his work without another word to her. Almost as if she ceased to exist now he had rescued her from Finch's Creek.

Perhaps I can win him over—given time, she thought hopefully.

After dinner that first night, Tom took Lisa outside again so she could see the homestead by night light.

It was a beautiful sight with the tree shadows between the pools of silver.

'No wonder nobody knows how to find Pardalote,' she said. 'You just can't see it, can you? I mean, not even from the air? The State does a lot of its surveying by aeroplane doesn't it?'

'I've only seen a plane come over twice. Then it was too high up. Sometimes you see one way over to the east, or the west.'

'Why not the north or south?'

'North there's nothing but barely charted river beds; gorge country. It's empty land except for the cattle pads to Wyndham. Rugged too. South is the way you came in. Then the desert.'

'So nobody comes this way at all?' Lisa asked.

'They wouldn't know the way, unless they were shown,' Tom said with a short laugh. 'Only the Ransome people,

46

over to the west valley, bringing in strangers. "Old-fella" does very occasionally. He's got a bunch at Knob Hill—' He broke off suddenly.

So now I know for certain—the nearest station to Pardalote is the one owned by Magool Ransome! Lisa's spirits lifted.

One day, if I stay here long enough—

Then she remembered someone called Imelda. If only she knew who Imelda really was! What claim had she that she could whisk Mr. James Magool Ransome out of his hospital bed and away at such short notice?

Two more days and two more nights passed and still 'Old-fella' Lindsay did not come back to the homestead. Lisa had had very little conversation with Mrs. Watson. This was because Mrs. Watson, not unfriendly but still watchful, appeared to take little notice of the newcomer. Yet there was a hint of concern in her voice when she spoke of 'Old-fella' to her son.

Tom too was often silent, but he was kind. On Lisa's second day, he saddled up an easy-going, not-so-young hack for her and took her riding. She was next to a novice, but knew she was going to love riding after the first ten minutes. Tom took her up the east side of the gorge so she could see the cattle browsing amongst the thinly treed slopes. In another far paddock there was a mob of horses. Away in the distance wild donkeys were scattering on the far plains.

'Grandfather rears horses too?' she asked.

'Breeds them and rears them,' Tom was sitting easy in his saddle, one leg thrown over the pommel. 'Blood strain that first came from India more'n a hundred years ago. They were brought here by the first Lindsay, along with a couple of Afghans and a camel train.'

'But where does my grandfather sell the horses?' Lisa asked puzzled.

'India. Where they came from first, they go back now.'

As they turned their own horses to ride back, Lisa caught sight of a wisp of smoke away over the west side of the range. As she watched, the wisp became a real column of smoke.

'Natives sending smoke signals?' she asked, not expecting
47

to be taken seriously. The smoke column was more the kind that rose from a chimney.

Tom Watson looked at the smoke through slitted eyes under the shade of his wide stockman's hat. So deep was the shadow cast by that hat-brim that his eyes seemed no more than two points of hard light.

'No,' he said, but did not explain. They rode on down the hill back to the homestead in silence.

Now Lisa knew one more fact. She knew the direction, *exactly*, where lay Nangardee, Magool Ransome's home.

She did not know why she was sure of this, unless it was something to do with the curious note in Tom's voice.

'Your grandfather is back,' Tom said as they trotted across the home paddock.

'You sound like Jimmy Come-up.' Lisa did not quite believe him. 'He liked to foretell—'

'Jimmy Come-up be blowed! "Old fella's" horse is grazing over there by the big tree. No one else ever rides Challenger. So if Challenger is around, then so is "Old-fella".'

Lisa was relieved, but a little shy of Tom's bluntness. 'Why do you call my grandfather "Old-fella"?'

'The natives do. Up thisaway it means *The Boss*—the lawgiver, in English. Like their tribal head is their top man. His father before him was "Old-fella". And that one's father before him. They have other native names meaning the same thing, of course.'

'I see.'

A native name like 'Magool' for instance? That word meant "Boss" too. Magool himself had told her.

Tom leaned over his saddle to open the gate. When they had walked their horses through he leaned down again to close it. Then he straightened up, lifting his head as he did so. He looked straight into the first red haze of sunset over the western range. His eyes, under the lowered brim of his hat, narrowed as the sunset deepened. Lisa saw the strange hard set of his jaw.

Then she too looked up into the wounding colour of the sky to where the range-top was black against its banner. So too were the mesa hill-tops, the stands of sentinel trees, and the cruel buttresses of barren rock.

Tom had been looking at the figure of a man mounted on *a horse*.

That man seemed faraway. So alone up there! A portrait in outline only. He and his horse were very still as he looked down into Pardalote's valley. At them?

Lisa sat still, bound by the kind of spell that gave her own face and sea-dark eyes that portrait look again. That man on horseback up there was a dark outline against the vivid blaze of the western sky. Lisa felt a pang to her heart because he reminded her of a tall strong man lying inert, and made so vulnerable by nothing more than a prick from a hypodermic needle. Now he was only a still black form, alone against the crimson back-drop above the sunset land.

Magool Ransome. It had to be. From his own kingdom on top of the range he was looking down in silence on herself and the horseman with her. Would he recognize her?

Tom turned his head.

'What goes with you, Lisa?' he asked.

'The sunset. No one would really believe it unless they saw it, would they, Tom?'

Her eyes came down from distant hills and met his. They were troubled, yet believing in miracles. Magool was up there. And *no one* was with him! Had Imelda gone away?

'What were *you* looking at, Tom?'

'I guess I spotted an eagle.' He lifted his rein and gave his horse a shove with his boot. 'Now's the hour to look out for such things. They're predatory, and hang above the range—after prey.'

'Eagles?' Lisa asked puzzled.

'Keep clear of the range tops, Lisa. Eagles can be dangerous things.' He looked directly at her. 'Specially the kind that watch for young birds,' he warned. 'They hunt alone. They keep one piece of plunder hard-by for future needs; then come after another. They're that kind of bird.'

Lisa blinked. Was Tom talking in double meanings?

They rode on to the stables. He took her reins from her and wound them round a timber upright, then helped her dismount. As she slipped from the saddle into his arms he held her just that extra second too long.

49

'Beware of an eagle,' he said again, half joking this time. He grinned and changed the subject. 'Maybe "Old-fella's" waiting for you up at the homestead. Don't be too hard on him, Lisa. Don't dicker with his enemies. He has them, and they're "*takers*" too.'

She stared at Tom in surprise. She couldn't believe he meant—what she *thought* he meant. He, too, had seen Magool Ransome on top of the range! She was sure now. '*Me* be hard on "Old-fella"? It could be the other . . .'

'Well, go and see him. Play your cards right. He'll be the one wanting favours. Accept that from me, Lisa. You could be on a running win. You never can tell, can you? If I were in your shoes I'd keep the game in hand; close-up. And play it from there.'

Lisa was so puzzled she never quite knew how she slipped out of Tom's arms, and out of the stables.

A minute later she forgot all about him. The homestead living-room light had come on, and through the wide deep-set window she saw her grandfather sitting in the arm-chair. His face was no longer closed-in and arrogant. It was *tired*. And old. Even a little sad.

He looked up at Lisa as she came in through the open door. What his eyes saw was a young girl with her cheeks glowing and a light in her eyes.

'Oh, Grandfather! I'm so glad to see you.'

She paused, longing for a welcome yet afraid of saying the wrong thing. 'You've come home!'

He put his hand inside his shirt and pressed it against his heart. She thought he winced.

She ran across the floor to him.

'Grandfather! You are all right?'

'Of course I'm all right,' he snapped. 'A bit tired, that's all. Generally speaking I'm never tired.'

His free hand dangled by his side fondling the ears of a black and tan kelpie.

'What a lovely dog!' Lisa exclaimed, dropping to the floor beside him. 'May I pat him? I mean, will he let me?'

'He'll let you, if I say so.' The old man seemed mollified by Lisa's quick attention to the dog. He saw by her eyes and eagerness that her admiration was genuine. 'There Sept!' he said speaking to the dog. 'Let the lady pat you.'

'Sept?' Lisa asked, puzzled, as she patted the dog's smooth shining head. 'What a strange name ...'

'Not at all. He's seventh in the line. All born and bred on Pardalote. Look at the pads on his paws. Tougher than hide. Can walk anywhere. Good as any dingo.'

The dog eyed Lisa with toleration while she lifted a front paw and rubbed the pads of his foot with her thumb. His eyes were friendly.

'He *ought* to be as good as a dingo,' she said firmly. 'Kelpies are partly descended from dingoes, aren't they?'

'So you know that much, do you?' Some of the coldness and harshness had gone from 'Old-fella's' voice. Lisa knew instinctively that he loved this dog very much. He had allowed her to come a little closer to him because she too admired Sept.

'Of course. I think I learned that at school.' She gently rubbed the dog under his chin, watching and waiting for the first thumping wag of his tail: a sign of approval. 'I love beautiful things,' she added. 'Sept is a beautiful dog.'

'In that case, what do you think of this?' 'Old-fella' had taken his right hand away from his chest. He drew something out of his shirt pocket and held it out to Lisa. In his palm lay a beautiful shining six-sided stone, an inch and a half long, with a pyramid cap to it. It was a mauvey-blue, the colours fading from depth to a cloudy blue and white near the base.

'Oh, but it's beautiful!' she cried, her eyes shining. 'It's a crystal, isn't it? It's natural too: just as Nature made it?' Her eyes gazed in wonder at the stone. 'Six exact equal sides,' she marvelled. 'And that perfect pyramid on top! It's like a sort-of miracle, isn't it?'

'Well, what is it? Name it' he demanded.

She shook her head. She would so like to please her grandfather by *knowing*.

'I've no idea,' she confessed.

'Beryl,' he said. 'That's what it is called. *Beryllium*. Very valuable. There's plenty of it back in the ranges, though no crystal found as big as this one yet.'

'On these ranges?' Lisa asked, incredulous.

She did not have time to hear an answer for Mrs. Watson came hurrying into the room. The older woman was in a different guise now, for her manner was bustling and busy: almost fussing.

'What are you doing worrying "Old-fella"?' she demanded. 'Can't you see that ... ?'

'Rot and rubbish!' 'Old-fella' interrupted, back to his earlier self. 'Your son will be in a minute, Mrs. Watson. Go look after him. He'll be needing his food—if I know anything about his appetite.'

Lisa looked from one to the other in surprise. How different these two people were all of a sudden. And who in the world of wonders could imagine Mrs. Watson fussing in a mother fashion over *anyone*? More puzzling, what had made her grandfather change his attitude to her, his granddaughter? Had some miracle of enlightenment taken place out there over the ranges—or wherever it was he had been during his absence?

Old-fella's hand was inside his shirt again, gently massaging the area over his heart. His eyes were closed, but there was a tiny satisfied smile on his lips almost as if he were enjoying having spoken to Mrs. Watson so sharply.

Lisa, still kneeling beside the dog, looked anxiously at Mrs. Watson. That lady for her part was looking at 'Old-fella', first with concern, then with exasperation. She turned away to the stove as if to hide the fact that something was worrying *her*. Grandfather's sharp words?

Lisa gazed into Sept's golden brown eyes and gently shook her head.

'Being wise and shrewd like all good kelpies, you know the answers,' she thought. 'As we don't know each other's language, Sept, I guess we can't communicate. Well, not just yet ...'

The dog thumped his tail on the floor. Lisa lifted her head. 'Old-fella' had one eye open, watching the girl and the dog. His free hand was caressing the lovely gemstone. When he saw Lisa looking at him he quickly shut both eyes again, leaned his head back on the head-rest, and gave himself up to being wan and tired again.

Just how cunning can everyone be around this place? Lisa wondered. *Are they all playing a game or something?*

5

The next morning, as Lisa was dressing, she heard men's voices coming from the north-side veranda, outside her window. She had risen very early and was happier this morning, for her grandfather clearly had recovered his energy in the early evening. He had once again been snappy and terse, but mostly aloof. Lisa was actually relieved. 'Old-fella' was back to form. In an odd way she found this quite a deliverance from an obscure sort of anxiety in herself. When she had first woken she had thought it might be a helpful idea to put the good things that had happened yesterday against the not-so-good; then balance them out.

She had seen the 'sunrise land' to the east. That had been wonderful. She had seen a column of smoke rising beyond the range opposite—from the 'sunset land' to the west. That was more wonderful. Her mother had talked mostly of the 'sunset land'.

It was over *that range*, where the sun went down, that her father had lived and worked.

Lisa could almost hear her mother's voice—*From a high look-out one can see the homestead in the valley below*.

Some time, somehow, she would go and find that 'sunset land' for herself.

Then about that dinner meal last night? Well, it hadn't really been too bad. Tom had occasionally passed a fleeting half-smile in her direction. Grandfather had been the same sort of person he had been right from the time he had come to Finch's Creek; but he had seemed *well*. Not tired and pale as before dinner. Lisa had discovered that he could *love* things too. His beautiful beryl stone, and his kelpie dog, for instance. Maybe she could . . . if she kept trying . . . Well, if not love, then perhaps recognition?

The voices outside were continuing, so Lisa put her head through the window to see who was there.

Standing at the veranda edge were three men—her grandfather, Tom, and another stockman.

'You didn't take her up the west side?' her grandfather was asking Tom.

'No,' Tom answered. 'I took her down the valley, along the Jinga-track to the east. Far enough since she's no rider—yet.'

Well, that's true, Lisa thought ruefully, knowing they were talking of her. *Still with practice—who knows? Maybe Tom—*

Her grandfather's voice was going on.

'Well, keep away from the west side,' he was saying. 'I've given those orders before. It's dangerous up there for more reasons than one. You can give Lisa the old mare Nellie to ride. I'll send Nellie in some time. Sam here is taking out the rest of the hacks to the out-camp to-day. Meantime, if my granddaughter goes wandering too far—warn her off dangerous places. You understand, Tom?'

Lisa thought this a very long speech for her grandfather, but she detected some symptoms of kindness in it. In spite of his indifferent aloof voice, he really wanted something interesting for her. He was going to send in a nice quiet old horse for her to ride! And he'd spoken of her as 'my granddaughter'! His prohibitions about 'dangerous places' might have something to do with Tom's remark about eagles. Were these eagles up in the far north dangerous to humans? She had never heard so. In fact she had gained the impression Tom just didn't want her to go up there, anyway. Maybe it was because her own mother had found someone to love over there in the west. Tom would be echoing her grandfather's feelings. That way, over the range to the west, 'Old-fella' had lost his runaway daughter!

But it had a call for Lisa! From that way, in the 'sunset land', her father had come!

Lisa went back to the dressing-table and finished brushing her hair. She looked at her face in the mirror.

What had Tom seen in this face yesterday? When he had lifted her down from the horse he had held her . . . just that minute too long.

Outside the window Tom was saying—'Okay "Old-fella"!'

Strange how Tom called her grandfather 'Old-fella' to his face! Did everyone do this? Even Mrs. Watson?

Out in the living-cum-kitchen room Mrs. Watson was grilling man-sized steaks and frying eggs by the dozen. Seated round the table, each reading one or other of the outdated newspapers brought back from Finch's Creek by 'Old-fella' Lindsay were *four* men. Lisa's eyes rounded. So Pardalote was really populated after all!

All four men were in workmanlike khaki clothes and wore riding boots—low-cut in the calf but high in the heel. The row of stetsons—shabby and dusty—were in a straight line at the far end of the table. These men were stockmen.

They looked up slowly as Lisa came in. Then each ducked behind a newspaper as if he had seen an apparition.

Lisa went to the stove where Mrs. Watson was hard at work.

'May I help, please?' she asked cautiously.

Mrs. Watson did not look up. For one long moment she did not answer either. Then she said—'Well . . . you can try. Put a steak and four eggs on each plate. Six eggs for the big fellow on the window side. After they've finished you can wash up. "Old-fella" and Tom have eaten.'

Mrs. Watson, like 'Old-fella', was back to form again this morning.

Lisa began to slide the cooked eggs on to the plates of steak waiting in the oven.

'Thank you for letting me help,' she said, hoping, though rather weakly, to dent Mrs. Watson's early morning armour a little.

'You can fix your own breakfast when the men have gone,' Mrs. Watson said in her toneless voice. 'Hot bread rolls are in the basket on the floor at the end of the hearth. When you've done you'd better go out for the day. Take a look around the station. Take yourself for a walk.'

'Of course. I'd love to do that,' Lisa was juggling two plates of the hot breakfast in one hand, and bending down to pick up the basket of bread rolls with the other. 'There's so much to see—'

Mrs. Watson stopped frying eggs, and looked at the girl closely.

Lisa's good intentions and her early morning snippets of happiness began slipping quietly from her.

'Don't go far,' Mrs. Watson advised. 'Some tracks are bad. The men are going out to the muster. Tom too. Won't be in for days.'

'Oh . . . well . . . Thank you for telling me—'

'Take yourself some food in a lunch box and keep out of *my* way. It's best like that. *You'll see*!'

Lisa, plate-laden and basket-laden, drew in a breath.

So Tom was going to the muster! She wondered where it was: in what distant reach of the valley? Her grandfather was really gone, she supposed. She didn't have the courage to ask. She'd be left alone in the homestead with Mrs. Watson, probably, for a day, or days!

Yes indeed—Lisa would take that walk!

She carried her burdens of food to the table. The men were only pretending to read. As Lisa had turned towards them every head had ducked down again.

She put the basket of rolls in the middle of the table and the two plates she carried in front of two of the men.

'Good morning everybody,' she said as brightly as she could manage. 'I'm Lisa. Lisa Tonkin.'

The men really looked up now. They were sun-weathered as Lisa had never seen men before. They were slim and hardy: and their faces were lined. These were people who lived for ever in the outback. They probably never left it. She smiled again, this time because of the shy wondering in their eyes.

Their faces creased a little as if they wanted to smile too, but were so unused to this exercise their cheek muscles wouldn't work. They gave up and went deadpan, then reached for bread rolls.

'I'll be back again in a minute with the other plates,' she promised.

When the breakfast was over, Lisa did as she had been told. She cooked herself some breakfast during Mrs. Watson's absence at the dairy. Next she set about washing up all the dishes, then scrubbing down the wooden work-table at the side of the stove. She made sure the griller and the frying pan were so spotlessly clean not even ten Mrs. Watsons could have faulted them.

She swept the kitchen floor, then went to her own small room and tidied that up. She swept the outside veranda, but did not go near the office nor her grandfather's room: nor the rooms belonging to Mrs. Watson and her son. She was much too nervous to intrude in those directions, yet.

She was also too unnerved by Mrs. Watson's half dismissal at breakfast time to go to the dairy and offer help there. She had really done quite a big job in the kitchen and thereabouts. It wasn't long after sun-up but the heat was coming across the ranges already.

If she was going for that walk—as directed—the earlier the better. Spelled out in one word she had permission to *escape*.

A walk meant to explore, and there was so much to see. Where was that old baob tree her mother had told her about? And the grove of tall paper-barked cadjebuts at the bottom of a creek-fall in a narrow gorge? Where were all the birds? The myriad finches and the black-winged parrots as well as the brilliant red ones? Her mother had said that hundreds of them came through the valley at times. Often at sunset.

If only she could find a bower bird's courting ground!

Yes, she would go for a walk and take her lunch too.

Lisa put slices of cold meat between two of the bread rolls and wrapped them with long curly leaves from a lettuce fresh from the garden. She took a tiny orange-sized rock-melon from the patch by the water-bore. There were two canvas waterbags hanging from nails on the veranda wall so she took one and filled it with water. Together with her food bag, she slung the waterbag over her shoulder.

She had put on her cotton shade hat, and now finally added a belt to her shorts, and tightened it.

Lisa felt 'girded' for exploration, and very happy. Free.

There was no one to whom she could say good-bye. Mrs. Watson, it seemed, had not come back to the homestead since she had left the kitchen earlier. She might have gone to any one of the outhouses scattered along the fence of the home paddocks. All was silence. There was no sight or sound of anyone anywhere in the old house: or of anyone in the world.

So, head-up and one shoulder a little weighted down with food and water, Lisa set out to see *her* world: this world her mother and father had known—oh, so long ago—

When Lisa reached the far side of the station square she turned her head—to see again just what the homestead looked like with its backside wedged into the hill, its wide verandas on three sides, and the blazing slashes of orange and purple bougainvillaea against the walls of the dairy and smithy. It was all so beautiful in its still, sleeping, sun-dusted way: a kind of a dream of a lost home come true.

Then, as she paused and looked she saw a *face* at one of the windows.

Mrs. Watson had not gone out, after all! She was watching Lisa's departure. But why?

Lisa, unable to answer that one, turned again to the timber rails of the home paddock, and climbed over them. The horses were all gone. The kelpie dog was gone with her grandfather. Everyone and everything was gone. The world of her grandfather's home, and her mother's home stood still in absolute silence—under a sky whitening with heat, as if it, like that face at the window, watched in silence as the last child of the Lindsay line set out to see a kingdom.

Lisa wasn't so sure about feeling so very happy now.

The outback could be frightening when it was like this. Waiting, moveless, silent; belonging to no one, no Lindsay, except to Time, and itself.

Lisa walked northwards, yet imperceptibly her feet carried her in a veering direction towards the west side of the valley, almost as if something outside herself drew her that way. Over there were trees. Perhaps birds. Beyond that range top had risen, yesterday, a column of smoke from a *chimney*. That meant people!

There were *people* over there—in the Sunset Land!

Happiness came back, slowly at first but completely.

A fold in the land led off the main floor of the paddocks. It was a small lead-away depression, like a wide trough.

Here were beautiful trees with spreading leafy arms. This 'little side valley' meandered about, and soon Lisa was not sure of her direction. But she didn't worry. She could always follow the fold back. How strange and wonderful, and different it all was. So cool and shaded.

A creek burst out of the red-brown rock-sides on Lisa's left. Wild-flowers, mauve, white and yellow, poked their heads from rock crevices. In the leafy tree-tops a world had come alive with colour, and sound: the movement of dozens of tiny birds.

Lisa, looking about her, found herself staring at a narrow path that led in between the trees and hummocks of grass: upwards to the gorge-top. Somewhere up there the path disappeared behind great boulders and rocky outcrops. Then, farther up, it reappeared above them.

Lisa climbed the rest of the gorge by the path.

She came out on a sort of natural platform between two huge walls of rock. She stood quite still, and looked down into the next valley. There were wooded slopes, and green grass down there. Against the far hillside stood a homestead, with smoke rising column-wise from the chimney, through the tree branches.

It was *another* Pardalote—old and beautiful, with the rear side built into the rock face for the sake of coolness. The high cadjebut trees were in different places, but they were the same kind of trees.

But one thing was different. Lisa held her breath as she gazed, and gazed—

By the front veranda stood two vehicles. One was a dusty Land-Rover. The other was a beautiful modern overlanding car.

The hot sun overhead was shining straight down on this long low-lined car. Things about it shone as bright as arc lamps. It must have been recently cleaned of the all-pervading dust that gathered on everything travelling. So the car perhaps *belonged*! *Or was there to stay*? This mattered because two figures were leaning on the boot-end of the car. Lisa couldn't quite see who or what, but she thought it was a man and a girl. Everything down there in that valley was tiny because of the distance. Even the homestead was a doll's house.

A flurry of dust meant a dog had run across the front gravel to the two standing by that car.

Lisa looked and looked. It was like staring into a fantasy place—a child's toy of built-up pieces—so pretty, and so unattainable.

Nangardee! Magool Ransome's homestead! *It had to be!*

Because her father had come from there Lisa thought she was looking at *home*. Part of her had come from there, just as another part of her had come from Pardalote.

The column of smoke from the chimney spiralled upwards in a wind drift reaching higher and higher. Yes. This was the place from whence she had seen the smoke while out riding with Tom.

Something near the homestead stirred, and frightened a flock of birds from their tree roosts. With a wonderful sweeping movement they rose, swinging and winging high above the homestead, then away from it coming towards where Lisa stood statue-still now. She did not want the birds to tell tales on her. They winged overhead—small birds of most glorious colours. Red, green, yellow, purple. They wheeled and swung back to the valley, over the homestead, and settled once again on their tree. *Had* their look-see visit told tales on her?

Lisa felt she was watching magic.

Alas! It was all too far away, and she had not been invited to come to the party.

She had not been invited to come to Pardalote either! She could understand how Mrs. Watson must look upon her as the 'outsider'. The one who did not belong.

6

A minute later Lisa forgot her sadness. She remembered something. The little path by which she had climbed the gorge had, in fact, wandered on to higher levels. It must lead somewhere.

She darted back to it, climbing it now in such haste she

60

kept stumbling and slipping. She felt, by some magic instinct, that it led somewhere important.

The track swung round an outcrop of rock and finished up between two massive wall-like boulders. These boulder walls themselves opened outwards to the sky on the far side.

Lisa edged inside this strange sort-of eagle's eyrie. Then she came to a sudden standstill.

She stared and stared. She could have rubbed her eyes for she could hardly believe what she saw. In front of her, right in the middle of the aperture, was a wooden bench-stool *exactly like those in Pardalote's kitchen*. It could have been one straight out of the homestead.

In front of the stool was a *telescope*, upright on a fixed stand, its barrel pointing outward and downward into the beyond on the far side of the range.

Lisa approached the bench almost on tiptoe. Her eyes, wide and incredulous, were fixed on the telescope. She could see that it wasn't all that dusty. It must have been used some time not so very long ago. But by whom?

She slipped on to the seat, still apprehensive, as if afraid of fork-lightning or some god-visit from on high. She put her eye to the telescope.

First she had to adjust the sight, and dust the glass with her handkerchief. Then, like a slide on a magic lantern, the valley below came slowly into view. It was the same valley and the same homestead. She could see it in detail now.

First the chimney with its column of smoke appeared. Then, as she tilted the telescope, the roof, the veranda, and last a shining limousine with the man and woman standing beside it.

Lisa held the telescope steady. Also her breath.

The man was Magool Ransome! Jim for short! He was talking to and smiling at a wonderfully good-looking person who might be Imelda! Could it be? She was leaning against the boot of the car, making gestures in a graceful but quite emphatic way, as she demonstrated some point. From the distance Lisa was sure she was beautiful. Her figure was beautiful anyway in its simple, but perfectly tailored linen-like dress. The whole effect was beautiful.

Magool Ransome didn't appear quite the same as he had

in pyjamas, and with bandages round his eyes. But he was the right height—tall. His hair was dark and the lower part of his face was the same. So were his shoulders, and his arms with the hands tucked in the belt of his khaki trousers. Undeniably, indisputably and for ever, *he was Magool Ransome*—the impatient patient! His manner, too, was his and his alone, for he was smiling at the picturesque female with him—teasing her, laughing a little, yet somehow still with the air of the king of the earth. He teased the very adult-looking girl down there just as he had teased Lisa. Yet, as before, he was master of the situation.

He had been the lone rider sitting his horse on the top of the range yesterday, at sundown! He had visited Pardalote. She was sure of it! Why? He would have seen her riding with Tom! He had been so *near*!

Marjory Dean had said his eyes were grey—very slitted. Well, they weren't very slitted just now. Lisa couldn't see the colour but she could see their owner was enjoying himself with the girl leaning against the car in front of him.

Meantime her own heart was beating very fast. She was too excited to account for *that*.

Lisa could have stayed watching for ever, but already time was creeping on and she'd better be gone herself. The way home was long and roundabout, and she had not even eaten the lunch she had brought with her.

If only she knew why those two down there were standing *by the car*. *Was* Imelda going away somewhere? Lisa rather hoped she was. Far, far away! If Imelda had been a really nice person she would have gently pointed out to Magool Ransome that it wasn't very polite of him to leave the hospital without saying 'good-bye' to everyone. In the case of absentees—if he couldn't wait for them to come home—then a nicely-worded note would have been appropriate.

It was Lisa who had watched over him, and attended to his smallest needs during his eight bandage-blind days at Finch's Creek. Not Imelda.

Lisa dropped her hands from the telescope and stood up. Now, she felt a sort-of sadness. It was like a hand pressing on her heart. She felt quite desolate.

Slowly she turned her back on Magool Ransome's valley and went out between the upright slabs of rock.

'He'll have forgotten I ever existed, by this time,' she thought. 'He probably didn't recognise me yesterday. How stupid can I be?'

Outside, a few yards away, Lisa now noticed yet another one-man track leading off as if it too led down into her own Pardalote's valley. It seemed to go straight down, in a near perpendicular way. It could be shorter—

She decided against trying it. It could have been a path once used by 'Old-fella', but now too steep for him to climb. That involuntary way he had slipped his hand in his shirt, and massaged his chest! Had that been meaningful?

Lisa had lost the will to venture on fresh discoveries to-day. It was better to go home the way she had come, she thought. She would try this new perpendicular path another day. When she was fresher—

She watched that her feet did not slip on the loose stones of the more familiar track. She did not realise she had already set her mind on another visit another day.

She had quite forgotten she had been, in effect, warned off Ransome territory. In addition to the matter of the new path to be explored, she was thinking of Magool Ransome himself.

How different he had looked through the eye of the telescope! He had been upright on his two feet. Tall, powerful, and wonderful to look at. He had moved as he talked, and she could see he had a sort-of hidden, yet easy-seeming strength about him.

Her heart lifted once again, and she banished the doldrums. Just living so near, he gave her something to think about. Maybe—*it was possible*—she might actually meet him again some day.

With, or without Imelda?

Lisa couldn't answer that one. And didn't try.

In spite of the long way home, Lisa was wrapped in her thinking so much she not only had forgotten to eat, she appeared to come upon the little creek unexpectedly, yet it was really two hours since she had left the range top. Now it seemed only minutes later that she was crossing the home paddock—which was ridiculous. *Then* it had been mid-day. Now it was darkling along the eastern side of the valley.

Mrs. Watson had come out of the homestead and was going towards the vegetable garden. When she saw—through the dusk—it was Lisa—dusty, somewhat dishevelled, and limping—she stopped and waited till the girl came near.

'Are you limping?' she asked. 'Are you tired? You must have walked too far. You've been gone all day. There's no time to spare to look after frail visitors on Pardalote, you know.'

Lisa's heart dropped with a clang.

'I have a pebble in my shoe, that's all,' she said simply. She had had an exciting day and she felt Mrs. Watson's non-welcoming words like a douche of cold water. 'I've only just a minute ago felt the pebble,' she explained. 'I was waiting till I reached the veranda to shake it out. It's easier . . . sitting down . . . That is . . .'

'No one does things the easy way up here in the North,' Mrs. Watson said quietly. 'You'll have to get used to that, Lisa—*if* you're going to stay long. I'm afraid it's a hard country.'

'I hope I harden-up soon,' Lisa said with dignity. 'I'll certainly try.'

Lisa reached the homestead and she sat down on the veranda edge, not only to shake out her shoe, but to rest. She was more tired than she had thought. She sat there, quite still, and waited while Mrs. Watson—having cut a lettuce and several ripe tomatoes—followed her to the homestead. It was near dark—except for the last pink glow over the Sunset Land.

'Most of the men won't be in for dinner to-night,' the older woman said, looking at Lisa as puzzled now as she was possibly critical. ' "Old-fella" should be back, though. You never can tell with him. As Tom says—he's a law to himself.' She paused, then added—'You'd better get yourself some dinner, late though it is. I'll wait for "Old-fella"—in case he comes. I'll put the home-paddock's lights on.'

'Yes, of course,' Lisa agreed. Actually she was relieved that she wouldn't have to sit down to a twosome meal with this strange woman. Yet she would rather have waited for her grandfather. She was sorry to have come home so late.

'Is there anything you are keeping that I *mustn't* touch? I could make a mistake—'

'There's chops in the cool-safe. The fire's alight,' Mrs. Watson said. She stepped up on the veranda and went to the switch-board. She turned round—when she had switched on the outside lights—as if there was something more on her mind.

'Did Tom treat you the right way when he took you out?' she asked, her eyes curious. Lisa was taken aback but unexpectedly she felt a little sorry for the other woman now. That question had literally been torn from her.

'Of course,' Lisa did her best to smile. 'It was very good of Tom to take me out. He was very kind. And thoughtful too—I enjoyed myself—'

Mrs. Watson, her hand on the screen door, cogitated this answer.

'That's all right,' she said at length. 'You best take notice of *Tom*. He seems to like you. He's the one who's stood by "Old-fella" these ten years, you know. He's the overseer. You understand what that is? Tom knows what goes on with the cattle more'n "Old-fella" does, these days. For what he's done on this station he's . . .' She broke off, clamping her lips together to prevent them physically from saying more. She turned away to enter the house. 'It's a compliment that Tom likes you, Lisa,' she finished. 'He doesn't take to girls much—generally. It's best you know that.'

Everything said—from the subject of frail delicate visitors, to the hard life at Pardalote, and Tom's importance as overseer—was double aboriginese to Lisa. She was glad Tom liked her but she had no idea what was in Mrs. Watson's mind, nor why she would have spoken this way. Almost in *warning*—

Except for the lights down the valley it was dark outside now. Even more than at home, night came down as fast as the drawing of a curtain.

Lisa had a shower, put on a clean frock, then went looking for chops in the hessian cooler on the back veranda. These chops, heavy cut from some old wether, reminded her again of toughness. Almost an hour had passed since she had begun to cross the home paddock. She *ought* to feel hungry. Specially as right now she should be going to bed.

At first, as she prepared her chops, she thought Mrs. Watson was in her own room. Then a shadow seemed to flit across the corner vision of her eyes. Mrs. Watson, in soft house-shoes, had gone to the west veranda. Waiting and watching?

In a way Lisa began to feel uneasy too. While the chops were sizzling loud enough to distract all attention, she herself went to the door.

Outside the valley was very dark, except where the lights made a path of gold. The moon had not yet risen. Against this frail glow of the lights Lisa could see Mrs. Watson pacing up and down on the path below the veranda. Every now and again she stopped and bent her head on one side in a listening way.

Mrs. Watson was watching and waiting for her grandfather in this strange, anxious manner! 'Old-fella' was a law to himself about his comings and goings. Mrs. Watson had said so herself. Lisa shook her head in puzzlement. Maybe people in the north were different! Actually the lawyer who had seen her about her mother's Will had said that *everyone* north of Twenty-six was *different*. They were a race apart. They made their own rules.

Lisa realized there was something very personal, and private, about Mrs. Watson's watching-and-listening attitude —alone out there. A little shamefacedly, because she herself had innocently witnessed it, Lisa went back to the kitchen table and her meal of chops and fried potatoes.

She sat down at the table, and pushed the potatoes aside with her fork. She had never really liked potatoes done this way. Yet so short a time ago she had been hungry enough—

The wire door from the outside opened and Mrs. Watson came in. Lisa could see worry written clearly in her face.

'How you could calmly go on eating—at this hour— while your grandfather . . .' Mrs. Watson began. Then suddenly she stopped. There was a long blank pause. 'Very well then, go on with it—' she said in a steadier voice. 'After all it isn't any worry of yours, is it? You and your mother never thought about him these twenty years . . .'

Lisa's knife and fork were down on her plate.

'We didn't know about him,' she said. 'I mean, *I* didn't know about him, except he was alive somewhere way up here in the Never—' She broke off.

'You could see for yourself last night that he'd overdone it,' Mrs. Watson went on. She was now at the stove pushing and rattling about frying-pan and pots in a pointless manner. 'I'm always telling him—*You stay out there too long these days*, I say. *Get in before dark*. Heat above the century in the day and temperature way down below— forty or fifty degrees sometimes—at night. It's all right for the young men. I've told McPhee at the Outcamp time and again to keep an eye on him . . .'

She stopped, suddenly aware that she was not just thinking angry thoughts but was actually speaking them aloud.

She turned round abruptly.

'Get on with your dinner, Lisa, and go to bed,' she suggested, more quietly. 'After all, it has nothing to do with you. What made you come . . . ?'

She broke off; listening again.

Listening for 'Old-fella' coming home too late—Lisa thought, sad for Mrs. Watson. *Why, she cares! She cares about someone other than Tom!*

'My grandfather seemed quite all right at dinner last night,' Lisa said thoughtfully, anxious herself now.

Mrs. Watson did not answer. She was standing upright and very still. The frying-pan was in one hand and the kettle in the other now. She was *listening*—not to Lisa, but to some sound outside.

Lisa too bent her head.

She could hear something . . . the faint beat of a horse's feet coming nearer and nearer.

'Tom?' she asked brightening. 'Better still, "Old-fella" himself?'

'It's not Tom's horse, and it's not Challenger.'

They listened again.

'How can you be so sure?' Lisa asked, trying to be reassuring. 'It's such a long long way away—the other side of the home paddock . . .'

'I was born with horses,' Mrs. Watson said flatly. She had not moved. The frypan and the kettle were as before —held rigid in her hands.

Lisa too, sat silent, her back brittle-straight as she too listened.

The horse beats came closer and closer. They were quite clear now. There was one pause, followed by the thump of a horse landing after a jump. The rider had not waited to open a gate. He had cleared the fence. What a good job the lights had been switched on! The hoof beats did not lessen in speed. Again, a minute later, Lisa could almost *feel* the half pause, then the gathering of a horse's legs beneath him to make yet another fence jump. It was the home fence this time.

Outside silence was banished, for the horse thundered along the side stretch by the vegetable garden, then across the gravel square. It pulled up with a scatter of small pebbles: It came to a dead stop in its own speed. Through the open door and wire window Lisa could hear the animal snorting and blowing deeply through its nostrils. It rattled its bridle, as its rider flung the reins at the saddling fence. Seconds later there came the sound of heavy boots striding towards the veranda.

Neither Lisa nor Mrs. Watson had moved. Their eyes were fixed on the door.

'Old-fella' would never have ridden in like that! It was beyond him at his age. The footsteps too! But Tom . . .

Someone strode across the veranda, and the screen door opened.

A man came in. No 'by your leave?' He stopped a foot inside the doorway. He did not look at Mrs. Watson, but at the girl sitting at the table instead.

Lisa, for one long moment, thought she was dreaming. Or had gone mad. It seemed so short a time ago that he had been standing with a beautiful girl by a gleaming car —in *another* valley. But of course that was more than half a day ago!

Magool Ransome was standing there!

Out of the nothingness of his arrival, he actually smiled. He was real. She was not mad after all.

'Good evening, Mrs. Watson,' Magool said to the older

68

woman, taking his hat from his head and wiping his brow with his sleeve.

Mrs. Watson turned away from him and placed the fry-pan and the kettle in their places on the stove. He turned to Lisa. His grey-clear eyes were wrinkled at the corners, as this time he looked at *her alone*.

7

'And good evening to you too,' Magool said with mock courtesy. There was something faintly sardonic about his smile.

Lisa hoped he might not know who she was. She had described herself as daffodil-tall with piles of golden curls on top of her head. That was when he had been blind-folded at Finch's Creek. She had been 'having him on' then for the fun of it, and to punish him for his arrogant ways. Now she was to be hoist with her own petard, so her smile to him was only half lit.

In the midst of this lightning passage of thoughts, she realised something *was* indeed wrong. There was an urgency about the way he had come in uninvited.

'My grandfather . . . ?' she asked. 'Is it because of him you have come? What has happened?'

Magool came across the room, and put his hat on the end of the table, brim down, as Tom and the stockmen had done. He moved out a chair from the table with the toe of his boot. He sat down opposite Lisa, looking straight into her face.

'Yes,' Magool said slowly, speaking carefully, as if he did not want to alarm. 'Your grandfather—*Miss Lisa Tonkin*—has had a slight accident. Or so it seems. How-ever, not to worry. Not for the moment anyway.'

Lisa, confused and worried now, was silent.

'Where? What?' Mrs. Watson demanded, coming to the table. 'How would *you* know?'

Magool stood up again and drew out a chair for her. Mrs. Watson ignored this gesture.

'Jabberdee brought me the news,' he said. 'You know Jabberdee? He's the same tribe as your people up on the east side. He—'

'What has happened?' Mrs. Watson interrupted sharply.

Lisa realised, in a startled way, but for sure, that Mrs. Watson had indeed been worrying about 'Old-fella'. Somewhere inside that seemingly luke-warm heart the other woman had an affection for her employer.

'Do please sit down, Mrs. Watson,' Magool said, 'You'll feel easier that way. There's nothing to cause real anxiety *as far as we know*—as yet.'

Mrs. Watson sat down.

'Go on,' she demanded.

Lisa sat quite still, her wide eyes fixed on Magool Ransome's face.

'Jabberdee found Challenger astray,' he said. ' "Old-fella's" horse was hobbled out on the range near the Number Four Outcamp late in the morning. *This morning*. There was no camp smoke and no sign of the old man. So Jabberdee followed "Old-fella's" tracks down the granite slide and found him sitting with his back to the cliff wall. He was apparently unable, or unwilling, to move. He was quite conscious, and his usual snapping dictatorial self.' He paused, then added—'No broken limbs. Jabberdee left food with "Old-fella" and made off across the range to our muster camp. They radioed from there to Nangardee homestead.' Magool paused again; giving Lisa and Mrs. Watson time to take this in. The smile was gone. He was all authority now. His speech was a mixture of quick-fire and drawl. He took out tobacco and paper from his pocket and began to roll a cigarette. He glanced at Lisa.

'I instructed my men to send out a rescue party and bring him in,' he said. *'Whether the old man was willing to come or not.'* He finished rolling his cigarette, then added —'In other words, with or without his co-operation. I've enough faith in Jabberdee's witch-doctory to know there is something wrong with "Old-fella". Though perhaps nothing disastrous.'

'You sound very hard,' Lisa said, troubled.

'Not hard. Determined perhaps.'

'Why didn't you go and find out for yourself?' Mrs. Watson asked bitterly. She had forgotten that five minutes

70

earlier Magool had not been welcomed into Pardalote's homestead. 'You could have—'

He cut her short but not impolitely.

'I did what had to be done, the best and most expedient way. Please understand. I was at the homestead when the message came shortly after two o'clock. I arranged for reliable men to bring "Old-fella" home *here*. Where he belongs. That's why I'm here myself, and not *there*. You forget, Mrs. Watson, that only someone with authority, or a relative, may call in the Flying Doctor Service. Being stubborn, "Old-fella" doesn't have a transceiver service here at the homestead. You have to rely on McPhee. He's too many miles away.'

'If my grandfather is ill, how can we call the Flying Doctor?' Lisa asked quickly.

'I've already done that—from Nangardee. Before I set out, I'm here to tell you what has happened. Also to fix flares down the far end of your valley so Dr. Anderson can see to land. That is, if he decides to come to-night.'

'What impertinence!' Mrs. Watson exclaimed standing up. 'If "Old-fella" appeared his usual self, then there's probably nothing wrong with him. You've taken *him over* because he's an old man, and now you think you can take over Pardalote too. That's what you've always wanted, isn't it? *Tom's the overseer*. He'll raise trouble when he gets here. So will "Old-fella". They won't like more interference. Not from Nangardee.'

'Forewarned is forearmed,' Magool said mildly. 'In that case I'll ask Dr. Anderson to produce some man-sized hypodermics to put "Old-fella" to rest. The kind of hypodermics Miss Lisa Tonkon was fond of advocating at Finch's Creek.'

His eyes looked into Lisa's, and he actually smiled. At least his eyes smiled. They were commanding eyes, grey and not a bit slitty as Marjory Dean had said. They were clear and not blinded, thank God. They didn't even show wound scars.

For one guilty minute Lisa's thoughts strayed from 'Old-fella's' plight to take in the Impatient Patient in the role of a station owner. One who could successfully push around people like her grandfather, *and* Mrs. Watson. In a very ruthless way too.

'Shall I make you some tea? I could perhaps cook you something?' she said, jumping up, eager to ease her embarrassment: also to show gratitude for his coming with the news. Mrs. Watson was outraged by this suggestion coming from Lisa.

'I'll do that, if it is necessary,' she said shortly. 'I'll—'

'It's quite all right, thank you,' Magool replied. 'I've had something already. If you'll excuse me I'll get along and attend to the flares for the Flying Doctor. This, I repeat, is only in case it is necessary for him to come to-night.'

'There aren't any of our stockmen about,' Mrs. Watson said. 'They've all gone out to the muster.'

'I've Jabberdee, in company with his cousin Nooma from your way. I called a few more of the bush people from your east side. I left them putting down markers when I came in.'

There was a suspicion of a smile again in Magool's eyes as he glanced at Lisa.

'You did *what*?' Mrs. Watson asked. 'Those people are *our* aborigines. They take orders from no one but—'

'But someone like Jabberdee? He is someone they know has "Old-fella's" welfare at heart,' Magool said, still mildly. He pushed back his chair, reached for his hat and stood up. He moved towards the door. 'In case the old man is in need of bedside attention, you could perhaps get his room ready,' he reminded her. 'A bit of a meal for Dr. Anderson too. He may have an assistant-pilot if he has to come in at night. Depends *when* he is coming.

From the door he looked back.

'About Dr. Anderson—' Lisa began.

'I'm sure with all your hospital experience, Miss Tonkin,' Magool said, mocking, 'you'll know what to do with him when he comes. No bandages for the eyes, of course. But hypodermics without a doubt.'

'I'll see you out—' Lisa said with sudden determination. 'Excuse me please, Mrs. Watson. I won't be long.'

For once she was standing firm on her dignity. Magool Ransome had left too much unsaid.

He held the screen door while she went through.

Outside it was quiet night now. The sunset was lost long since over the range top for yet another day. Magool

72

stubbed out the butt-end of his cigarette on the gravel below the veranda as he jumped down, leaving Lisa standing alone, above him.

'Well?' he asked. 'Are you coming the long way down the valley to build small beacons and play it's Guy Fawkes night, Lisa?' he asked. 'Or are you going to wait for your grandfather here? Maybe you could show him a little loving kindness—*however* much he might pretend he has no time for such things.'

'I will wait here for my grandfather, of course,' she said. 'Please don't misunderstand me. I only wanted to ask you how you recognised me. I'm not as tall as I said. And I have dark, not fair hair: no curls—'

'Didn't I tell you back at Finch's Creek?' he asked, surprised, but really amused. 'I must have overlooked it. Matron, Sister Davitt, Nurse Dean, and even Gertie—all described your appearance to me. At intervals, of course. From time to time, as it were!'

'I didn't think of that! How stupid can one be! Why should they tell you about *me*?'

'I asked them, of course.'

'Oh!'

Lisa was deflated. Why should he have wanted to know—from others—what she looked like? He hadn't accepted what she said.

He kicked dried mud from his boot against a foundation stone. She could see his outline against the first pale light of the coming moonrise. Looking at his shadowy bent head had a curiously 'catching' effect on her heart-strings. It had something to do with his past helplessness when they had pushed those despised needles into him on the first and second day after his eye operation. That had touched her deeply. Big, strong, impatient, self-willed men like Mr. Station-owner Ransome were not meant by God, or nature, to be helpless.

'Then there is your voice—' he was saying as he looked up again. 'Even if I hadn't recognised you earlier I would have known your voice.'

Lisa said 'Oh!' again, in a very awed way.

'My voice is all right, I hope?' Her eyes, hidden by the shadows, were anxious and curious.

'With so many orders given, who wouldn't remember the

voice?' he said obliquely. He took his matches from his shirt pocket and lit yet another cigarette. She could see in the flare of the match the full oval of his face and a gleam in his eyes. 'Once a teacher of children—always a teacher of children!' he finished.

Lisa's back straightened.

'I was an "aide" not a teacher,' she reminded him firmly. 'I would have liked to have been a teacher. I didn't have the right qualifications.'

'I seem to remember you did tell me that before,' he remarked lightly.

'If you'll excuse me, I'll be going inside.' Lisa had a sudden compulsion to be gone. 'Mrs. Watson may need me. Besides, if you have really come to help my grandfather—'

'One minute, Lisa. Please. One cannot make haste in this situation. Distance, time and nightfall will prevent anyone bringing "Old-fella" in for quite some time. So let us be calm for our own sakes as well as for his sake.'

She had turned away, but now turned back. He stood on the gravel below the veranda, being very logical. She had to admit it. Moonrise was nearer now and the sky was lighter. She could see he'd clapped his hat back on his head.

'These preparations we are making here are in *case* they bring "Old-fella" in to-night,' he said. 'It is not at all certain that they will. Actually the terrain between the Number Four Outcamp at Knob's Hill, and the homestead, is extremely difficult.'

'But the Flying Doctor will come?'

'Not till he gets a further call from me. The beacons will be made ready, but not lit till I give the word. I didn't explain all that to Mrs. Watson because I felt she had to digest and accept my presence here. She needed time for the digestive process to get to work.'

'We haven't a transceiver set, and—'

'And McPhee's too far away: inaccessible at night anyway. Yes, I've thought all that out. I've a team of experts from down south working on some mineral veins on the Nangardee side of the range. There's a car with a two-way radio standing by, and can keep contact with Nangardee homestead. The message will go through to the

Flying Service base that way—as soon as Jabberdee brings in the word that they've got "Old-fella" as far as Pardalote boundary. I did mention before that he was in his right mind, had no broken limbs, and was his usual obstinate self? He's not in grave danger as yet.'

Lisa felt ashamed now, not only at her own impatience, but because she and Mrs. Watson had shown such poor hospitality in the face of the complicated organisation Magool Ransome had set in train. In such quick time too.

'When you've seen to the beacons you must come back here to the homestead,' she insisted. 'You can't stay out there all night. The temperatures drop—'

He had moved to the shade-tree and was loosening the reins of his horse. His laugh was a low teasing echo of his 'better' days at the hospital.

'I thought of doing just that myself,' he said.

Again Lisa was taken aback. While she had been giving her invitation she had been girding herself to the need to be persuasive. It hadn't been necessary. There wasn't anything he hadn't planned, even to the lengths of spending a night under Pardalote's roof. This in the face of Mrs. Watson's prohibitive dislike too! What kind of a man was he really?

With a vaulting movement he had mounted his horse. It side-stepped in a restless way to the veranda's edge. His teeth flashed in the shadow of his sun-browned face. He was smiling again—probably at women's foibles, for he guessed her embarrassment.

'Dear Lisa,' he said with a touch of irony in his voice. 'To make sure I get any message from the car on the other side of the range, or from Nangardee, I *also* have a two-way radio. Right here on my own saddle. You see? Nothing overlooked. You could break the news about modern gadgets to Mrs. Watson, like a good girl. She won't like it, but it'll save her a lot of worry in the long run. What with trackers, smoke signals, didgeridoos and transistor radios, "Old-fella" is not so very far away. And is being well and truly cared for.'

He slapped the reins on his horse's neck. A minute later he was no more than a dark silhouette against the home paddock lights galloping away down the valley.

Lisa watched him go, listening to every hoof beat until

75

she could no longer hear one sound in all the valley's silent world.

Magool Ransome was an enigma. She had better settle for that. How much easier to deal with someone blunt and straightforward like Tom Watson. If only Tom were here he would take over and she herself would know what to do: and how to do it so as not to offend his mother. Tom would be blunt about things: and that would be that! No quandaries!

Meantime she had to go and forewarn Mrs. Watson of Magool Ransome's possible return.

Oh dear, oh dear!

Inside the kitchen Mrs. Watson had finished grilling chops for her own meal. She had just placed them on a plate, together with some fried potatoes, and was putting the plate between her knife and fork on the table. She had this minute decided now was the time for her to eat, after all. It was something to *do* while one waited.

'So?' Mrs. Watson said, sitting down and not looking at Lisa at all. 'What were you talking about outside? What plans could you and that man from Nangardee be making? Don't you know your grandfather is not likely to have anything to do with those people over there? He hasn't trusted them for twenty years or more. Not that he's spoken of it. I just *know*.'

She attacked the food on her plate as if it too were the enemy. She wasn't very hungry, that was clear.

Lisa went to the stove and stirred the coals under the kettle. She put tea-leaves in the pot at the side.

'He was not being an untrustworthy neighbour to-night,' she explained quietly. 'I'm sure of that. He was doing an awful lot to see that "Old-fella" came in safely. And that he'll get attention—'

'You mean he left him to be brought in by the stockmen and aborigines? Meanwhile he's riding his horse up gorge and down slide over here? He should be out on the range doing something for "Old-fella".' She clattered her fork down on her plate. 'Bursting in our door without knocking—' she continued. 'What *manners*—'

'I have a feeling,' Lisa added, trying to placate, 'that

Mr. Ransome might have thought we would not open the door to him—once we saw who was there. My grandfather was more important to him just then perhaps than *our* feelings.'

'I'd have bolted and barred the door if I'd known who was there,' Mrs. Watson declared illogically.

In spite of the worry and anxiety of the moment, Lisa could not help one little smile as Mrs. Watson went on. It was all so illogical. If Magool Ransome had been bolted and barred out they would not have known what had happened to 'Old-fella', nor why he had not come in to dinner.

The tea hadn't drawn for very long, but Lisa guessed that its appearance in a cup would be a solace to Mrs. Watson. A cup of tea was always that to herself. She poured out two cups and brought them to the table.

How to break her news that they might have a visitor for the night? And that visitor—the terrible man from Nangardee?

Lisa sipped her tea. After a minute she put her cup down, her elbows on the table and her chin on her hands. She decided to tell Mrs. Watson the 'Magool Ransome way'—Make a statement of fact, straight from the shoulder! Maybe it was the only way.

'As we don't seem to have a spare room around—unless we could use Tom's room,' she suggested, 'I think we'd better make up a stretcher in here. We're likely to have a visitor.'

Mrs. Watson's head went up with a jerk.

'You mean the Flying Doctor? Dr. Anderson?'

'Goodness me! I forgot the doctor! How dreadful! He might not necessarily be piloting his plane himself—so Mr. Ransome said. He might have an assistant. That would mean *three* stretchers. Have we three stretchers?'

'You mean has "Old-fella" three stretchers? I have not been told that you own anything here, Lisa. There is no occasion for the "we". In any case why three? Even with an assistant, Dr. Anderson is not likely to sleep in two beds at once.'

Lisa sipped her tea again. She had an uneasy feeling she was making a mess of this, after all.

'I was thinking of Mr. Ransome,' she said, with an effort of being matter-of-fact. 'We could hardly expect him to sleep on the floor . . . Well, not after all he's done.'

Mrs. Watson was silent for five explosive seconds.

'Mr. Ransome? You mean that man from Nangardee?' she demanded at length. '*Sleep* here? Over my . . .' She broke off, swallowing hard. ' "Old-fella" would die before he was carried over the threshold *if he knew*. He won't allow it.'

' "Old-fella",' Lisa reminded her gently, 'maybe could be very ill when he is eventually carried over the threshold. In any case we don't know what would happen to him if it weren't for all that man from Nangardee is doing.'

Whatever Mrs. Watson had been about to say, she did not now say it. She folded her lips together as if to close in her own words. She looked at Lisa with suspicion and an obscure sort of anxiety in her eyes.

Lisa drank her tea slowly, watching the door as she did so. In an irrational way she wished or hoped that it would open, and that magically Magool Ransome, with 'Old-fella', would be standing there.

The silence was long and not very golden, so after a minute or two she glanced at Mrs. Watson. The other woman had stopped eating; her hands were on her lap, moveless. She was looking at the far end of the table where 'Old-fella's' place was still set, as for dinner. His chair was drawn up before it. Her face was shadowed.

Behind the veneer of crossness and jealous guardianship, Mrs. Watson had a heart after all. At least, Lisa thought so. With relief too.

For the first time since Magool Ransome had come in with his frightening news, she herself wanted to relax herself. She'd had quite a day! Come a long way—in mind as well as body.

Meantime, three beds were to be made up. One for the Flying Doctor; one for his pilot—if any.

One for Magool Ransome.

There was much to do.

8

Minutes dragged by that evening. And so did the hours.

Mrs. Watson took to baking as if preparing for an invasion. The fire was stoked up, and out came all manner of mixing bowls.

'The beds—' Lisa reminded her. 'Shouldn't we . . . ?'

'We shall do nothing till we see who comes. If "Old-fella" comes first he will make the decisions. It's his homestead.'

Lisa felt flattened, not for the first time.

'Well,' she suggested, 'will you please let me help with the baking? I'd love to do that. And I really can, you know. My mother taught me—'

She broke off. Mrs. Watson was staring at her over a mountain of pastry dough on the floured board. Over the rolling pin too.

Lisa was saying the wrong thing again. All the same, Mrs. Watson was being deliberately unkind.

No, she wasn't quite all that. She had minded very much that 'Old-fella' was somewhere out on the range; and that there was something wrong with him. Lisa, too, minded. Very much. But alas, she had to do everything to hide the fact. She was not allowed to care about her grandfather, that was clear. Nor mention her mother.

'I'll go and get my mending,' she said in desperation at last. 'I'm always breaking the shoulder straps on my underclothes, and we can't buy little gold safety-pins up here, can we? No shops!'

She caught Mrs. Watson's eye, and her spirits sank.

Saying the wrong thing again! Talking about gold safety pins, indeed.

Lisa fled.

The night hours crept along, one by one. Nothing could be heard outside but the occasional cry of a night bird. The silence almost shouted, it was so noticeable.

Even as Lisa was thinking this, she saw Mrs. Watson stiffen and turn her head as if listening. Lisa too lifted her head and listened. There was a new sound in the distance. It was the fast clip-clop of a horse coming up the valley.

Neither spoke until the sounds came nearer. Mrs. Watson dropped her shoulders for a moment, then began, almost as a protest, to rattle and bang the cooking utensils as she put them away. Whoever this was coming up the valley, she patently did not approve. Lisa, less accustomed to recognising sounds in the silences of the North, knew the visitor would not please, nor be welcomed.

She dropped her head over her sewing again—to hide her hope that the rider in the still night might be Magool Ransome coming to the homestead again. He would be company! And might be bringing news!

The horse came to a halt by the cadjebut tree outside. For the second time that night, strong meaningful footsteps crunched across the veranda. Lisa recognised them this time. She did not wait for Mrs. Watson's reaction, but dropped her sewing and went to the screen door. For the sake of good manners, she thought, and for no other reason at all, she could not let him come in unwelcomed twice in one night.

She reached the screen door as Magool came from the veranda. They stood looking at each other across the shadows through the wire mesh.

'Any news?' Lisa asked, trying to sound impersonal as she opened the door.

'Yes,' he said briefly as he came in. He glanced at Mrs. Watson's hostile face. 'The situation is much the same as before. They won't be able to get "Old-fella" off the range to-night, I'm afraid. He's not particularly willing to come, you know. And the gorges are dark and treacherous up along those parts.'

'But he is all right?' Lisa persisted anxiously. 'Please, will you come and sit down? I will make some supper—'

'Yes, he's all right,' Magool said wearily now. He walked to the table and put his hat at the far end again, just as he had done before.

He's making himself very much at home, Lisa thought with relief. *And so he should—considering* . . .

Aloud she repeated her question. 'But my grandfather is all right? How do you know, Mr. . . . er . . .'

80

'Magool,' he prompted, glancing up at her and nearly smiling. '*Jim for short*. I did mention that before, didn't I? There were no "misters" at Finch's Creek. Remember?'

Mrs. Watson looked from one to the other, startled and suspicious.

'How do you know he is all right?' Lisa repeated, not quite knowing how else to answer him. Her own eyes were dark pools and her face had that stillness about it that hid her vulnerability.

'The two-way radio, infant. I thought I mentioned that little modern gadget earlier. Didn't I?'

'You mean you could contact someone on top of the range from out there? From right down the valley?'

Mrs. Watson was listening, her face keen and sharp, her heart wanting news too, but not forgetting her suspicions of these two and their knowledge of each other at another time, and elsewhere.

Magool sat down on the same chair he had sat on before. He pulled a small rectangular box out of his hip-pocket and put it on the table.

'There it is,' he said. 'Try it for yourself, Lisa—' He looked up and this time she saw real tiredness, like a dull cloud, at the back of his eyes. 'I would like that cup of tea,' he added. 'Did I dream you mentioned it?'

Lisa felt compunction but she dared not show it.

She longed to take up the radio and gather news for herself. Instead she went to the fire and lifted the simmering kettle to the middle of the stove.

Mrs. Watson moved to the end of the table and stood looking down at her seated unwelcome guest. Magool made a gesture as if to rise, but she stopped him.

'You may continue to sit,' she said. 'I prefer to stand. I want to know what your news is. And *now*.'

'I did tell you, Mrs. Watson,' Magool said with the kind of mildness that could mean anything from a cat purring to a lion roaring. 'Everything is as it was before. "Old-fella" is resting out on the gorge-side about a mile from the Number Four muster area. Jabberdee and his off-siders are with him, and are looking after him. He couldn't be in better hands. They report nothing serious except the old man's stubbornness. Or could it be . . . ?' He broke off, letting the question hang, ominous on the air.

There was a sudden silence in the room.

Could it be that 'Old-fella' knew better than even Jaberdee?

Lisa poured boiling water into the tea-pot. She brought cups and saucers to the table.

Mrs. Watson moved at last. She went to the work bench near the stove and put hot biscuits on a plate.

'Or could it be *what*?' she asked, dully. 'What were you going to say?' She was no longer angry nor unwelcoming.

Lisa, pouring the tea, guessed the thought that lay unspoken between Mrs. Watson and Magool Ransome. *A game old horse stays game; ruler and sire to his paddock; then one day a stockman comes in and reports—'The old stallion is down!'*

In such a case the station-owner silently takes down his rifle, and with a certain sad deliberation goes out to the paddock.

The only sound in the kitchen was the fall of a live coal in the stove.

None of them looked at the other for quite a minute.

Mrs. Watson sat down on the chair at her end of the table.

'I'll have a cup of tea too, thank you, Lisa,' she said. All the enmity, anger and dislike had gone out of her voice. It was empty.

Magool drew his cup and saucer towards him.

'So you see?' he said gravely, 'until we get a doctor to see him there are always possibilities. Meantime it is best to be prepared. At the same time, let's remember that "Old-fella" may be no more than over-tired. Taking a rest *his* way. And, as usual, resenting interference.' Magool glanced from Lisa's quiet face to Mrs. Watson. 'We just can't take a risk, can we?' he asked. 'We'll have to treat him as a casualty until he proves to us he's not. I think he will do that quickly enough if all is reasonably well. These biscuits are the best ever, Mrs. Watson. I'll have to introduce the recipe to Nangardee. That is, if you'll be good enough to give it to me.'

Mrs. Watson did not reply. Possibly she did not register his last kindly words. Her eyes were on the small rectangular box on the table. Lisa too, as she took a bite of biscuit, looked at it as if *it* was the problem child of their anxiety. It knew all the secrets of what was going on out on the range. It could hear all, from over the top at Nangardee, and even what was going on down the far end of their own valley.

Magool picked the box up and turned it over in his hand.

'Would you like to hear me make contact, Mrs. Watson?' he asked. She very nearly said—'*No. Modern gadgets were not for the people on Pardalote. "Old-fella" would have none of them.*'

Magool saw her dilemma and understood it. He waited in silence.

Lisa spoke for her.

'Please, Magool,' she said. 'Yes, we would like you to do that. There might be more news. Even good news—'

He pulled the little silver knob out and with it drew a long slim rod. Each small length of this rod was partially cuffed over the next length so that when all was out there was about three feet of rod. By lifting a trap-lid at the front of the box, he revealed a kind of grating. With one finger he turned a small dial. The room was filled with crackling sounds. Magool adjusted the dial. Then the crackling ceased. There was a fractional silence before a woman's clear voice came through—filling the room with sound as if, magically, she was actually present.

'NS 215 here. That you PS 219?'

'Yes, it's me, Nellie,' Magool spoke into the box. 'The homestead closed down for the night?'

'Except for me. I'm listening-in till one o'clock. We've made a roster so someone will stand by the set through the night.'

'Good girl. Meantime have you heard anything from the camp at the top of the range since I last called?'

'No, except that Imelda made contact, just to make sure the air was open.'

To Lisa, concentrating on the magic box, the name Imelda startled her. She actually felt a stab. A real one. She had seen two-ways being used before. Taxi drivers used them to contact their base. She'd even seen men working on the tops of high buildings listening-in to instructions from the construction engineer far below at ground level. But she'd never dreamed of anything so small and therefore magical, as this tiny pocket-sized two-way in Magool's hand. And that this little box should pinpoint a sore spot inside herself so accurately—speaking that name 'Imelda' seemed stranger than fact.

She shook her head as if to move cobwebs. Why should Imelda—either transporting Magool Ransome away from the hospital, or being spoken of through this miniature box—bother her?

'Right!' Magool was saying. 'I'd call Imelda myself but can't make clear contact over the range from down here in the valley. I hope she doesn't mind too much about waiting around for hours. If she calls you again, thank her for standing by from me. And Nellie? Don't forget to give her my love, will you? She'll know what I mean. That's a password.'

'She won't mind standing by,' the voice came back. 'She's likely to do anything for you, Boss—bar miss her breakfast at the homestead to-morrow morning. Imelda's a pretty good scout—all things considered. Over.'

'Coming from you, Nellie, that's wisdom on the night air. She's a good scout all right. She'll keep watch. Over for now. Good night.'

'Over. Good night, Boss.'

Mrs. Watson was sitting transfixed, her eyes not leaving the radio for a single minute. She looked as if she was seeing the Aurora Borealis for the first time and being forced to admit there was such phenomena.

'We must fix up a bed . . .' Lisa said a little awkwardly.

Mrs. Watson shook her head and came back to the realm of Pardalote's kitchen.

'Yes of course.' Her voice was monotonous as if she was 'giving-in' to something, yet not understanding why she did so. 'That sofa over there between the door and the window. It can be made into a bed. We won't need any others now—'

Lisa wanted to suggest Tom's room. A sofa in the kitchen-living-room seemed to her poor hospitality for a neighbour doing good. She hadn't the right kind of courage to make such a decision herself.

In an uncanny way Magool sensed the dilemma. He pressed down the radio's mast, closed the side that concealed the mouth-piece, then looked up at Lisa. He was wearing his own brand of inimical smile.

'I like to sleep on a sofa,' he said. 'Specially one in a firelit room. I'm told they're worth a lot on the "colonial" antique market. I'll have the pleasant feeling of sleeping on wealth.'

Mrs. Watson had no idea how to take this. Lisa was suddenly sorry for her. Magool's presence in the homestead was relentlessly tearing Mrs. Watson into two people. One who was secretly relieved that this strong-minded neighbour, with his radio gadget, was looking after 'Old-fella'. The other who resented the intruder for being who he was: the enemy from over the range.

It was half an hour before they all settled down for the remainder of the night. Lisa made-up the sofa with bed clothes, showed Magool where he could find the shower-room, gave him Tom's pyjamas, and offered him yet another cup of tea. She did all this delicately so as not to affront Mrs. Watson's prior claim to be the suzeraine of 'Old-fella's' home.

The 'good nights' were quick and perfunctory, for by this time, Mrs. Watson was back to being a closed shell. Magool looked as if he was barely hiding the irritating fact that he was enjoying a kind of amusement at Lisa's expense.

There was one compensation. Lisa decided that Magool could not have looked like this—producing a prize-size series of good manners, and been near to teasing form again—if he did not feel sure that all would go well with 'Old-fella'.

He couldn't have been that heartless.

In the morning the whole world of the valley changed.

Magool was up and showered first and had made tea for

all—including Mrs. Watson. The two-way radio had told him shortly after sunrise that the men were already bringing 'Old-fella' in. It would be another two hours, they thought, before they got him to the lower end of the valley. There had been no change in his condition.

'My *aide-de-camp* over the range has taken things into her own hands and contacted the Flying Doctor, Mrs. Watson,' Magool said over the top of a tea cup. 'Can you prepare for an invasion by mid-morning?'

Mrs. Watson pushed back her chair and moved away to look at the state of her fire in the stove.

'Yes, so long as they don't make a mess about the place,' she said almost ungraciously, back turned.

The absence of bad news concerning 'Old-fella' seemed good news so far as she was concerned. Her manner indicated the invasion from Nangardee should be over and gone as soon as possible. She would see to that.

Lisa tried being cheerful.

'What a good thing you did all that cooking last night, Mrs. Watson. I mean . . . the cakes and biscuits. The soup too. They'll love that. Specially Tom. I can't help being sure Tom must have heard *something* of the news, and he'll come riding home again. I have a feeling—'

'How would he hear the news?' Mrs. Watson asked. '*He* doesn't have one of those radio things Mr. Ransome was so anxious to show off last night. "Old-fella" wouldn't allow it—'

'Do I detect a note of triumph?' Magool asked—gently teasing even Mrs. Watson. 'Tom, like the good overseer, is doubtless minding his own business out at the muster. Goings-on in homesteads when the big muster is on would be of no concern to him. First things first—with Tom?'

'Most of the year you would be right, Mr. Ransome,' Mrs. Watson said abruptly. 'But any mishap to "Old-fella" would concern Tom. It's his business. Besides . . .' She stopped and glanced at Lisa. A new thought had entered her mind. A thought that would settle Magool Ransome for his aspersions against her son. 'Besides—' she repeated meaningly. 'We have a *visitor* with us now. Lisa. That makes things different doesn't it? Tom approves of Lisa. He has taken her riding. You can see for yourself she hopes he will hear the news—*and come home*. Tom isn't *all* cattle, musters, and sale-prices. I can tell you that for sure, Mr. Ransome.

Lisa's eyes widened, then once again became still pools that even Mrs. Watson could not fathom. It was the same 'waiting' expression that had so concerned, yet bewitched, the staff and patients at Finch's Creek. Lisa sat very still. Her face in its quiet gentle way was so very still too.

Magool watched her thoughtfully.

'So Tom the overseer,' he said slowly, 'has his *charms* for some? Is that what you are telling me, Mrs. Watson?'

Lisa did not speak. She was thinking that Magool Ransome also had his charms for some. They were reciprocated, if his *aide-de-camp*, whom he had called a 'she', was prepared to stay out on the range half of yesterday and most of last night to help him. That 'she' must be the not-so-mythical *Imelda*. She was only continuing the role she had begun by whisking Magool away from Finch's Creek. Imelda was the one who had seen to it Magool had ceased to be a patient and become very much a gone-away man. *He hadn't even said good-bye—*

Magool put down his cup and began searching for cigarette makings in his shirt pocket.

'Why so silent, Lisa?' he asked quietly.

'Was I silent?' She looked up, perplexed.

'Very much so. You were "not-with-us". Were you dreaming of a beat of horse-hooves coming up the valley— Tom riding homewards from the muster?'

'Why yes, I suppose I might have been.' Lisa was not thinking very clearly. She wondered just what she really had been thinking about. Something to do with Tom hearing the news. And about Imelda. About Finch's Creek and people who helped one another. About those who just went away. *Someone called Imelda.*

Imagined visions of Imelda's reputed beauty clouded Lisa's eyes. Someone at Finch's Creek had called her 'stunning'.

But, of course, she couldn't tell Magool all that. Thoughts were very private things—even when they were muddled.

So Lisa only blinked her eyes as she looked back into his grey ones.

Mrs. Watson came to the table and picked up the tea-pot.

She looked at them both sharply. She, also, was thinking her own thoughts.

'That's to let them know,' she decided, '*about Tom thinking a lot of Lisa*. The sooner Tom gets in the better. If I had one of those two-way boxes I'd get in touch with McPhee. He'd let Tom know what's going on here. That man from Nangardee sitting in Tom's very own chair! Lisa making him welcome! She ought to have told him to sit in a different chair. Gadgets or not, I'll tell "Old-fella" to get a radio—' Her thoughts broke off.

Ah, but if 'Old-fella' were really sick! What then?

Her face looked tired, as if she hadn't slept well. There was no one to see this expression except the fire flames licking up as she stirred the wood in the stove. Her back was turned on the two at the table again.

'Well, if you'll excuse me, Mrs. Watson? Lisa?' Magool, making a snap decision, was getting up and retrieving his hat from the end of the table as he spoke. 'There are things to be done down the far end of the valley. I can call the beacon watchers off.' He paused for a fraction of a second. 'Thank you for putting me up,' he added.

He did not look back as he went to the screen door, opened it, thrust his broad-brimmed slouch hat on his head, and went out.

Gone-away again! Lisa thought. She wondered why she minded.

She listened to his heavy booted feet cross the veranda, followed by a thump as he leapt down to the gravel below. *Gone-away again!*

She pushed her chair back and stood up. There was much to do. She mustn't sit here idly: day dreaming! The sofa had to be cleared of bedclothes; the room straightened. Everything had to be made clean and shining for 'Old-fella's' homecoming. She doubted if he would notice it. She had a kind of feeling that he had settled long long ago for the kept side of the homestead as being 'fit only for women's work'. He was that much of a patriarch.

For Tom too—if he did get the news and come in?

A clean and shining home would be a good thing altogether.

All men, she had been taught, were thankful for a home-coming that was cheerful and good; all things done that ought to have been done.

Then there was Imelda, of course, *if she came*. Supposing she really did? No single Imelda in all the world was going to find one speck of dust, one thing out of place, in Pardalote's homestead!

Oh bother Imelda! She's probably a hundred miles away!

He had gone-away, again. Just gone-away!

Mrs. Watson was so deep in her thoughts she did not notice Lisa's busyness, both in the kitchen and elsewhere. Lisa was thankful for this aberration, for otherwise she guessed she would have been forbidden to do this and forbidden to do that.

Mrs. Watson was jealous of her own rights in her own provinces.

It was half past eleven when the silence of the valley was broken again. A stockman rode up—a stranger. A man from Nangardee. He slipped his reins on the saddling-post and rolled, very bow-legged, towards the side veranda. Lisa and Mrs. Watson were already there waiting for him.

'We fetched "Old-fella" down as far as the foot of the cleft just south of the wait-abit patch,' he said. 'The chaps are bringin' him across now. Where's the Boss?'

'You mean that man from Nangardee?' Mrs. Watson asked coldly. 'He's . . .'

'How is my grandfather?' Lisa asked quickly. 'Please Mister . . . er . . .'

'Plain Bob, Miss. That's my name. The old man's kinda okay, in a way. Jes' his same rakin' bad-tempered red-kangaroo-self, excusin' my language. But he won't walk. Not a step. Could be no more'n plain stubborn-like. But what for? Well, he's not tellin'. Jes' won't get up an' walk.'

'It was good of you to bring us the news,' Lisa said. 'He can't be too bad? Too *ill* I mean?'

'Well, sick-like, if you know what I mean. It's a good sign he's blowin' his trump an' raisin' all hell when we make him turn on his side the way it's easiest to get him down the gorge. Shows he's not kinda dying, anyway. That's for sure.'

'I'll get my hat and come at once,' Mrs. Watson said.

'That's jes' what you can't do, lady,' the stockman said. 'Beggin' your pardon for givin' orders round your own place. We gotta get this old man over here ourselves, or the mob'll beat us to it from Nangardee. Like they reckoned they'd bring 'im in first. Then words 'ud fly. Fists too. Too many bosses around, if you ask me. I jes' came in to say "Old-fella" Lindsay's on his way. If Boss Ransome comes in will you kindly tell him all's okay?'

He looked at Lisa. His brown tight-skinned face was dead-pan but his eyes had a hint of a grin in them.

'You bein' "Old-fella's" gran'daughter,' he added, 'you'll tell Magool, will you? Fer sure? I don't want to get taken to pieces, like he can do when he wants. Very particular is Magool. An' some more too, if you get what I mean?'

'Yes, of course *we'll* tell him,' Lisa said, smiling her sunshine smile for the first time in days. 'We have everything prepared here. Magool has a two-way on his saddle. You could perhaps contact him that way—'

'Maybe have Miss Bossy from over at Nangardee pick up the message? Then come licking up the dust in that glory-be limousine of hers? Make one Boss too many—too soon, that would. Not that she won't be here soon enough anyway. She's kinda like that. Gotta be in on the kill *first*. Well, this time we got her beat. Square an' fair.'

Lisa puzzled over what he meant by this last—almost as if there was a race on. He reeled away in his born-in-the-saddle walk to the saddling-post where his horse was tethered.

With one vault he was in the saddle and a minute later was no more than a thunder of hooves and a cloud of dust, racing away to the west.

'How will we get his message to Magool?' Lisa asked helplessly.

'All to the good if we don't,' Mrs. Watson said shortly. '*I* will look after "Old-fella" till the doctor gets here. It is not the first time I've nursed sickness on this station. We have no further use for those people from Nangardee now.'

'Oh . . . but . . .' Lisa protested. 'They have been very

good. Specially this man and the others bringing in my grandfather. What would we have done without them? Oh . . .' She broke off because Mrs. Watson had gone inside while she was still speaking. *If only I could go to meet my grandfather!* She told the empty air. *Why not? Even on foot—except that I would offend everyone. Specially Mrs. Watson.*

What a ridiculous situation!

She looked down the distant reaches of the valley, and immediately forgot her irritation. A tiny speck in the sky, between the two wall-ends of the valley, was becoming larger second by second. The light caught its wings—way up there, and something gleamed mirror-like. Sunlight was glancing on the sides of an aeroplane.

Below, along the floor of the valley was a fast moving cloud of dust. Another horseman was coming—this time from the north end. It had to be Magool. He, with that two-way, would have known the Flying Doctor was about to arrive.

Suddenly everything was all right. 'Old-fella' was on his way home, and please God, coming to what Magool had called *loving* kindness. The Flying Doctor was coming. Magool was coming. All was well in this strange world, after all.

Lisa turned to run in to tell Mrs. Watson. Then she stopped and stared, for a movement from the opposite end of the valley had caught her eye. That was the way she had driven in from Finch's Creek with her grandfather. It was yet *another* dust cloud coming. Being a big cloud and moving very fast, this couldn't be another horseman. It was a car!

The stockman's rival helper from Nangardee? One more of the 'too many bosses'? Would it be the 'good scout' dust-flying along in a glory-be limousine?

Right inside Lisa a tiny inner voice went into conference with itself.

'Here,' it warned—and rather like the stockman, not being very glad about it. 'Here comes Imelda. *If it really is Imelda who is the "good scout".* Now what are you going to do about this, oh Lisa, dear Lisa?'

The rider from the north and the car from the south would meet, any minute now, right in the gravel square by the home paddock.

Lisa couldn't bear to see it.

She went inside.

She would rather experience an earthquake than watch Magool Ransome kiss Imelda.

9

From outside came the thrumming sound of the plane flying low overhead.

Lisa watched it through a window. It circled over the homestead, then swooped low into the air-stream from the south. Down the valley the engines cut low. Then out.

Lisa breathed out again. The Flying Doctor was safe and down on the ground.

She went to the dressing-table and began to do things to her hair and face, without quite knowing what she did: or why. She dropped her hands to the table and stared at herself in the mirror.

'I'm not doing this for me,' she thought. 'Not for Dr. Anderson, either. He won't remember seeing me at Finch's Creek. It's not for my grandfather. He wouldn't notice, on purpose. It's certainly not for Magool Ransome. That goes without saying. But Imelda—*if it is Imelda*?' Well, Marjory Dean said she was beautiful. One girl looking at another was not always as kind as she might be. Maybe the Indians put on war paint for courage. She couldn't win in a battle of 'looks', of course. She only wanted to pass scrutiny unimpaired, as it were. Match-up just that little bit! Not feel small! Oh blow! What could it matter anyway!

Lisa went back to grooming her hair, and examining her mild-seeming make-up. Nothing too noticeable. That would be fatal. Everyone would wonder *why*.

She changed her shirt but not her shorts; and her scuffs for sandals.

She felt better. *Prepared* as it were. A Spartan before

Phillipi—that was Lisa on the moment before meeting Imelda.

She went back to the kitchen. Mrs. Watson was already poking the fire coals and refilling the kettle.

'So many people outside!' Lisa said. 'A car came. And I think Magool Ransome on his horse. Did you hear the plane come in? Shall I go and see?'

Silence.

Lisa's spirits dropped one inch.

'Shall I put out cups and saucers then? And some of the cakes and biscuits you made yesterday?' She ventured a second try at being helpful.

'Yes, do that. Don't touch the special cakes I've put in the blue tin for "Old-fella".'

'You've made special ones? Oh, I'm so glad you did. He'll need the feeling of *home-coming*, won't he?'

'They're bringing him across from the west side now,' Mrs. Watson said. 'Half the area's tribe is with him. Strange how all these people manage to arrive *at the same time*. Something peculiar about it.'

'Not peculiar. Maybe—' Lisa suggested lightly, as she set out cakes on two plates, then put them on the table. 'It's that two-way radio. Magool Ransome is quite an organiser, isn't he?'

Mrs. Watson turned and stared at Lisa coldly.

'Don't mention that name *Magool Ransome* when "Old-fella" is brought in,' she advised. 'It will make him angry.'

Lisa had the sugar bowl in one hand; somehow suspended in air.

'But . . .' she said, puzzled. 'He'll have to know won't he? I mean—my grandfather will have to know how he was rescued. Magool's been quite wonderful really. He's done so much—'

'You don't know what you are talking about, Lisa. No one from Nangardee has ever done anything except for an *ulterior* motive. Something to be gained from it. That man Ransome has been trying to mix-in with Pardalote affairs for a long time. He's up to something for his own gain. I'm sure of that. 'Old-fella' says nothing of course. But that's his way with everything.'

'But . . .'

'Don't argue with me, Lisa. And don't ask questions. Just mind what I say. If you have to talk to someone it had best be Tom. Tom's the overseer and he knows what's best for Pardalote. "Old-fella" isn't so sure of things these days. Tom's trustworthy. You must lean on *him*, Lisa.'

Lisa was so surprised at this news she didn't know what to say next. There was quite a silence except for the rattle of a cup on saucer as she put it in its place uneasily.

Suddenly she lifted her head. From outside came the noise of many voices. It could have been a real corroboree of bush people out there.

'They're coming,' Lisa said, glancing hopefully at Mrs. Watson. She would have given anything to run out to meet her grandfather. Somehow she knew Mrs. Watson would resent it if she did.

'Please Mrs. Watson, do let us go outside? He will be expecting us . . . At least, expecting *you*, I'm sure. He'll be looking forward to the special tea you make him. And those cakes.'

Mrs. Watson untied the strings of her apron. Lisa thought how nicely groomed the housekeeper was this morning. Not one prim hair out of place. No lipstick, but just the smallest dash of powder.

She really does want to give grandfather a welcome, Lisa thought. *She's not all hard words and cold looks. Underneath she does have a heart!*

'See that the kettle is kept boiling,' Mrs. Watson said. 'And watch the scones in the oven. I made a new lot—'

She was moving away as she spoke, so neither she nor Lisa heard the sound of footsteps. Shadows were thrown across the screen door. Two figures were standing there.

Magool, more polite than yesterday, knocked with his knuckles on the door frame. Then, unbidden, he opened the door. He stood aside to let his companion enter first.

'May we come in?' he asked. Neither Lisa nor the housekeeper answered, for they were wholly absorbed looking at the young woman he had brought with him.

Lisa tried hard not to *stare*. Her way of covering her surprise was for her face to go very still and picture-like again. She was at a loss—and thinking. Her sea-blue eyes were luminous and questioning, yet they said nothing: only *asked*.

'Miss Imelda Bannister,' Magool said. 'Mrs. Watson, Pardalote's housekeeper, Imelda. And this mouse-quiet girl over by the table is Miss Lisa . . .'

'Don't tell me,' Imelda interrupted. 'Let me think . . . !'

She was, as Marjory Dean had said, quite stunningly beautiful—in a sun-touched outback way. She wore a marvellous simple, yet perfectly tailored, tan-coloured shirt and khaki slacks. On her bright brown head sat, slightly angled, a fashion version of the bush hat. Her face was a silken smooth tan, oval, and brightened by a kind of professional smile. Her eyes were hazel. Dazzling gem-like hazel eyes—

Lisa's heart dropped. Why had she, herself, bothered with that hair-comb, and the modest make-up.

'Don't tell me, Jim—' Imelda implored again, making a striking staying gesture with one hand held high in the air. 'She's—? Now, let me see. What *did* they say about her? It will come to me in a minute.'

Lisa simply stood and stared.

'My dear girl,' Imelda said, in a comforting way as if to a child. 'What on earth are you looking at? I'm not an apparition, you know. You really are taking quite an interest in me, aren't you?'

Disdainfully Mrs. Watson went through the door to the veranda. Clearly she did not approve of the company. She had gone, *and gone alone*, to meet 'Old-fella'. His granddaughter was not wanted, at the moment.

'I'm sorry,' Lisa said. Her eyes had a 'lost' look in them for a fraction of a second. Except that Magool had opened the door for Mrs. Watson, no one seemed to mind that the housekeeper had gone without a word to either guest.

Imelda sat down at the table, casual-like, but in a graceful way. She was quite at home. Lisa waited for Magool to say something. Even *do* something.

'Well, here we are, Lisa,' he said—too casually to be true. 'You have met Imelda, haven't you? Imelda Bannister? She came to the hospital at Finch's Creek and met all my nurses—'

'No,' Lisa said quietly. 'I must have been out.'

Imelda's beautiful eyebrows shot up.

'Out,' she asked, incredulous. 'Where is there to go "out" at Finch's Creek?'

'Walking, I dare say,' Magool suggested, watching Lisa with that 'amused' smile again. 'This is Lisa from Pardalote, Imelda—if that is what you were trying to recollect. She's very much given to walking. She's only been on the station a very short time, and I'm sure if she's already walked east, south, and north of the valley—as well as *the west side*—why then she's not yet walked quite round the earth.'

He had underlined the west side, and Lisa heard the underlining. *He couldn't possibly know . . . or could he?*

Her eyes asked a question but he was fishing for his cigarette makings in his pocket. He was no longer looking at either his subject for jest, or Imelda.

Lisa's eyes came back to Imelda's face. The visitor had idly picked up a biscuit from a plate and nibbled it.

This is Mrs. Watson's kitchen, Lisa wanted to say. *Mind your manners!*

'For goodness sake!' Imelda demanded between bites of the biscuit, 'why must you look like that? I'm just an ordinary visitor, you know. It's always pleasant to visit the more remote homesteads. Isn't it, Jim darling?' She glanced up at him in a very companionable way. 'Is her face moulded, or something, Jim? Does she find it difficult to talk? She's quite pretty really, isn't she?'

Lisa was wearing her 'portrait' look, but had no idea of it. Magool, lifting his head from the ritual of cigarette making, observed it with interest.

'Not moulded,' Lisa answered for him, quite gently. 'I sometimes laugh. And sometimes I've cried—oh, quite a lot. I suppose my muscles must have worked then—'

'Good for you,' Imelda laughed. She turned her head to Magool. '*Got it!*' she said with delight. 'Now I remember. This is the girl who was asking her way to Pardalote —across the North. *The girl no one came for at Finch's Creek.* Good heavens!'

Magool wet the cigarette paper, slowly drawing the whole thing along the line of his lips. He looked over the top of his handicraft at Lisa: and really smiled, almost like a conspirator. Except it couldn't be that.

96

A wintry smile, barely seen then gone, came back in response.

'Someone clearly came for her in the long run,' he said. 'You didn't walk here by any chance, Lisa? I know you are very good at climbing.'

So he *did* know she'd been up the west side? But how?

Her chin lifted fractionally. Her pride, already wounded by Imelda's words, came steadfastly to her aid.

'I didn't walk, Mr. Ransome,' she said gravely, her face a still-painting of itself. 'My grandfather came for me at Finch's Creek. I was always sure he would do that—when he knew exactly where I was.'

'For heaven's sake, Jim!' Imelda exclaimed. 'She sounds like a text out of a book, or something.'

Lisa's eyes came back to Imelda. How perfectly Imelda was dressed even for mountain ranges in the outback! The clothes were dead right. Her face had a kind of luminous shine to its tan: the colour in her cheeks was natural. Her hair under that fashion-version of a bush hat was a bright gold-brown. Not quite a natural. But then everybody did things to their hair to make it shine! Lisa forgave Imelda that artifice; but not the words *'the girl nobody came for'*. They had cut deep.

Imelda looked at Lisa again with a sort-of amused curiosity. She laughed. 'She really is out of this world, Jim. Quite naïve, but sweet. She didn't come out of an orphanage by any chance?'

'Did you, Lisa?' he asked, that small smile still on his lips. She thought, or dreamed, there was almost a promise of help-at-hand in it. Yet . . . ?

Oh well! It was a pleasant dream all the same.

She shook her head so lightly that only Magool Ransome saw she was negating some fleeting fancy.

'No,' she said aloud. 'I told you when you were a patient at Finch's Creek, Mr. Ransome, exactly who I was. It was you who asked the questions then.'

'Quite right. I remember distinctly!' he said. 'You were a kindergarten teacher! That's it! I'm right, aren't I?'

'No,' Lisa said slowly, and extra quietly. Two could play at this game, she thought. He was being the wilful patient once more. His heart and mind were bandaged this time, not his eyes.

'A kindergarten *aide*. I cut out pictures for the children. I played games with the children, and generally helped to keep them amused. Like one does for *some* patients in some hospitals—'

'Good for you, Lisa,' Magool laughed. 'I brought that one on myself, didn't I?'

'You certainly did, Jim dear. You deserved that!' Imelda said. 'These are gorgeous biscuits. Anyone mind if I have another? Ghastly for the figure of course—'

'Please do have another,' Lisa said. 'I'll make some tea now.'

'You can cook as well as look, can you?' Imelda watched the other girl with arched eyebrows.

'Yes. But those particular cakes and biscuits were made by Mrs. Watson. Oh! My goodness me . . .!' She fled to the stove, picked up a cloth and opened the oven. She drew out a tray of hard brown scones, and looked at them as if she could cry. 'Mrs. Watson will never forgive me—'

'Whip up another lot,' Imelda advised from the table-end of the room. 'That wry-faced dear won't be back for ages if she's gone out to join the welcome party. By the way, what goes with her? Not very pleasing I'd say. Jim! *Do* sit down, there's a dear. You positively worry me throwing a shadow across my shoulder like that. You know I'm superstitious—'

If he heard he did not answer. He went across to Lisa and took the oven tray from her hands.

'I'll empty these out,' he said. 'And to hell with making another lot. Mrs. Watson will be in such a state of excursions and alarms when she comes in with 'Old-fella' that scones, fresh or burned, won't interest her.'

'Thank you,' Lisa said gratefully. 'I think I'd better fill the tea-pot first. My grandfather would think Pardalote's hospitality very poor if he found I hadn't given you some refreshment.'

Imelda stood up.

'Thank you, but *no*,' she said. 'No tea. I only came across to give Jim a message. It had nothing to do with "Old-fella", lost or found. A very private personal message! Hence my intrusion. Are you too young to understand that *private-personal* generally means *at once*, Lisa?'

Lisa shook her head. She guessed the one time school

shirt, and her short shorts, made her look younger than she was. Imelda, in her amused condescending way, was so very down-talking.

'I understand,' she said.

'Then don't mention my visit to "Old-fella". Not unless the housekeeper *dear* gets in first. That's a pet. Well, I'll be off. I'll have a word with Jim, with or without the tray of burnt scones, *outside*.'

With a wave of her hand, and another flashing smile, she was through the screen door. And gone.

Not for the first time that morning, Lisa stood quite still and drew in a breath. Then slowly expelled it.

The noise of the bush people outside—chattering and calling to one another—suddenly increased.

'My grandfather is coming *now*,' Lisa thought. She pressed one hand to her cheek. 'Please Guardian Angel up there—if there is one—make him be pleased to see me. And thank you, Magool—Jim for short—for taking out the burned scones and hiding them.'

10

Lisa went out to the veranda.

The land-breeze had fallen away, as it did each day by mid-morning. The heat was settling on the land like a vast hot oppressive cloud—from sky line to sky line.

A hundred yards away was a milling circle of people that made Lisa open her eyes wide. She forgot Imelda. Where had they all come from, the people? Pardalote had been empty.

Over there were a dozen aborigines, men, women and children, sitting under a shady tree. Near them three stock-men and one of the bush people were lowering a bough litter to the ground. Mrs. Watson and Magool Ransome —Imelda too now—were stooping over the figure lying propped on a pillow of bush twigs and leaves.

From everyone—those under the tree and those around 'Old-fella'—came the music of excited chatter.

Lisa longed to jump from the veranda and run across to

join them. 'Old-fella' was *her* grandfather. If he belonged to anyone he belonged to her. Yet she was afraid to move for fear of offending Mrs. Watson to the point of some irrevocable quarrel. She reasoned, reluctantly, that Mrs. Watson's possessiveness in relation to all things Pardalote was fair enough. It was her home, and she'd been keeping house for 'Old-fella' for many years. It was Lisa who was the stranger.

'So too is Imelda!' she thought. 'Why should she be there—and not me?'

Alas, it was petty thinking that way. If she had been an 'Imelda' type of person she wouldn't now be fixed to the veranda floor like a wax doll!

Magool Ransome turned his head and looked back to the homestead. He broke away from the group and came towards Lisa. His near-smile, apart from his height and his brown-ness, was the most noticeable thing about him as he came across the gravel.

'All's well, Lisa,' he said. ' "Old-fella's" colour is good, and his vocabulary is bordering on the lurid. Your mind at rest now?'

'Yes. Thank you for coming and telling me. I'd like to go over to him, but—well, I'm not sure—'

'Too many people smothering him already? Mrs. Watson's proprietorship? You're quite right. Besides—'

He broke off looking at Lisa for quite a minute.

'I'm sure the sight of you—patiently waiting *here*—will be the best reception you can give him, Lisa,' he said abruptly. He looked away, frowning now.

'I suppose Dr. Anderson will know *why* my grandfather just sat down, and then wouldn't move?' Lisa asked doubtfully. 'There has to be a reason, doesn't there?'

Magool's eyes came back from outer space.

'Of course the doctor will know,' he said, almost tersely. 'He's used to bush-wacky people. Your grandfather's been that since I first knew him, Lisa. I was a tree-climbing boy at that stage. He's independent and a law to himself—' He broke off. 'I'm sorry Lisa,' he said after a moment's hesitation, 'I withdraw all critical remarks. Will you consider them unsaid?'

'Of course.'

'Talking of tree-climbing and flying doctors'—Magool was looking down the valley—'here he comes now.'

Lisa shaded her eyes with her hand. Three figures were walking towards the homestead, each leaving a faint trail of dust-cloud behind him. High over their heads a mass of brilliant coloured birds flew in from the east. They too added to the chattering and excitement of the scene. These birds, in turn, swung round in a great arc, circling the valley. Then finally they too disappeared into the stringy-barks at the foot of the west-side range. Great was the colour, rustling and gossiping amongst twigs and leaves. All the world seemed to have come to the party.

Magool caught Lisa's eyes again. She had made a move as if to step down from the veranda, but he shook his head.

'No,' he said. 'Wait here, Lisa. It's better this way. I think you know that.'

She nodded.

'Yes,' she said reluctantly. 'I think I do.'

The men had picked up 'Old-fella's' litter again. They were bringing him to the homestead. It was like a triumphal march. The bush people scampered out from the shade of the trees and came tagging along too.

Imelda walked away towards her car. It was dusty but still magnificent—right up from the kangaroo bars in front to the sun-visor over the windscreen: and to the studded leather mudflaps behind the wheels and the water-bags on the bumpers. It carried an aerial mast high above the roof. Her *radio*, of course.

The procession carrying 'Old-fella' arrived at the veranda's edge. Between the litter-bearers Lisa could see 'Old-fella's' face. It had a faint grey tinge about it. Behind the group, wary and dignified, walked Sept, 'Old-fella's' dog.

A hush fell over everyone. Each and all of them knew, in his outback-telepathic way, that this was a special ceremony.

The girl on the veranda—with her beautiful still face, and watching eyes—was 'Old-fella's' granddaughter. She was his blood. Was he going to show he was pleased to see her? Had the old feud with his own daughter, Lisa's mother, died its long hard death?

It seemed as if the station hands held their collective breath while the sick man and the young girl looked at each other. Both, it seemed, had forgotten they were not alone.

The dog stood still, pricked-eared, watching. Mrs. Watson stood watching too. No one could read the expression in her eyes.

'Grandfather?' Lisa began tentatively. Her voice, always soft, could hardly be heard.

'Old-fella' stared back at her, lips clamped together, his eyes distant as when she had first seen him at Finch's Creek. Then—quite suddenly—something happened to him. A cloud might have crossed the face of the sun, or was it just a shadow in his eyes? The stockmen were dead-pan. The bush people took in yet another breath, almost in unison. Their great black eyes stared hopefully from 'Old-fella' to Lisa.

The shadow in 'Old-fella's' face passed and a light crept in his eyes. A struggling smile cracked the tight lips. Lisa stepped down from the veranda and went close to him. He held up one hand. Lisa took it, holding it tightly. There were tears at the back of her eyes. Waves of messages passed between those two clasped hands. It was the aboriginal people, and the dog Sept, who *knew* what messages. Faces broke into spontaneous grins, and the old ones nodded to one another in a knowing fashion. Sept gave one wag of his tail, and sat down to scratch his ear. Looking up, Lisa's eyes met Mrs. Watson's across the litter.

Without speaking a word, a truce was declared—temporarily at least.

'Mrs. Watson has made a grand welcome home for you, grandfather,' Lisa said. 'You've never seen such cakes and biscuits. There's cream in the cooler and the very best beef in the meat-safe under the trees. Tom sent it in.'

'Always one for thinking of your stomach, weren't you, Lisa!' 'Old-fella' grumbled. 'Well get on inside and set to laying the table. I haven't eaten in two days. See that Sept's fed too.'

Even the stockmen looked surprised. 'Old-fella' hadn't exploded and, more important, he was interested in food. Must be feeling better— the old *bartoo*.

Lisa did as she was told and went back in to the homestead. Her step was light for she was certain her grandfather had communicated an understanding to her. There was not going to be any war between them—for a breathing space anyway. He was grateful she hadn't started wringing her hands and asking questions about sickness or health. Instinctively she *knew* her grandfather's pride in his health had suffered a blow. To be brought home on a litter was the last indignity of an elderly man.

Five minutes later the homestead was full of people. Where had they all come from? Lisa added more cups and saucers to those already set out. Mrs. Watson had been the wise one after all. When the news of 'Old-fella's' sickness had come in, she had set to baking—not wringing hands, nor wailing either. Firelight in the stove, and food on the table made a homestead look, smell, and feel like home to everybody—the litter-bearers too. Mrs. Watson had seen to it that that was how it would be.

Magool Ransome, having seen Imelda off, and said whatever vital thing it was he had to say to her, returned and came into the living-room with Dr. Anderson. Five minutes later both were closeted in 'Old-fella's' room with the patient.

Mrs. Watson and Lisa—no words wasted between them —set to work to give a meal to all. First to the stockmen who had brought 'Old-fella' home from the range, and then to those who had met Dr. Anderson when the plane landed. Cakes, bicuits, dried fruits—and a huge billy-can of tea—were sent out to the bush people still conducting their wongi out under the trees by the homestead square. Sept was fed at the kitchen door.

Ironically Pardalote seemed to be in a festive state. This, in spite of the fact that its master had been brought home under emergency conditions.

For Lisa the world was different. It had come alive!

She was so busy passing plates, re-filling cups of tea, finding her way to and from the stove through clouds of cigarette smoke, she did not have time to wonder what was going on behind that closed door down the end of the passage. Her spirits were almost festive too. Intuitively she had put her faith in the wisdom of the bush people. They *knew everything*. This time it had nothing to do with smoke-signals or thrumming music through the hollow bough of a tree. They were gay, talkative and happy, so everything must be all right with 'Old-fella'.

Sept too would have known if there was danger in the air. He'd gone to sleep with his nose on his forepaws: his paws on the kitchen doorstep. Unconcerned.

Fed and filled, the stockmen wandered outside to the veranda.

Lisa was alone in the kitchen with Mrs. Watson. She wanted badly to say something to the older woman, but Mrs. Watson—a closed shell again—would not look her way.

A little later, striding boots clattered along the passage. Magool Ransome came into the kitchen.

'All's well,' he said briefly. ' "Old-fella" became dizzy. It seems he has a special phobia about dizziness. Dr. Anderson said the records back at the hospital show that his father died of a stroke which came on with acute dizziness.' Magool looked from Lisa's face to Mrs. Watson's, then back again to Lisa. 'Your grandfather,' he said, 'does not show unduly high blood pressure, Lisa. But it's a shade above normal. The doctor says he'll need watching for a short while. What he really had was a fright. I think you'd better go and see Dr. Anderson now. He'll give you the drill.'

Lisa started towards the door. Then stopped. She turned and saw that Mrs. Watson's face had gone sheet white. Her almost dark eyes were glowing with anger, not fear. She was taking off her apron. It was *her* province to discuss 'Old-fella's' treatment with the doctor! Her face said so.

'You go, Mrs. Watson,' Lisa said very quietly. 'You know my grandfather better than I do. You are more experienced—'

Before she had finished speaking, Mrs. Watson had flung her apron over the back of a chair and gone to the door. She paused as if to say something; then changed her mind, and went out.

Silence reigned in the kitchen. Magool broke it.

'Why did you do that, Lisa?' he asked curiously. 'Your grandfather needs kith and kin, right now. You are all of that in one person. In spite of the façade, he's a very frightened old man.

'Did he ask for me? Specially?' Her eyes were dark sea-blue and quite fathomless. Her face was still and patient and listening.

'No,' he said, weighing each word. 'He did not ask for anyone. He's not the kind of man to ask any single being on earth to do anything for him. Do you know that? It doesn't mean he hasn't a need: feelings too. He's plain stubborn that's all. It was Dr. Anderson who asked for you, since you are a relative.'

'Mrs. Watson will follow the doctor's instructions carefully,' Lisa said tonelessly. 'She is like that. Everything is done well. She's a perfectionist in practical things.'

'You think she'll be better for "Old-fella" than *you*, his granddaughter?'

'Yes.'

'I see.' He went to the tea-pot on the stove exactly as if he were in his own homestead. 'Do you mind if we get something to eat for Dr. Anderson? He had a difficult time getting here. He had to make a skilful landing on rough ground. Add to that the fact he's working hard at keeping "Old-fella" disciplined.' Magool glanced round at Lisa. 'No easy job that—' he finished. 'The old boy doesn't react well to doing as he's told.'

'I'll make some fresh tea,' Lisa said. She was avoiding his eyes. How could she explain about Mrs. Watson's rights? 'I made some sandwiches earlier—specially for Dr. Anderson. They're under the cover on the bench.'

'So you *have* been doing something useful meanwhile?' It was more a statement than a question. Lisa had her back to him as she put tea leaves in a smaller tea-pot. Her hands stayed still for one long minute.

'Yes,' she said. She couldn't bring herself to tell him that Mrs. Watson also had feelings and rights. The Chinese word for 'war' was a pictograph of two women in one kitchen. For all she knew the same people might paint the same pictograph really lurid—to mean two women in a battle of wills over a sick man's bed.

He watched her while she busied herself again with kettle and tea-pot.

'Will you excuse me for a few minutes, Lisa,' he said at

length. 'I need to check something on my radio. If Imelda is able to pick up a call I'll know how far she's got. She went off quite suddenly. There was something important I wanted to see her about. She was to give me an answer to a matter of great importance to me.'

'Perhaps she didn't know it was important—' Lisa said, meaning to make a kindly excuse for Imelda.

'Oh yes she did, Lisa.' He had moved as if about to go to the door. 'When two people are thinking about a common venture the woman's intuition will have been at work. Do *you* believe in woman's intuition?'

Lisa turned round. Magool had stopped in his traces as if deliberating. His face had become thoughtful.

'Why yes,' she said. 'I think I do. But Imelda would believe in that too—'

'That's what I thought. Imelda can be very tantalising at times. I'm afraid "Old-fella's" fall from grace came bang at the wrong moment for me. I must go. I'll be back later to help with "Old-fella".'

Mrs. Watson, arriving at the kitchen door at the same time, met him face to face. She was glowing with satisfaction, and puffed with a certain importance.

Here was one more *changed* person. Lisa felt a pinprick of envy. Actually, she could have cried. 'Old-fella' belonged to Mrs. Watson, while she, his granddaughter, was prisoned in the kitchen to a routine of tea-making. Magool belonged to Imelda. He had to dash off to her to clinch this '*common venture*'? What was more common or more of an adventure than love and marriage? It must be that. They had been so much together. It was so apparent there was something between them. Everybody else seemed to belong to someone else. Ah well! Lisa's own little daydream had gone the way of all soap bubbles! It was her own silliness, of course. Nobody had *asked* her to daydream. She was the uninvited guest! Mrs. Watson, for her part, had looked after 'Old-fella' for years. As for Magool—one had to face it—Imelda certainly *was* a dazzler.

Magool was now standing aside to let Mrs. Watson come into the kitchen.

'All well?' he asked.

'Yes, thank you. I've come to make "Old-fella" his special

106

brew of beef-tea. He likes it a certain way. Not too strong and not too weak. A pinch of mustard in it too.'

'I'm sure you'll make it perfectly,' Magool said dryly. 'Now, if you don't mind I've some urgent business to attend to. Nothing to do with the patient, I assure you. This is entirely personal.'

At that moment footsteps could be heard crossing the veranda. One of the stockmen who had brought 'Old-fella' in, put his head in the door.

'A message for you, Boss,' he said to Magool. His manner seemed too knowing. 'Miss Bannister said to tell you she's taken two of our men back to Nangardee with her and she'll see you over there. *Soon*, she hopes. Leastways that's what she said.' He paused and grinned. 'Seems she has something personal she wants to talk about and it can't be done over the two-way. Said she'd be willing and waiting as soon as you've settled the problem with this lot over here.' He caught Magool's expression and his grin faded. He was suddenly uncomfortable. Magool's eyes had fixed him with ice picks.

'Say, Mrs. Watson!' the stockman said, with a lame attempt to cover-up his tactless remarks. 'You might like to know Tom is headin' home. So Jabberdee tells me, any-way. Seems Tom's heard the news and will get in some time later. I guess Jabberdee and his mob'll be lighting out straight away. Tom won't be all that happy to see 'em witch-doctoring round his stretch 'uv country—'

The expression on Magool's face became unreadable.

The stockman was not exactly making amends, however much he tried. Mrs. Watson decided now was the moment to make her own stand with those 'foreigners' from Nangardee.

'You see, Mr. Ransome!' she said, looking quite pleased with herself. 'You had better go and join Miss Bannister. She seems to have strong claims on you. We don't want to detain you over here unnecessarily. You agree Lisa, don't you?'

Lisa, fixed to the spot on the floor in front of the stove, did not know what to say.

Mrs. Watson saw her dilemma and broke the small silence herself.

107

'Thank you for your help, Mr. Ransome. We won't keep you from your own affairs any longer. We do need a man in the house, of course, but Lisa and I will have *Tom* now. We've been hoping he'd come. Lisa's been waiting for him out here in the kitchen—just in case. That is so Lisa, isn't it?'

Lisa was astonished. All this was news to her. She looked from one face to the other. In Mrs. Watson's face there was victory. Magool's face was inscrutable.

'I will be very glad to see Tom home,' she said, at last, her head down as she carried cooking utensils to the cupboard. 'We do need him. It will save you, Magool . . .' Her voice broke off. She longed to say something different—because her heart *meant* something different. But Mrs. Watson's words and their implications practically silenced her. Actually, she had never heard Mrs. Watson utter one really long sentence before—and what did it all matter anyway? Waiting for Tom might be better than waiting for no one at all. Tom was kind. That was *something*.

'Thank you, Magool—that is—for all you have done—' she stammered, turning round and looking at him across the room. 'Please . . . You did say you would have some tea? Won't you wait? I'll be quick with it so as not to keep you. I promise—'

She broke off again.

You can't catch the tail of a rainbow with words, she thought sadly. Why don't I go play draughts instead?

'Not to worry, Lisa,' Magool said, faintly sardonic. He came back to the big table. 'Now I come to think of it, Nangardee will still be there in an hour's time. For sure I'll have some tea. Waste not want not. How's that? Do you suppose Dr. Anderson will mind if I share his sandwiches, Mrs. Watson?'

'Probably not.' She was taken aback by Magool's change of manner. Change of intention too.

'Like the beef-tea that you and you alone can make to please "Old-fella",' Magool went on steadily, yet managing to imply he was 'up to something,' 'I think the sandwiches might have a special flavour about them. Only an idea of course—'

Mrs. Watson was completely baffled by the man. She looked at the visitor with suspicion.

'Please have your tea, and some lunch by all means,' she said a trifle shortly. 'Don't forget your message from Miss Bannister will you? Not that you're likely to do that. She has a special place in your scheme of affairs I'm told.'

'Quite right,' Magool said. 'Your informant is correct. Meantime, while that tea is drawing, I'll go and send a radio message. In code of course. I like my tea hot, strong and black, Lisa.' He had moved towards the door again. He paused.

'By the way, Mrs. Watson,' he added, 'in case you're concerned for Tom's comfort, I'll move my horse out of his way. I've probably tethered it to his particular post. The ground there appears to have been much stamped on lately. It couldn't have been Challenger, so I assume it must have been done by Tom's horse coming in from the muster often?'

He turned to the stockman who had been leaning against the door jamb, fascinated by the last five minutes of conversation. Translated, his thoughts were—*These people here in this homestead are plain nuts! What goes with them?*

'*Sam!*' Magool said sharply. The stockman sprang upright and put his weight on his own feet. '*Scram!*'

Sam did just that. He scrammed.

Outside all lay inert and still in the hot noonday silence. Not a bird moved, nor an ant, nor a lizard. Overhead a colourless heat-dazed sky brooded over the ranges on either side. Over Pardalote homestead too.

Far, far down the valley, a rising dust cloud behind a lone rider signalled that Tom Watson was coming home for sure. He was riding at a quiet, not-to-be-hurried, even pace too.

There was a girl in the homestead waiting, and 'Old-fella' was down on his stumps! It doesn't pay to seem too eager!

He'd allow himself plenty of time—as he came riding home.

He didn't believe in rushing his gates. Every horse he'd ever handled he's taught to take it quietly. Same with the cattle, when they were nearing water. No stampede that way. No broken traces. No locking of horns.

And Lisa was a mighty pretty girl!

109

So his ordered logical thoughts followed one upon the other to the rhythm of his mount's hoof-beats, and the steady beating of the pulse on his right temple.

Magool Ransome ended up sharing lunch with Dr. Anderson. Later, Dr. Anderson, to Mrs. Watson's barely suppressed indignation, took a look at Magool's so lately wounded eyes. In public too! Over by the living-room window, in fact. He had lifted one eyelid and made mumbling noises to himself: then lifted the other and made further unintelligible sounds.

'I suppose all that means I pass fit?' Magool asked with a grin.

'You do. But you've only one pair of eyes, so throw that shot-gun away. For myself I always prefer a rifle. You're either dead or alive with that. Nothing messy.'

'Ug-huh,' Magool said and went back to the table. He picked up the last sandwich, and ate it with an air of complacence.

Dr. Anderson shook hands with Lisa and said 'Yes—he remembered her at Finch's Creek. Yes, the appendicitis case was well: and the same went for the two tonsil patients. If she ever went through Finch's Creek again old Jimmy Come-up would give her a royal welcome. Now he must be going. He had that so-and-so plane to get off the flaming track down the north end of that wretched valley.'

True to his word, he went. Magool Ransome went with him, first to see him off, then to depart himself. If he came back to say 'good-bye' Lisa did not know, because at long last she could now go and see her grandfather. This time it was without by-your-leave from anyone. Mrs. Watson had gone to see Tom's room was ready for him.

'Old-fella' Lindsay's door was ajar, and Lisa opened it quietly for fear of waking him—if he were asleep. 'Old-fella' was far from that. From his bed on the far side, under the window, he watched the door opening inch by inch. His face was in the shadow so Lisa did not see his eyes first lighten, then deliberately switch themselves down to half-shut again, as he saw the girl, with her gentle friendly face, and anxious fathomless eyes, looking across the space at him.

110

'Grandfather?'

'Well, come in, if that's what you've come for. Don't be so slow about it. Shut the door behind you. Didn't your mother teach you to shut doors when people were sick?'

'Not in the heat of the tropics, grandfather,' she said coming to the bedside. 'Besides, you're not so very sick you know. Not at all, if you take care. Dr. Anderson said so. So did all the aboriginal people: those fram Nangardee as well as those from the east side here at Pardalote. They *know*, don't they?'

His eyes lightened again.

'The aborigines said I'm not too sick, did they? Humph! Well, they *ought* to know. Never knew anything they didn't know first. I'll have a sharp word with them when I get out of this bed, and out of old mother Watson's hands. Confounded busybody—'

'Not really, grandfather. She cares about you quite a lot. In fact I didn't come in before because I knew she wanted to be *first* to look after you. She was anxious, you know . . .'

She sat on the edge of his bed and leaned forward to straighten the cover sheet under his chin.

'Don't fuss around me girl,' 'Old-fella' said, crabby as a jag-edged crag now. 'I suppose you learned that nonsense at the hospital—'

'Yes. And how to make an arm-chair set with pillows. Much more comfortable than lying straight like that with just two pillows flattened under your head. Shall I show you?'

She didn't wait for permission. She was up on her feet looking round the room for cushions or more pillows. He watched her in silence, his sharp pale eyes taking in every detail of her appearance. Her face, her hair, her neat young body. Her air of intention.

'Just like your mother,' he said caustically. 'Have to have your own way. Is that it?'

'About making you comfortable, grandfather? Yes. Will you excuse me a minute. I think I know where I can get some more pillows.'

Feet as light as a bird's—he said gruffly to no one in particular. *Like her mother's. Like her mother's mother too* — He broke off, then added as if forced to play one card for the kitty-pool of his disapprovals. *Well, it's something*

111

better than that woman Watson crunching about: and Tom thundering up and down the passage all hours of the night.

Yet even these last reflections were not said—in his mind —with either anger or dislike. Dr. Anderson, taking a look inside his head, would have seen not rocks, but a slightly alarmed elderly man. There was a creeping gratefulness in his heart, but also too much stubborn pride to admit this to himself. Well, not aloud anyway. He didn't want to hear about such virtues as he might or might not have himself.

He'd always been the way he was, and the way he was going to be to the end.

Lisa, taking pillows from the cupboard in the passage, was thinking, once again, how each belonged to another in this world of Pardalote and Nangardee.

'Old-fella' belonged to Mrs. Watson—whether he agreed or not. Magool belonged to Imelda, and had wished to hasten off to find her. She, Lisa, was alone.

But now Tom was coming home!

She was surprised at how glad that suddenly made her feel.

She didn't *have* to be a lonely one. She did have someone!

11

Lisa came through the door. All 'Old-fella' could see of her was a neat pair of legs, a neat pair of tan-coloured shorts, and her chin resting on a multiplicity of pillows. Over these pillows her blue, blue eyes, and her dark shining hair, were looking at him in quite a bewitching way.

'Where'd you get those pillows?' he demanded crossly. 'I'll wager Sept for that dingo half-breed of McPhee's, that Mrs. Watson didn't give you the store keys.'

'No she didn't, Grandfather. Besides, I wouldn't have had time to get over to the store and back again. Now would I?'

Her blue eyes had an imp in them as they looked at him over the cushiony pile. A soft hand touched his heart as, for one moment, a soft hand had held his when those half-wits from Nangardee had brought him home in that thundering-bad litter. Nevertheless he was not prepared to admit any surrender to his granddaughter *yet*. Not by a long shot!

'You wouldn't expect any of that Nangardee mob to know how to make anything, let alone a decent litter, now would you?' he asked aloud. 'Slip-shod. Slung together. That's their way. Anything's good enough. Like women —they're contrary. I'll tell you something, girl. When I want a female to do something, I tell her to do the *opposite*. Being contrary she does it *my* way. Handle 'em with cunning like you would a dingo. Give 'em a taste of their own medicine. That's the way to handle 'em—'

He was wrapped in his cloak of anger again so Lisa made use of this preoccupation by lifting his arms and pulling his head and shoulders forward while she turned the two pillows already in place. Next she deftly put two more pillows long-ways, one on each side of the others: half on them and half off them. She eased these new ones into a V shape at the top. Then pulling 'Old-fella' a little forward she slipped a small cushion under the small of his back.

'Now. Lie back, Grandfather, and tell me how that feels.' She was smiling down at him.

'Lot of confounded rot . . .' he began. Then stopped. His upper part was cradled in an arm-chair of pillows. And it felt good.

'Not so bad, considering—' he admitted. 'You thought you were fooling me, pulling me about like that, didn't you? Well, for the good of your stay here, Lisa, you weren't. No one fools me. You hear me?'

Lisa sat on the edge of his bed. She longed to pat his hand but thought it might be going too far—too soon.

'Not slip-shod or slung together?' she asked solemnly.

'Now look here, Lisa! I'll have no nonsense about what I think or say of that mob over at Nangardee: or of women. I've my opinion and I'm sticking to it.'

'But Grandfather, they were so helpful. Magool Ransome came over here—'

'*Who*?' he roared.

'Magool. You live so near him, you must know him well.'

'You mean Jim Ransome? What's he doing calling
113

himself "Magool"? You know what that name means? It means "chief". The "boss". It's an aboriginal word and I won't have it said round here. *I'm* the "boss". The Lindsays, over a hundred years ago, beat the Ransomes to these ranges by six months. Upstarts and outsiders, that's what they are.'

'Yes, Grandfather. I'll remember,' Lisa said. 'But if ever I meet him again, round these ranges, you won't mind my thanking him for his help, will you?'

'*Thanking* him? Now you look here, young lady. You don't know anything about North-west business. If you had a man's head on your shoulders I might explain. But you haven't, so I won't. Sufficient to say that that man's already had a lot out of me. He's had concessions—but that's as far as I'll go. Just now anyway. There's a limit. You understand that? Not an inch further. I'm not dying yet—'

'Nobody thinks or fears you are dying, Grandfather,' Lisa said mildly. 'The aborigines are deep in a wongi—and enjoying it. They're in great spirits. Sept has gone to sleep. Mrs. Watson and I—and the Flying Doctor—agree with their collective opinion. We are quite happy too.'

'Then what the blazes is wrong with me?'

'A touch of dizziness. It's a little bell ringing in your head and saying—*It would be fine to have someone around to talk to, now and again. It would be fine to rest up a bit, from time to time: and have a bit of women's care.* You were so annoyed at the message, Grandfather, you sat down and wouldn't get up again; just to show that no one or nothing—not even a little bell in your head—gives you advice.'

The old man lay back in his arm-chair of pillows and stared at his granddaughter.

'The first minute I clapped eyes on you,' he said at length, 'I said to myself *This one runs deep. A regular one for talking, if I give her half a chance.* So I didn't give you a chance. Now did I?'

Lisa laughed, hugging her knees and rocking her slim young body to and fro.

'No you didn't give me even a quarter of a chance. Do you know what I said, Grandfather? I said—*This one's a non-talker. I'd better mind my ps and qs for quite a while. That is, till I get to know him better.*'

114

'Old-fella' lifted himself from his pillows.

'Now look here, young lady—' he began. Then over Lisa's head he saw Mrs. Watson come into the doorway. She was carrying a small tray with a steaming bowl sitting in the middle of it.

'Beef tea!' she said. 'The way you like it—I've always made it for you when you've been a bit off—'

'Me *off*?' he roared. 'You're talking out of the top of your head, woman. I've never been "off" in my life.'

'No,' Mrs. Watson agreed. She placed the tray on the chair beside his bed. 'Not what you'd call really "off". Not once these fifteen years. You just like beef tea now'n again when your stomach gets sick of mutton, beef and lamb. Vegetables fresh out of the garden too—'

Lisa eased herself off the bed, then out of Mrs. Watson's way. *Why!* she thought, making yet another discovery. *Mrs. Watson can be quite kind and gentle! How different she looks when she doesn't scowl! She really means to take proper care of 'Old-fella'. She likes to have him depending on her!*

Mrs. Watson pummelled Lisa's pillows and tucked a napkin under 'Old-fella's' chin. He was arguing with her: ordering her about. At the same time, he let her minister to him. He had forgotten Lisa was there.

She slipped out of the room. She was suddenly so happy she almost skipped as she ran down the passage. She pushed wide the kitchen door and flung herself forward—into a wonderful future, she thought.

Actually it was straight into Tom Watson's arms.

'Whoa! Steady!' he said.

He had caught her and now held her firmly. She stared into his face, surprised.

'Why, *Tom*?'

'Hallo, Lisa! I didn't know you could smile—a real rainbow smile—like that. You're a very pretty girl, Lisa.' He looked down at her—still the outbacker who drawled when he talked, and whose expression was half shrewd, half withheld. He was taking more than a common interest in holding the warm slim body of this young girl close to him.

'Oh Tom!' Lisa said again, gently freeing herself. 'I'm so sorry—bumping into you like that. Very clumsy of me. But I'm so *glad* to see you.'

115

'You're glad?'

'Oh yes. Thrilled! Now we have a man in the house —to help us look after "Old-fella". Shall I tell you something, Tom? Don't laugh, will you? I was wondering how in the name of wallabies your mother and I were going to manage bathing, or even washing-down "Old-fella". It was a real think-problem, I can tell you.'

Tom laughed, showing fine strong teeth. Suddenly he was looking quite handsome, even in his dusty brown-stained mustering clothes. Lisa put her head on one side to make sure she was seeing right.

'If I hadn't come in to fix that side of affairs my mother would have managed, don't you fret,' he said. 'I never knew anything she couldn't manage. Even "Old-fella". Though he wouldn't thank anyone for saying it.'

'You must be hungry—' Lisa made a movement towards the stove for the umpteenth time that day.

'Not so fast, Lisa,' he said. 'Like "Old-fella" and my mother, I'll eat when I'm good and ready. I want to know something—'

'Yes?'

'What was that chap Ransome doing over here at Pardalote? He wasn't needed in the long run, was he? Slept the night too, I'm told—'

'He organised it all. My grandfather's rescue I mean. I suppose you would call it a rescue?'

Tom avoided an answer to that.

'You look different, Lisa,' he said, watching her closely. 'Sort of bright and happy. Why's that? Not "Old-fella's" cheerful conversation I'll wager! Nor my mother's—'

Lisa shook a strand of hair from her eyes, and tilted her chin quite proudly.

'I'm happy because now everyone's *home* at Pardalote. Me. You too, Tom. We're all here, and everything's going to be fine now. It is, isn't it? I was nervous when I first came—'

The strand of hair had fallen again. Tom tossed it into place with the tip of his finger.

'Nothing to do with that fellow Ransome being here then? You knew him out there at Finch's hospital, didn't you?'

'He was one more patient,' Lisa said with dignity. 'Besides he had—'

'He had Imelda Bannister coming and going for him. That what you were going to say? She came after him over here too. From Nangardee?'

'Tom. You're like the bush people, and Sept. You know everything. Smoke signals?'

'Maybe. I'm not telling. So that pair went back to Nangardee, did they? Well, good luck to them. They're not welcome here.'

Lisa slipped away from the hand that was holding her.

'Let's forget them,' she said easily. 'Who'd have thought so much talk could go on about so few people so many many miles apart. Besides, this time *he's* gone *after her*. Back to Nangardee, as you said.' Lisa paused, then added— 'Tom, you said you'd eat when you wanted to. Is that *now*?'

'When I've had a shower.' He went to the door then looked back at Lisa. She too had turned, and their eyes met across the distance. He smiled, and so did Lisa.

'Tom, I'm so glad you're home,' she said again. 'Did I say that before? I was afraid of being lonely.'

'I'll tell you something, Lisa. I'm glad I'm home too.'

The rest of the day passed in a whirl of activity, most of it revolving around 'Old-fella', his needs and complaints. There were moments when, at his most blustering, Lisa sensed something a little piteous, way far-off at the back of his eyes. At the back of his voice too.

He's afraid he might really be ill, she thought. *Perhaps for the first time in his life he is afraid of something.*

She knew that Mrs. Watson was aware of this pinpinch doubt in the old man's heart. Mrs. Watson, for once, was tactful in all she said not only to 'Old-fella' but to Lisa too. She was a different person now she had 'Old-fella' to look after. In a way this knowledge moved Lisa to pity. This time it was for Mrs. Watson. 'Old-fella' would get over this touch of high blood pressure. She believed this because she had come to believe in the bush people: in the kelpie dog too.

Lisa, in her lonely moments before 'Old-fella' had been brought home, had taken to talking to *things*—in her

117

head, and just for the sake of talking to *something* because it couldn't be to *somebody*.

This evening it was the sunset's turn to be her confidant.

'What do you say about it all now?' she asked, looking at the blazing banner across the skyline. 'I think that, maybe *I've come for keeps*. Come *home* for keeps. Well, maybe . . . I mustn't be too hasty, of course. It was stupid of me to go thinking so much of those days at Finch's Creek. As Nurse Davitt said—"patients come, and patients go!"—It's having a *home* that matters.'

The dark trees pencilled against the crimson at the top of the range seemed, to her imagination, to catch her message and signal it on. It would be wonderful if smoke signals took it up from there—and went on and on round the world for *ever*.

Hundreds of brilliant-winged birds were coming through the valley like an invasion against the foothills. Now if they would only spread the news too—up over the range and down into the next valley. Down to Nangardee's homestead!

'I've come to stay,' she kept repeating, as if by wishful thinking this might not only be a message, but a fact too. 'I have a home now.'

She stayed there watching the sun disappear like a golden ball over the range-top, her heart full of the happiness of hope.

'Golly, I'm getting bush-whacky! Or is it bush-mystic?' She had better go and find if Tom were free from the long 'sit-down wongi' he had been having with 'Old-fella'. With Tom she would have someone to talk to.

When Lisa went indoors Tom had disappeared. He must have gone out from the far side of the house, she thought, through the living-room door—the way 'Old-fella' had brought her in that first day. That door was open and the wire screen beyond it had just clanged-to as Lisa came in the kitchen end.

Five minutes later, as she was peeling potatoes for the evening meal, she heard galloping hooves—disappearing in sound and distance down the north end of the valley.

That must be Tom! Where was he going? Not back to the muster surely? *Not without saying good-bye!* What about 'Old-fella's' bath?

Not another gone-away person!

Oh, how she wished she knew what Mrs. Watson would like her to put on for dinner. And for how many. What could or would 'Old-fella' eat?

The sound of Mrs. Watson's footsteps were coming down the passage. She came into the kitchen carrying a bowl.

'I've sponged "Old-fella's" face and hands again,' she said. 'It's very refreshing to be sponged every hour or two. Specially towards evening—'

'Yes, I know,' Lisa agreed. 'We did that at Finch's Creek. I could see at once how good the patients felt—' She broke off.

Mrs. Watson was staring at her again.

'At Finch's Creek? Goodness me! You were there little more than a week, and you are a nurse already!'

Lisa's blush was flame-coloured as she turned back to the potatoes. 'I meant that I sort-of gave a hand while I was there,' she said apologetically. 'I sponged the children . . . just to help the nurses. They were short-staffed—'

'You don't have to explain yourself to me, Lisa. Your affairs are your own. Move that pot away will you, so I can put this pan of milk to scald. I'm glad to know you were a help. It was kind of you!'

'Then what will I do to help you with dinner?' Lisa was a little nonplussed at Mrs. Watson's hint of kindness on her own part.

'Get yourself something to eat like a good girl. I please myself what I'll have and when I'll have it. I've told you that before! Don't you remember *anything*, Lisa? There's no need for all those potatoes, you know. Tom won't be in, after all. I'll get "Old-fella's" meal. I always do. I understand what he likes—'

'Of course!' Lisa agreed. She dared not ask why Tom had gone off again. Such a question might break up this moment of 'understanding' between them.

'I would like to see my grandfather again to-night,' she said cautiously.

119

'You can take a look in the door later. You must do that of course. He will expect the courtesy of a "good night" from you. No talking, mind you. People whose blood pressure is up should be kept *quiet*. We must *both* watch that.'

'Oh yes. Of course. I won't disturb him, Mrs. Watson. I promise. I hope I didn't excite him earlier—'

Mrs. Watson's eyes met Lisa's as they both turned away from the table.

'Well, come to think of it, you *are* rather quiet, I must admit,' she said in a more friendly tone. Lisa realised Mrs. Watson was really thinking out, and measuring up, what was best for 'Old-fella'. 'You're not exactly an exciting person, Lisa,' Mrs. Watson went on. 'When we have sickness in the homestead that's all to the good!' She paused and considered the girl who was now removing the potatoes from the pot and wrapping them in a towel. 'No, you're not exciting, thank goodness,' she repeated. 'Not like that Imelda Bannister. You're quiet as a mouse, compared with her. Of course, *she's* brilliant. Showy, if you care for that kind of person. Which I do not. She'd have had a very bad effect on "Old-fella". I'm glad she went off.'

'Yes, she is brilliant,' Lisa agreed.

'I'm glad that Ransome man went off after her too. Quite a pair, they make. All's well that ends well. What do you think?'

'Yes . . . I expect so . . .'

'I don't expect so,' Mrs. Watson said firmly. 'I know so. He's welcome to that kind if exotic entertainment— *if that's what he needs*. Two of a kind! That's what I thought. Well matched. As long as they keep it the other side of the range.'

Lisa's face was picture-still again as she now dried the potatoes so they wouldn't be spoiled by their dip in the pot. Her thinking eyes were sea-sombre, but Mrs. Watson did not notice that because the dark head was bent over the work the hands were doing. Lisa had never heard Mrs. Watson make so much conversation before. That in itself was a surprise. It sounded as if there was a friendly purpose behind it. She meant to give Lisa some wholesome advice perhaps.

'Well now,' Mrs. Watson said quite brightly, 'where did I put that cloth? Oh, here it is. A dust-up will freshen "Old-fella's" room. I must make his bed again too. That will leave him comfortable for the night.'

She was still talking as she disappeared through the door.

Lisa's hands ceased working. She wiped the back of one hand across her eyes as if to brush veils away.

How everything had changed! Mrs. Watson was being conversational. She was happy because she had 'Old-fella' pinned to his room and letting her look after him.

Lisa hoped that some of the happiness came from the knowledge that Lisa herself was not attempting to take her authority from her: or 'take-over' 'Old-fella' because she was a relative.

Yet Tom had gone, so unexpectedly! Why did no one mention this? 'Old-fella' must have told him in pretty strong words that the muster was more important. But, alas, Tom had not left a message. Mrs. Watson showed no sign of disappointment.

Everything seemed so *quiet* now.

Such a little time ago the homestead had been vital and happy. It had been full of people, talking and laughing —none of them really worried about her grandfather. Now the homestead was nearly empty. Even her grandfather was being sort-of guarded. In a well-meaning way, of course!

What a see-saw her spirits were, this day!

Lisa didn't have any appetite for grilled chops to-night. If Tom had been in for dinner that would have been different. She would have shown him she was quite a good cook. As it was, she settled for an omelette.

How funny people were! One minute they were all here, and the next they were all gone. Very much like Magool Ransome, when one came to think of it. He was the kingpin of gone-away men. They'd all followed his example—the aborigines, the stockmen, Imelda, Tom. All gone!

She was left on her own, and was a bit of a saddo.

Well, she would have to do something about *that*!

Later that evening Lisa went to 'Old-fella's' door to bid

him good night. She had promised not to go right inside so she waved her hand to him, and smiled her smilingest best. The overhead light caught her eyes and put sparkles in them till they shone like the old man's beautiful gem-stone—the six-sided crystal of *beryl*. Lisa did not see this, but, looking across the room at her grandfather, she remembered—unexpectedly and out of the blue—it was not only for his care and interest that she had come to Par-dalote.

There had been that peculiar 'third share' mentioned in her mother's will. She had no idea why this thought came to her at this time, but it affected her in one way. *She decided never to think of it again*, if possible. The lawyer had referred it to the Public Trustee, and both had been sceptical about the existence of any third share. Her mother, they said, might have thought that one day . . . if she lived long enough . . . she could inherit something. They would look into the matter thoroughly.

All that was over now. Finished.

If she herself could stay on at Pardalote it would be for her grandfather's sake—much more than for her own sake.

This had something to do with the dishevelled state of his pillows, and the knowledge that he had *liked them her way*, when she had fixed them into an arm-chair arrangement.

She longed to go and fix those pillows now, but had promised not to go in.

She waved her hand again.

'Good night, Grandfather,' she said in her gentle, soft voice. 'Sleep well.'

'Old-fella' lifted his hand and waved back. He had a certain something in his eye too. It was almost con-spiratorial.

His face, surmounted by its cap of grey hair, was sud-denly impish, as if he and she had been plotting together, and between them had some secret. He was very pleased about this secret too. All very strange; yet pleasant.

'Good night, child,' he said gruffly.

Lisa forgot that her grandfather must have sent Tom away—and deprived her of some glad company. There was something between them! Hurray! Some day it would ripen.

'Good night again, Grandfather dear,' she said, so gently it was only a whisper.

She would be careful to do every thing she could to please Mrs. Watson as well as 'Old-fella'. That way there would be peace, and kindness too, in the homestead.

And Mrs. Watson was kind in some ways. At least where her grandfather was concerned. There was something to be guarded—for everyone's sake.

Lisa kissed her hand to the old man. She thought—for a split second—that his eyes were suddenly misty.

She went down the passage with a light step! Happy again. *Funny*, she thought, *but do-gooding is really quite a selfish occupation, after all. I make up my mind that I'll see only the good things all around me, and who's the one feeling happy?*

Why me!! Very selfish.

All the same, I'm still on a see-saw!

12

Several days had passed since 'Old-fella' had been brought in by the men from Nangardee. He was much better—quite lively too, except when he remembered to appear as an invalid again. Poor health had, for the moment, its allurements. He discovered it commanded a great deal of attention. More easily and more willingly given than when blustering orders went forth.

'Please, Mrs. Watson,' Lisa said once, 'do let me make Grandfather's bed for you. And do out his room. That's *heavy* work—'

'Since when has a girl from the city known as much about hard work as someone who has lived in the outback all her life?' Mrs. Watson asked, more or less cheerfully.

Oh dear! Another clanger! Lisa thought.

'I suppose I put that a silly way,' she admitted. 'I thought you might like a change. I mean vary the jobs . . .'

'You mean you want to vary *your* jobs? What you want is a day off, I expect. Like the farmers in the southern districts? They never work seven days in the week. I've never known Tom *not*—'

'Why don't you take a day off for a change, and be like a southerner, Mrs. Watson? *Why not*? I can manage here. Besides, Tom told me you used to ride to the outcamp once a week.'

'Tom talks too much,' Mrs. Watson said shortly. 'Besides "Old-fella" needs me here. He doesn't need you, or Tom, or anyone else. He needs *me*. I understand him.'

'Yes, I think you do,' Lisa agreed. 'You are very good to him.' She longed to add—*As his granddaughter I'm grateful to you*, but this she knew would be the red-kangaroo of all clangers.

She went on with the breakfast wash-up. Then, when Mrs. Watson had literally run off to answer—a condamine cow-bell—that 'Old-fella' kept by his bed, she gathered the teatowels and Mrs. Watson's hessian aprons and took them out to the laundry.

In the distance she could see Nooma, the bush-girl, turning the skins along the rails of the drying fence under a shed-roof. She had met Nooma in the laundry three days before. Since then the two girls had exchanged smiles and waves whenever they caught sight of each other. Each smile and each hand-wave made them closer friends. In fact, if it hadn't been for Nooma—always somewhere between the laundry and drying sheds—Lisa would have been lonely all over again. Mrs. Watson, except for an odd spurt now and again, was not always conversational.

As for her grandfather? Sometimes he wanted Lisa to talk to him, but most times he dismissed her with—'Off you go. There's work for idle hands round Pardalote. Always was. My blood pressure's up to-day.'

Lisa knew very well his blood pressure was not up, and that he knew it too.

For her part, Lisa was contented with the wave of the hand he gave her as she stopped at his door last thing at night.

On one or two occasions she caught a sudden watching gleam in his eyes after he'd been specially curt with her. Her heart lifted when she saw those lights, for she was sure he was playing some sort of 'testing' game with her. He

124

was not to be won over in a day, and he was letting her know it.

Fair enough, she thought. *But two can play at that game! Both playing a cat and mouse game. I certainly have his very own blood in my veins.*

The next morning after Lisa had had her conversation about varying jobs with Mrs. Watson, 'Old-fella' sent for her.

'Good morning, Grandfather!' Lisa wore her best fine-weather smile. 'Mrs. Watson said you want me. I mustn't disturb you before ten o'clock, generally. By that time I feel—'

'Never mind what you feel, Lisa. That wretched fussing woman out there doesn't bother what anyone *feels*—'

'Grandfather, you are wrong,' Lisa said gently, but firmly. 'Mrs. Watson fairly runs—when you ring that bell so loudly. The birds down the valley could hear it—'

'It was made for the birds to hear, *as well as the cattle*. The best bells came from Condamine. They were made by an artist. There's music in them. The cattle would sing to them if they could. The stockmen do. The birds too.'

'Yes, Grandfather. But even without the bell Mrs. Watson is not a "wretched woman". She's devoted to you! And she's very kind. I hope she knows you don't mean ...'

'You stop *don'ting* me, young lady, and *don't* give orders round here about bells. Or what I choose to call "women". I've said it before. Women are all contrary. One and all. I give the orders round here. Are you listening?'

'Yes, Grandfather,' Lisa said meekly—but only to placate him.

'Good. Then I'm giving you an order now. Get out in the fresh air. No complaints about the heat either. A young girl like you should be out and about—'

'But—'

'Silence. Do as you're told. Learn to be active. Learn to walk distances—the way I walk—twenty miles in a day if so I want. Harden up! That's the thing. If you're going to stop here long you'd better be tough. It's a tough life out-back.'

His ice-blue eyes were watching her, but actually she thought there was more wariness than ice in them this

125

morning. Her ear had caught, and her heart held that phrase 'going to stop here long'.

Now what, she wondered, *is my grandfather up to this morning? Mrs. Watson told tales on me, kindly, I hope. For some reason it suits his order-book—for to-day.*

'Well, what have you got to say for yourself?' he demanded.

'I'd like to go out and toughen-up, Grandfather. I'd like to go for a long long walk—though I don't think I should try twenty miles till I train for it. As soon as you've finished with me I'll get my hat, and something to eat and drink—and I'll go.'

'Old-fella' did his best not to look startled. He hadn't expected her to take up his challenge. Lisa's sea-blue eyes were looking into his light blue eyes. Hers smiled: and the ice in his melted just that much.

He put out his hand and took hers.

'Good for you!' he said. 'I see you have some Lindsay in you—in spite of that Nangardee jackeroo that took your mother off. Mind you, she had spark in her too—or she'd never have gone.'

'I wouldn't be here if she hadn't gone, Grandfather.'

'Yes . . . well . . . that's as it may be . . .'

He dropped her hand to push the cover sheet lower. The day's heat was already rising.

'Not that anyone asked you to come!' he finished, back to his old form.

'But you're glad now that I did—'

'Glad?' he almost stuttered. 'Tom-fool rot!' His eyes caught hers again, and this time wavered. 'Go and get your hat and a tucker-bag and go, girl,' he said. 'Have a day out. Right out. Get away from this old woman's parlour of a homestead.'

'Yes I will, Grandfather. And thank you for telling me. I haven't really explored Pardalote yet. You will take care of yourself?'

'*Take care of myself?*' he exploded. 'Anyone 'ud think someone was ill in the place. Tom kept telling me that. I sent him off with his come-uppance. That very moment. Counting his money before he'd earned it, is Tom. Thinks I don't know what his little game is. Like you, Lisa. *You* think I don't know your little game. Well I do. You wait and see. I've got it all worked out. You'll have a surprise . . . that's what you'll have, my girl. Now will you get out of here and let me go and take a shower?'

'Yes, Grandfather, I will.' Swift as the touch of a bird's wing, she bent down and dropped a kiss on his forehead. 'There you are!' she said. 'I've been wanting to do that for ages!'

She caught the look of astonishment in his face. Then she fled. 'Old-fella' was the last one on earth who would bear to see one of these 'contrary' women with tears in her eyes.

Lisa climbed the west side gorge again on her holiday walk that day.

As she crossed the valley with her sun hat on her head and her lunch in a bag over her left shoulder, half of her hoped her grandfather would not ask her, later, where she'd been this day. That half of her feared the explosion that would follow. The other half hoped that he *would* ask her. She would like to tell the truth. Then the chips would well and truly be down. He himself might also oblige with a little telling. Why, for instance, was there an unspoken law—almost forbidding her any interest in the west side? There was not another runaway jackeroo waiting over there for another Lindsay to go follow him. That was certain. Maybe grandfather had been tantalising her. Punishing her for her mother's wrong-headedness! There wasn't any jackeroo now. Only Magool Ransome was over there.

And Magool had Imelda. Had they become engaged yet? Lisa was sure they had been teetering on the brink when the 'affair of "Old-fella" ' had temporarily called a halt.

How Magool had hurried after Imelda, that day, back to Nangardee!

Grandfather, like the bush people, would know that. So why worry about Lisa—*the girl whom nobody came for?* Grandfather might also tell her *what* were the concessions he said he had made to Magool Ransome—the man with whom he would have nothing to do. Why the paradox?

Lisa wondered about these things all the way across the

valley, but once she began to climb the gorge she thought of other things. Things like—Would the telescope be there to-day? Who would have moved it, if not? What would she see of the homestead down in the valley? Would Magool be there? Even Imelda?

It was a long uphill pull for it was even hotter to-day, and she'd rested longer by the little creek in the valley fold.

When she reached the top she approached the lookout —or as she now called it—'the eagle's eyrie', quite slowly. She would be so disappointed if *IT* was not there.

But it was there. Hurray! The telescope stood where it had stood before. The bench seat, like the ones in Pardalote's kitchen, stood in front of it.

Lisa dropped her lunch bag on the ground and sat down quickly. It took longer to-day to adjust the barrel and the sight, but that was because she was in too much of a hurry.

Suddenly, there at last—like the slide in a magic lantern —was Nangardee's homestead! It stood there sleeping, so very still in a dreaming valley. Everything was still. Perhaps because *no one* was there at all! No Magool Ransome stood, or walked, or talked near the shade trees or by the big shining car to-day. There was no sign of Imelda. There were no stockmen nor horses about. Nothing—

Then, suddenly, in the nearer distance there was a movement. Lisa adjusted the barrel. A young aborigine was hoeing away at the garden with fine sweeping strokes of his arm. Alas, there was no other sign of life of any kind. The world in the valley down there was only a dream world.

Actually Lisa could have cried—except she knew she was being foolish.

So long a walk, and climb. Then nothing. *Nobody*!

Where had they all gone? Magool away to a muster maybe: with Imelda? Could she ride as well as drive?

Magool had left Pardalote hastily enough when she had slipped off without him! Had Imelda done that to tantalise him? Maybe he was *very much* in love. Mrs. Watson had said Imelda was an *exciting* person, and she, Lisa, was —in effect—only a mouse.

Way up on the opposite hill, far far away, Lisa could see

spurts of dust rising between the boulders and low stumpy trees. She supposed these would be made by the stockmen mustering-in the strays from the bush. Maybe that was where Magool Ransome, *with Imelda*, had gone to-day.

She lowered the barrel of the telescope, and abandoned the bench-seat. She turned towards the opening that led to the track. A little further down she had seen a cave in the hillside. She would go and explore *that*. She might even find a much sought-after prehistoric rock-painting. People did find such things occasionally.

She followed the track back a little, then scrambled a foot or two up the rocky incline to the mouth of the cave. She stepped inside cautiously. Then her eyes rounded with surprise.

Here were no rock-paintings, but instead a treasure trove of sparkling lights from a cave roof studded with tiny shining crystals. The whole area above her head was encrusted with hexagonal shapes that gleamed where the light caught them. Crystal gems!

They weren't like 'Old-fella's' lovely stone, but they were wonderful and beautiful in their difference, and in their smallness too. Some were a pale vitreous green, and some a light blue. Others were a silvery white. Their crystal formation was perfect and in this one way they were like 'Old-fella's' beryl. They were six-sided and each ended with a pyramid cap. Lisa gathered some that had broken off and fallen to the ground. She carried them outside the better to see the light shining through them in dozens of sparkles, and in many lovely colours.

Back in the cave again, she saw something she had not noticed before. At the side, by the rock wall, was a pick lying on the ground. Against the wall farther along was a small hammer with a pick-like back to the hammer-head. Lisa was certain she had seen the picture of such a hammer somewhere in a magazine or book. It was called a 'geo-logist's hammer'. *Geologists*, she knew, were people who had to do with precious stones. Precious minerals; and even things like oil, too.

These tools were 'Old-fella's' tools. She was sure of it. The bench-seat in the 'lookout' had been one of those from

Pardalote's kitchen. The hand-cut handles of these tools told the same tale.

Lisa stared and stared.

Why had 'Old-fella' kept a watch on Nangardee? Was it because here in this cave he hoped to find more gems like his precious *beryl*? And, since he did not trust the Ransomes, was he making sure they too didn't discover his treasure cave?

A new thought assailed her, and her heart felt a little sad for her grandfather. Until he had had his dizzy spell, and become afraid he was ill, he had kept himself aloof. And very alone.

That telescope overlooking Nangardee may have been a lonely old man's way of vicariously finding company. He wanted to *know* what the neighbours were up to—just for their company.

One thing Lisa was sure about. She couldn't now tell 'Old-fella' where she'd been to-day on her walk-about. Or ever mention the telescope or the crystal cave. His pride would suffer too great a blow.

She would just have to say she 'walked about'. Talk a little about the creek. And the birds. Seeing Nooma at the drying sheds!

That night, Lisa had barely slipped into her bed when she heard a knocking on her window. First she thought the branch of the tree outside had caught a whiff of the land breeze, and its leaf-ends were beating a tattoo.

The tap became more persistent and she realised *someone* was trying to attract her attention.

'That you, Lisa?' It was Tom Watson's voice.

'Tom? Is that you, Tom?'

She didn't know which she was *most*—relieved or glad. She had been lonely. Now she could admit it. Specially as 'Old-fella' had gone to bed without saying 'good night'.

'Put on your clothes and come outside, Lisa. I want to talk to you,' Tom said.

'Yes, I'll come, Tom. Please wait—'

'Hurry up then. I won't be here in the morning. I'll be

back in the muster camp. I've ridden in ten miles to see you.'

'Just give me a few minutes, Tom. I'll meet you on the front veranda.'

Ridden ten miles to see her! Somebody in all the world *cared that much about her!*

Like the crystal cave her own world was a sparkling world after all!

Lisa slipped into clothes, then swished a comb through her hair.

She tiptoed through the house to the front veranda. Tom was leaning against one of the creeper-hung posts—a tallish shadowy figure with a cigarette glowing in one hand. Lisa's eyes searching through the shadows could see he still wore his hat. His eyes gleamed a little in the darkness of his face as he raised the cigarette to his mouth and drew on it.

He un-leaned himself from the post and stood up straight.

'Good girl,' he said. His drawling voice unexpectedly had a new charm for her. 'Along there a bitaways we can sit on "Old-fella's" think-bench.'

This bench was a heavy slatted affair that must have stood on Pardalote's veranda since the old homestead was first built. Hand-cut—like the seats in the kitchen, and the one up on the range-top. Like the tools too!

Lisa sat down, and Tom sat down beside her. He stretched his long legs out in front of him. He had left a space between himself and Lisa that somehow seemed awkward. Lisa *felt* this awkwardness, but did not understand it.

With a flick of his fingers Tom sent the deadened butt of his cigarette flying past the gum tree that stood near the veranda.

'It was a long way for you to ride, Tom,' Lisa ventured. *'In the dark of night too!* Was it really ten miles?'

'Not a long ride for me; and it was all of ten,' Tom said slowly. 'It's longer by a hundred and fifty to go up Wyndham way—which maybe I'll do shortly.'

'I'm glad you came.'

'A man like me doesn't see a girl unless he goes for freight—maybe three times a year. The only places I know

131

where there's girls, are Wyndham and Darwin. Like I said, I'll be going up that way pretty soon now,'

Lisa hugged her knees.

'It's friendly of you to want to see this particular girl anyway,' she said happily. 'You know when I first came, I thought you were not going to like my being here one bit. You remember that first morning? In the kitchen?'

'I remember.'

There was a long silence, broken at last by Lisa.

'Of course you weren't to know what sort of person to expect,' she said. 'I might have been . . .'

'I didn't expect any sort of person. "Old-fella" didn't say why he went off to Finch's Creek.'

'Then I was a *shock*? Oh, I wish I'd known—'

'I knew someone was coming, even though "Old-fella" didn't say. I always *know*.'

'How did you know Tom?'

'From one of the men at the out-camp. He has an old pedal radio. "Old-fella" won't have those gadgets up here at the homestead, but he likes to pick up the news from McPhee sometimes. Never says so, though. A real one for keeping knowledge to himself, is "Old-fella".'

'Someone at the out-camp picked up one of the radio messages sent out from the hospital?'

'That's about it. McPhee's as close as "Old-fella" when it suits him. *We* just kinda knew the old boy was off to pick up somebody *special*. We knew that because he took the Dodge, instead of the Land-Rover. And dressed himself up like he does once about every ten years. We didn't know *who*. McPhee wasn't telling.'

'But the Land-Rover would have been better through that country—'

'Yes, but it wasn't special. It isn't that comfortable.'

Lisa unhugged her knees and dropped her feet to the ground.

'Tom, are you telling me that when my grandfather came for me he thought it *important enough* to dress up? I was someone *who mattered*?'

'That's about it.'

He leaned forward and broke a twig from the creeper and began to chew it.

'It's hard to believe,' Lisa said puzzled.

There was another long silence and this time it was Tom who broke it.

'My mother knew later. I guess McPhee told her. I could tell—afterwards—by her manner. She was worried. Didn't know what you'd be like.'

'Tom, please—' Lisa said. 'I didn't mean to come here and upset you all. I had no idea. I wanted to find my grandfather. That is all.'

'Ma's okay now,' Tom said. 'Softening up a bit.'

'Did *you* mind, Tom?'

'I was going to mind. I'll tell you that, Lisa. But I didn't. Not when I saw you, and heard you speaking—sort-of soft-like. Then the other day, when you came running in the kitchen door, I saw the way your eyes were shining. You looked prettier still. You ran right into my arms. I liked that.'

Lisa was surprised.

How Tom had changed since that first meeting over breakfast!

Her heart began to beat a little faster. Someone had wanted to see her enough to ride ten miles to do it! That was wonderful. And now he said things about her *shining* eyes. She wasn't such a mouse-type after all. Not to Tom. *She wasn't just the girl that no one came for*, either. 'Old-fella' had put on his best suit and taken the best car!

The thought that Tom and 'Old-fella' cared enough to do these things lifted her heart sky high.

The moon had been rising steadily out of the eastern sky behind the homestead. At that moment its first silver-bright sheen crept over the sturdy iron roof, lit the papery stems of the cadjebuts and dispersed the darkness from the valley.

Lisa did not know how to say 'Thank-you' to Tom. Or if she should say anything at all. She felt happy, but just that little bit embarrassed.

Tom was leaning back against the seat rest and rolling himself another cigarette.

'Tell me about the cattle pads that go up north, Tom?' she asked to break the silence which had become—like the space between them on the think-bench—a little awkward. 'Is it all trees and rain-forest?'

133

'Not on your life! There's pindan too. That's mostly scrub land. And savannah. North of that there's the most rugged country anywhere in the world. The oldest country in the world too. Desert ranges sprawling all over. Mesa-topped too.'

'Your voice sounds as if you like it. Even if it is rugged.'

'It's kinda exciting. Like you're alone in the world. You keep driving and you never reach the horizon. The ranges try to frighten you . . . but they don't. That's because you're one of them—in a way. I'm not good at describing, Lisa. You ought to see for yourself.'

She hugged her knees again.

'Oh, Tom. I'd love to. Do you think I'll ever be able to?'

'Can't see why not. I'll be going through in the freight truck for stores. Soon. That'll be the time.'

'I'd have to ask my grandfather, of course. I wonder if he'd let me go?'

'Leave it to me. I'll fix it. The best time'll be when he gets up off his back, and rides out to see those men he's got on top of the north-west range. He won't leave *them* alone too long.'

'Men? Stockmen, you mean?'

'No. They'll be the ones putting the finishing touches to the muster for me. The muster is my job. I'm the overseer on Pardalote.'

'Then—'

'The men "Old-fella's" got up there know about minerals and rocks and things. Maybe he thinks he's going to find gold, or something. A fool's chase, if you ask me. Cattle's the paying dirt in this country. "Old-fella's" getting a bit soft about such things as minerals. He's forgetting important matters.'

'Like cattle, for instance?'

'That's right. You said it, Lisa.'

'My grandfather wouldn't miss me, while he's away would he?' Lisa said thoughtfully. 'We'd have to ask him first though—'

'Leave it to me, Lisa. Too much noise round the muster at night time'll start a stampede. Take a tip from that. *Softly* does it. The same with the "Old-fella". Softly does it.'

'I think you're a schemer, Tom,' Lisa said laughing, hugging her knees even higher.

'With a pretty girl like you around? Why not?'

Lisa had not heard his last words. Her knees dropped to the ground and she sat up stem-straight.

The valley was a sheen of silver, but up the west side, the flanks of the range were dark with trees and shadows cast here and there from crags and buttresses of ancient worn-down squared-off mountains.

Had she dreamed that something moved up there? Even *called* to her! Alas, she was the one getting soft in the head. Not 'Old-fella'. Ever since she'd been here at Pardalote, one high hooked crag up there had been to her like a beckoning finger. Each night it had been stark, commanding, and black against the sunset.

Tom was saying something kind and flattering. Something about 'Tom and Lisa and Pardalote all three belonging—'

Belonging to what, and to whom?

She *belonged* to that range top! Not even to her grandfather *altogether*—

Funny how the moon takes the brilliance out of the stars, she thought. *Except that twinkling one by the crooked crag on the very top. It is still bright. Yellow bright. Shining.*

She stiffened.

It had moved. The star was not a star, but a light. Someone was carrying it. It flashed on and off as it passed behind a tree then came out again.

Lisa strained forward. She was deaf to the soft patter of Tom's drawling words as she looked farther along the range-top. There was another light there. It too flashed on and off as it passed behind trees. The two lights moved towards each other as if to a meeting.

Magool and Imelda?

It *hurt* that the mountain tops on a moonlit night were only for people like Imelda. The top of the world was for some people: not others. Perhaps it wasn't Magool and Imelda at all! But her own feelings stayed the same as if it were indeed them.

That meeting place up there belonged to Pardalote. It had been her mother's. And her own father's—the jackeroo from Nangardee. Now it was *her own*. Lisa's. Because she'd found a way up there by herself.

Something in Lisa wanted to make her leap forward and run. Run, run, run, across the valley and up the gorge path to answer that beckoning finger. It stood black against the moon-white sky and said that *there*, with it, was where her heart belonged. *Not anywhere else*.

But she was fixed to the think-bench with Tom; and to Tom's drawling voice and flattering words.

Lisa sank back against the seat-rest again.

She closed her eyes to shut-out the calling finger of jagged rock: and the thought of Magool being up there with Imelda.

Behind the dark shutter of her eyes, instead of the light and the beckoning crag, she could see *his* long lean frame, with the bandaged eyes above it, lying on the iron bed in the hospital at Finch's Creek. Instead of Tom's half-heard voice, she could hear that other amused, derisive one—'Well Tonky-teacher? What have you found for your wilful pupil's read to-day? Something juicy and slanderous I hope. I'm blind, teacher dear, so I can't see you blush. If I put my hand on your cheek I might *feel* it. How about that, Lisa? Shall I put my hand on your cheek?'

Alas, when he at last could see, it was Imelda's radiance by the bedside that had dazzled him. And taken him away too—without any kind of a blush at all.

'*But not to the top of my mountain range*,' Lisa said aloud; flatly. '*My mother's range and my father's range! "Old-fella's" range ...*'

Tom was startled.

'Lisa, what in the name of flying foxes are you talking about?'

She took his hand to show she was grateful for the kind things he had said; and as an apology for having been absent in mind and heart for this little while. He seemed to like her hand in his.

'Minerals and such things,' she said. 'You did say "Old-fella's" men were looking for that sort of thing?

Well, not on top of the west-side range. I have a "thing" about that place, Tom. It sort-of belongs—'

'Ye-es,' he said, still not quite understanding her.

'Second-best is not good enough, is it, Tom?' she asked, deflated. 'Please don't ever let me settle for second-best will you?'

Not having seen inside her head, Tom still had no idea what she meant. It meant nothing; he decided. All females were empty-headed—more or less.

'Second best sometimes turns out first-best—in the long run'—was all he said, dryly. 'That's the way it is with cattle. I reckon it's time to go in, Lisa. I've ten miles to ride back.'

'Yes, of course. You won't let me make you some supper?'

'No time. So it's all fixed, is it? You'll come on the freight trip with me over the cattle pads and through the wild country to Wyndham?'

'If it can be managed, Tom. I do hope so!'

But her mind had gone somewhere else again. Back to a very high place.

'I love Him,' she said inside herself—*not meaning Tom*. 'I always will, in spite of Imelda. I would never have admitted it but for the range-top—all dressed in black and silver, and taken over by someone else. Not that too! That at least is mine. It was my mother's, and my father's. Not Imelda's. I'll never let her have it—'

When Tom had gone, Lisa went to the cooler on the back veranda to get herself a glass of milk. She felt thirsty and a little hungry.

She stood by the cooler, sipping from the glass in her hand and looking out over the station yard to the stables. Then beyond them to the moonshine sweeping down the valley. Finally to the range-top again. All was still there now, and *all* the stars were twinkling quietly. It was hers again.

Everything stood still, and there was no single bright light. Perhaps she dreamed it. The tall trees by the home-stead and round the out-houses were statue still. Yet in the absolute silence—*there was something missing*. Nothing to do with the bright light either. Something to do with the valley.

Lisa had a bewildering feeling that something *ought* to be there, but was not. The soundlessness was too odd.

She finished her milk, made sure she had replaced the hessian drippers over the cooler's door, and went back into the kitchen. The moonlight flooded through the window, lighting everything so she could have read a book by it.

As she paused at her bedroom door, she *thought* she heard a sound. After all a leaf falling might have been heard in that brooding silence everywhere over all Pardalote. She turned her head and saw that the passage was not all that dark. She thought she saw a long thin line of blacker darkness—a small opening between a door and its frame. As she looked the wedge of darkness disappeared: the passage wall and its doors were all of the one plain surface.

She shook her head as she slipped into her own room, then later slid down between the sheets of her bed. She had imagined so much to-night. *Too much.*

She laid, her head turned on her pillow, drowsing off. Then suddenly she was wide awake. She knew now what had been missing from that midnight valley scene. It was Tom's horse carrying him back to the muster. There had been no *hoof beats* on the hard earth!

Lisa drowsed off again. What did it matter anyway? In the morning she would think it out. Or ask Tom next time he came in.

In the morning she had forgotten.

13

For Lisa—busy in the homestead—days passed quickly. Then, in no time, the days had become first one week, then another. And another.

'Old-fella' liked to have Lisa read the newspapers and magazines sent into him from McPhee at the outcamp.

Lisa discovered that McPhee, being more in contact with distant civilisation because of his pedal radio, always had the journals dropped by planes to him. No plane except the Flying Doctor's, or one off-course, ever ventured over Pardalote valley directly.

When McPhee had finished with his journals he sent them in by a stockman to 'Old-fella'. One stockman or another came in at regular intervals to report on the state of the muster, and the progress of the cut-out.

Sept kept one eye closed and one eye on guard outside the window where he lay sprawled on the veranda; not asleep, but watchful.

Sometimes Tom himself came in to give 'Old-fella' his estimate of the number of clean-skins and stragglers caught up in the muster.

'Why are they so important?' Lisa asked Tom one night, when he had come in, and they were sitting on the think-bench. 'You send the clean-skins off to sell, the same as the branded cattle, don't you?'

'Our share get sent off,' Tom said a trifle grimly.

'Why? Who else *shares*?'

'Who do you think? Who is the only neighbour? There are no boundary fences to Pardalote or Nangardee: so no one knows whose cattle produced the clean-skins. They've been fathered and delivered out on the range; or farther north in the spinifex. It's anybody's guess which belong to one station, and what belongs to the other.'

'So you *do* have some kind of meeting with Magool Ransome? Even if it is only once a year?'

'Not me! That's why McPhee lives at the outcamp. He's referee. Nangardee sends over three stockmen to the muster-yards out near the so-called boundaries. We send three. A man from each side takes it in turn to cut out a beast from the mob; and McPhee keeps the tally.'

'What a strange system!'

'It's not a system. It's a law. It's called the "*law of the country*" which means it's a widely used practice on all stations that are so big they can't and don't fence. What's more the "*law of the country*" holds good in a Court of Law, though it's never been written in to any Statute book, as far as I know. It's *custom*.'

'In that case,' Lisa said happily, 'I think it's rather

139

wonderful. The men don't have to quarrel over any one particular animal.'

'They don't even *talk*, Lisa. They cut-out and go. That's all.'

'Oh dear! You are strange people. It's almost like a silent war. I wish I knew why there was this feeling between the Ransomes and the Lindsays.'

'McPhee told me once that it's historical. Back a generation or two there was argument about boundaries. The Lindsays were here first and they saw no reason to have their boundaries surveyed at high cost merely because the Ransomes turned up months later, in the next valley.'

'But the government? Doesn't it interfere?'

'Not yet. It was empty land in the early days. No one wanted it. There were plenty of squatters last century, and early this one. Even some in the far outback still. The north might have been the other side of the world for all any-one cared a hundred years ago. Even thirty years ago. Now it's different, but "Old-fella" won't change his ways. As things stand, Lisa, *anyone* who could *prove* he'd reared cattle right here on Pardalote could put in a claim for the lease. He'd stand a ninety per cent chance of getting it.'

'*Anyone*?' she exclaimed. 'You mean McPhee, or one of the stockmen?'

'No. They've tended cattle. Not reared them.' Tom paused, then added—'In this generation there's only "Old-fella" and me who've reared and bred cattle: horses too.'

'I can't understand why my grandfather doesn't . . .' Lisa broke off for she had caught a nuance in Tom's voice.

'Old-fella' won't lease officially: but Tom could! But Tom wouldn't do that, of course. He is 'Old-fella's' over-seer. And has been taking wages, his share of sales, and had a home since he was a stripling.

Tom would be loyal. Staunch to the last day and last hour of 'Old-fella's' life. She was sure of that.

'What are you looking so anxious about, Lisa?' Tom asked. ' "Old-fella's" going to be okay again as soon as he wants. He could be that right now, if he had a mind to it—'

'Yes, I agree. I think he's enjoying himself—in a way.'

'He is. But there's more to it than that. He's nursing himself up so *it won't happen again*. He had a fright, Lisa.'

140

'I know.'

'I kinda thought for quite a while back that he was worrying,' Tom said slowly. 'It started about three months ago. Now I think he's stopped worrying. No one knows what goes on in "Old-fella's" head, but I'll wager the best mare on the place to any old dingo on the range, he's figured things out for himself.'

'What has he figured out for himself, Tom?'

'*Lisa, Tom and Pardalote*! He's bunched them—all three—together. He's said to himself—"I didn't have any son to carry on, but look what I've got myself instead. *Lisa, Tom and Pardalote*! *What the heck am I worrying about*?" Do you see it, Lisa? That's why he's not worrying any more. He's done a simple little sum.'

Lisa wrinkled her brow thoughtfully.

'That may be . . .' she said tentatively. 'He hasn't asked me to stay on permanently, though. I'm hoping every day that he will. Anyhow, the only thing that really matters is that he should be his old self. I would think he has years and years ahead of him. Actually I hate talking about him as if he's getting too old. Or that one day he might die. Please let's talk about something else, Tom.'

'Right. We'll talk some more about the track to Wyndham. You know something, Lisa? Those emus spot a fella in a truck racing across the plain, an' blow me if they don't start-up racing too. Right alongside. What's more they'll keep it up at sixty miles an hour. You have to see them to believe it. You wait and see. It's quite a sight—hundreds of emus racing across the plain, hell for leather.'

'I am waiting, and I'm longing to see,' Lisa said hugging her knees happily. 'We must pick the right time to ask Grandfather.'

'Leave it to me. I've told you I'll fix it okay, Lisa. I'll know just exactly how and when to tackle him. I can always tell with "Old-fella".'

'Tom, I am grateful to you for asking me. I'm sure it will come off.' She dropped her knees and stood up. 'I've the last article in that new magazine to read to grandfather to-night. I think he *likes* being read to sleep.'

'Okay, Lisa. It you get him off before midnight I'll still be here. I'll be waiting.'

'Please don't wait, Tom. You've such an awful long way to ride.'

'I said it, and I'll be here: just on chance!'

Lisa laughed.

'You're one for keeping your word aren't you, Tom? That's something my grandfather is lucky about. He has an overseer he trusts. And your mother too. She's the one who's really pushed him up on his feet again.'

'She would!' Tom said laconically. 'She's the only person on the place who understands him. And he knows that too. What he doesn't know is—when she wants it *she runs him*.'

'It's getting on, Tom. 'Bye for now. I must run or "Old-fella" will start roaring. His roar is really fine and healthy these last few days.'

She ran through the door as she finished. Reading to her grandfather had daily brought her nearer to him. Or so she hoped. She almost . . . but not quite . . . believed he had actually begun to like her as his granddaughter too. Well, if not to like her at least to put up with her. Specially round reading time.

If she didn't hurry now she'd be hearing that condamine bell for the second time to-day. Loud and sweetly clear. As 'Old-fella' had said, once one began to listen to the tones of that particular hand-made brand of bell, one was completely won by it. If the birds could sing to it, she herself certainly came running to it.

Lisa had barely arrived and seated herself on the little cane chair at his bed-side—magazine in hand—then 'Old-fella' said he didn't want to be read-to to-night. He wasn't in the mood.

'You sit there and do the listening for a change, Lisa,' he said. 'It's time I told you a thing or two. You don't know anything about Pardalote yet.'

Lisa was so pleased to learn something about the station, she all but wriggled in her chair.

'Yes, Grandfather. Please tell me. I'm longing to know.'

He looked at her obliquely.

'Like what, for instance?'

'Well, will you tell me about the Ransomes over at Nangardee, and why you don't like them? What did you

mean when you said you had given them some *concessions*?
Does that mean you meant to be more neighbourly? Please
do tell me, Grandfather.'

He was no longer looking at her, but scowling—deep in
thought.

'You see,' Lisa went on. 'I'd like to know what would
be the right thing or the wrong thing to do if Magool Ransome comes over to see how you are getting on. He might,
you know. He was so helpful the day you were brought
in.'

'You mean Jim Ransome? Didn't I tell you not to use
that name "Magool" round me? Being a woman you're
contrary and do the opposite to what I ask. Well, Miss, if
you want to know I bargained on that too—'

'That I'd ask you what to say?'

'No,' he almost roared. 'I bargained *that you'd be
contrary*, and call him by that name. I was right, wasn't I?'

'Grandfather, dear. I don't believe you ever gave it a
thought—after he'd gone.'

He twisted round in his bed and stared at Lisa with icy
blue eyes.

'Are you taking me to task, young woman? Now you
listen to me—'

Lisa wasn't a bit alarmed by the sound of anger in his
voice. In a funny sixth-sense sort of way she had an idea
that her grandfather was playing some sort of game with
her. His ferocity just might be phony. But she wasn't all
that sure.

'I'm listening, Grandfather,' she said—sounding docile on
purpose.

He lay back on his pillow and stared at the opposite wall.

'Very well then,' he said. 'Time passes. Are you too
young to understand that? When time passes, things change.
One makes concessions because it's the *sensible* thing to do.
Like it or not. My advice to you is—don't bother your head
about that Ransome mob over there. I'm fixing all that—
about them and me. Have you got that in your head? You'll
find out one day.' He stopped. Then went on. 'I'm not as
fettle as I used to be; and doesn't that Jim Ransome fellow
know it! Still, I'll give him this—he's up with the times. I've
kept my eye on him. On them, I should say. There's

143

only him and an elderly cousin who house-keeps for him. *And* that flashy person he's seen with, up and down and over the range. Flashy name she has. Amelia . . . or something.'

'Imelda,' Lisa corrected him gently. The old man turned his head and looked at her again. His eyes were still ice-blue but this time were looking at her questioningly.

'So you know that, do you?'

'Yes. She came the day you were ill. I think she too, wanted to help. But she went away—'

'Just as well. She doesn't know—none of them know —I've got a streak in me. Since you know so much, young miss, do you know what *that* is?'

'No, Grandfather. Please tell me. I'd love to know.'

'*Cunning*,' he said. 'That's what I have. A streak of cunning. You heard that dingo howling out on the range the other night? He survives. No one catches him. Not the stockmen, and not Tom. They've tried too. Time and time again. They can't catch him. Do you know why?'

'He's very fast? Perhaps he's young and very strong?'

'Young and strong, my foot! That fella's the daddy of the dingoes round these parts. *He has cunning*, Lisa. That's why. *Cunning*. That's why he survives. That's the way I —"Old-fella Lindsay"—survive. I've got cunning too. And I stay on top of that Nangardee lot.'

'Yes . . .' Lisa said gently. 'I'm sure you do.'

'Well that's one good thing you know.' He sounded appeased. His next words were tinged with regret.

'I'm getting on, so I don't have muscle. That young fella over the range has plenty of it.' He paused, and his spirit seemed to revive again. 'It's my *cunning* that gets me my own way in the end. They don't—any of them—guess it, because they think my way is the opposite to what it is. Do you understand that, Lisa?'

Lisa didn't, but she only admitted this in part. She wanted to humour him because she saw he needed it.

'I might be beginning to understand. Please tell me about your cunning, Grandfather. What have you been doing with it lately?'

'Oh no! You don't catch me that way, my girl! Trying to find out, are you? Well, I'm not telling you *yet*. You'll

144

know in the end. All in good time. It'll turn out the opposite to what you think, I've told you that already. I've worked everything out about what's to be done with Pardalote when I'm gone. Are you listening, Lisa?'

'Yes, of course.'

'I've been setting-up my plan for weeks. Don't forget I told you I had cunning, Lisa, when the time comes. I had to use it because it was the only way to make things work out. Times have changed. Things are different now.'

'Yes, everything changes doesn't it? The seasons do. And the crops. Even the cattle get bigger and fatter.'

'Have you ever played chess, Lisa?'

'No, but I would love to learn. Do you think I could? Is it very hard?'

'You spend your time learning things more useful to women, my girl. How to run a home properly—*that's* women's work.' He paused and took in a deep breath as if he needed air. Lots of it. 'Chess is for Army Generals organising wars—down to the last battle. And for people like me who know that when they want to reach a certain point they *don't* go straight at it, like a bull at a gate.'

'I think I understand—'

'You don't and never will. Women are contrary. They do the opposite to what they're told. Perverse—every single one of them. Your mother too. You'll be the same, Lisa. I'm allowing for that.' He paused again, to breathe in deeply. 'That's why I have to build a strategy of my own,' he went on. 'Now listen! If someone wants to reach a certain point, *he doesn't go straight at it*. Remember that. He goes round-about, feinting. Like the dingo does. He misleads people, on purpose. That's the way he wins. He tricks people into believing he means something that he doesn't mean at all. That way the other fella doesn't know what he's up to.' 'Old-fella' paused to breathe in deeply yet again.

'Grandfather,' Lisa said gently. 'Shall I take down the wire screens? You seem as if you'd like more air.'

'No, certainly not,' he said testily. 'That would let the mosquitoes in. I'm tired, that's all. Too much talking. Tom talked at me for nearly an hour. What he doesn't know is that he wears me out. Bores me. A very sound cattleman, though.'

'He's a good overseer, Grandfather. He feels it's necessary to keep you up to date with the muster.'

'Necessary, my foot! He can muster-up better than any man in the north, and he knows it. He knows I know it too. No, no, Lisa—I'm tired. I'll take a nap. You can finish that article in the magazine to-morrow.'

'Of course, Grandfather. Thank you for telling me so much. About yourself, I mean ...'

She stooped and kissed his forehead. He had shut his eyes and made no sign that he felt the warm soft lips on his brow.

'I wanted you to know that I'd worked it all out myself, Lisa. Now I've told you, off you go. Leave me to take my nap.'

It was all a little odd, Lisa thought. Yet she wasn't certain. Perhaps her grandfather was trying to tell her something, and instead of 'feinting' he really funked it at the last minute. He had so much self-assertiveness, yet, underneath was afraid that whatever it was he had planned might not come off, after all.

Lisa did not go back to Tom on the veranda. Instead she went to her own room. From there she could tip-toe up the passage now and again and take a peep at her grandfather. She thought he was—as he had said—only tired, but she wanted to keep a watch over him all the same.

Each time she looked in his room he was sleeping, and breathing regularly and easily. The only different thing about him was his face. It wore the expression of a guile-less—thought rather *smug*—child.

In fact he looked too innocent! Too pleased with himself by far!

All that talk about cunning? And round-about ways instead of straight ways? *What was it all about?*

He had said she would know when the time came. He had been up to something but clearly she was not to know *what*—yet.

Her grandfather did get up to tricks, Lisa had learned that already.

'He's quite a scamp really, under all that bluster,' she said on one occasion to Mrs. Watson. That lady had looked indignant at such disrespect for the invalid. After that, Lisa kept her own counsel as to what she sometimes thought of her dearly loved grandfather.

Two stockmen had come in late that night from distant places. They had slept at the quarters on the far side of the gravel square. The following morning they had come up to the homestead for breakfast. They had come, they had explained, to give 'Old-fella'—in person—an account of the conditions out-back of the range, northway. Mrs. Watson was busy with steak and eggs for the men so she sent Lisa into 'Old-fella's' with his breakfast tray.

'Oh, so it's you carrying trays, is it?' he asked quite cheerfully. 'What's Mother Watson doing, eh? Waiting hand and foot on those men? Well, the pair of you—Mrs. Watson and you, Lisa—are well rid of the homestead to-day. I've my own men here and they'll look after me if necessary. There's no room for women in men's talk. Off with you both. Out for the day. You tell Mrs. Watson I said so. My orders.'

'I could do with a day off again,' Lisa said cheerfully.

She had learned that 'Old-fella' thought more of her if she promptly took him up on his words. When he threw out a challenge he liked to be met with one on the boomerang.

She set the tray on the table, then pummelled up his pillow into an arm-chair position. 'It'll be a long long all-day walk, if you don't look out, Grandfather. You'll miss me, won't you?'

She glanced from the tray to his face. He was not amused. This time her boomerang had fallen dead on the ground.

'So? Blackmail, is it? Well, I'll tell you how I answer blackmail. You go. And for *the whole day*, my girl. I don't want sight or sound of you till after sundown. You hear me, Lisa?'

'Yes I do, Grandfather,' she said regretfully. 'I was only joking. You know that, don't you? They had a wilful patient at Finch's Creek and I used to sort-of humour him that way. I took him at his word . . .'

'A wilful patient! So that's it, is it?' the old man bellowed. 'Who was that may I ask? Not Jimmy Come-up! That Ransome rapscallion from over the range, eh? They told me you'd been waiting on *him*. So that's who you compare me with?'

'Please, Grandfather,' Lisa begged. 'I was being tactless. That's all.'

'Very well, but I'm the one who gives orders round here; and let there be no talk of *humouring the patient*! Both of you go off for the day. *Out*. It might occur to the women in this homestead that I'd like a day to myself . . . with my own men . . .'

'Yes, of course, Grandfather. I didn't think of that. But the *whole day*?'

'The whole day. Get your hat and a tucker bag and go look at Pardalote. What did you come here for? To moon around in a homestead? A fine outbacker you'd make!'

Under his scornful words Lisa detected a note of concern. He really wanted her to go. Perhaps Mrs. Watson too. For their own sakes, as well as his, he wanted them to take a holiday. Lisa dared not show understanding. Instead she went to the door looking appropriately foolish. As she reached the door she looked up in the wall mirror. 'Old-fella' was leaning back in his arm-chair of pillows looking pleased with himself. For an invalid, he was about to attack his breakfast with strange relish.

This time Lisa was certain. Her grandfather was 'up to something'. What it was she would probably never know. Useless to guess.

Back in the kitchen, Lisa told Mrs. Watson the orders 'Old-fella' had given for the day.

'Quite right,' Mrs. Watson replied unexpectedly. She was sorting out the used tea towels while the stockmen at the end of the table, fed and replete, were lighting up their first cigarettes of the day. Out of the corner of her eye Lisa saw the men exchanging grins with one another.

Are they all in some kind of conspiracy? she wondered.

'Do you think it is all right for *both of us* to leave him for a whole day?' Lisa asked Mrs. Watson.

'Certainly. He's much better than he lets us know. Besides, I haven't given my horse any exercise for days. I might go to the outcamp. McPhee could have some more newspapers or magazines for "Old-fella".' She looked up from her bundle of towels and considered Lisa, this time with something like a forced air of friendliness. 'Take some food and a Thermos,' she said. 'And your hat. Be back at sundown.' Finally she added—after further thought —'*Tom will be in to-night.*'

Again Lisa caught an exchange of grins between the men at the table. Life was just one puzzle after another! By the manner of people in the homestead to-day she'd have thought everyone wanted to get rid of her. She would also have thought Mrs. Watson would want to keep her beloved son a hundred miles away. Not sort-of offer him up as a temptation to be home at sundown.

Half an hour later, on her way out for her walkabout, Lisa took the bundled tea towels down to the laundry. Nooma, the pretty smiling aboriginal girl, was busy at work in a cloud of steam. The sight now of a broad smile of welcome did Lisa's heart good. At least someone in the homestead liked to see her around to-day.

'What-for you go walkabout longa you-self?' Nooma asked. 'How 'bout you wait thet-way stringy-barks eh? This one-fella Nooma come bime-by alla-same this fella towel finish eh? You got plenty tucker, Lisa?'

'You'll come with me? Oh, Nooma, I'd love that!' Lisa dumped her shoulder bag, tucker-box and all, on the floor, and pushed her hat to the back of her head. 'Quick. Give me those towels, Nooma. I'll help you finish here while you hang out the rest of the clothes.'

Nooma laughed her giggly laugh as she watched Lisa plunge her towel-laden hands into the soapy water.

'Okay, Lisa!' she said. 'Quick'um wash eh? Mis' Watson plenty busy longa two-fella come wongi alla-long "Old-fella" eh? Bime-by maybe Mis' Watson go outcamp see McPhee. Fetchum papers belonga "Old-fella" eh?'

'You seem to know most things in advance, Nooma. But not *all*.' Lisa started wringing then rinsing, then wringing again. 'Mrs. Watson maybe is going to the outcamp, but the two men in the homestead are *stockmen*.'

Nooma's giggle became a shriek of laughter. 'That one-fella Rep bin stockman onetime ten year 'go. No-more. He bin allasame prospector this time. That other fella Jack bin stockman onetime las' year for walk-about, tha's all, He bin make plenty money rouseabout roun' muster-time. Tha's all. No more any-time stockman now. He bin gottem job rouseabout alla-long those fellas diggin' up stones belonga cattle-pad. Thet-away—' She pointed north-wards down the valley.

Lisa's arms came out of the soap suds and she stared at Nooma. The dark girl tossed her curly head and laughed and laughed.

'Mis' Watson maybe think them two-fella come talk alla-bout cattle belonga "Old-fella",' Nooma said at last. 'Alla-same they come talk blue stones, maybe white stones, maybe little yella stones.'

'Nooma!' Lisa asked ceasing work. 'Do you know the name of those stones? Are they called *beryl*?'

Nooma shrugged.

'Plenty stone, alla-bout ebry place,' she said. ' "Old-fella" bringum plenty fella from thet-away down south tell him what-name this stone. An', what-name this other-fella stone.'

Lisa looked thoughtful.

'Yes . . .' she said slowly. 'I think I was told he had a team of geologists somewhere out on the other side of the range. Tom said . . .'

'Tom good cattleman,' Nooma said cheerfully. 'Plenty good. He no like stones. Boss Ransome, he likes stones alla-same "Old-fella" like 'em.'

Lisa was so dazed by this news, she let the bush girl take the towels from her hands without noticing.

Funny, she thought, *how everybody knows something about something, if not about everything. But I don't know anything. Well, why should I? I'm just the stranger round here. What business is it of mine?*

'Okay, you ready, Lisa?' Nooma said when she had emptied and wiped out the troughs. 'We go now. Alla-same walk-about, you'n me. I show you how blackfella track, eh?'

'Yes, please, Nooma. I'd love that. I hope I'm not too dull a pupil to-day. Half the time I feel it—'

Nooma only laughed—*knowingly*—had Lisa noticed it.

Together, chatting happily, the two girls walked across the floor of the valley to the west side. When they reached the creek Nooma would not dally beside it. She had some other purpose in mind.

'I show you plenty good track up this-fella way, Lisa,' she said. Yard by yard she led Lisa upwards and crosswards then upwards again, towards that beckoning crag on the range-top. Though Lisa paid a sort-of mesmerised attention to Nooma's tracking lessons, her other self—standing by and watching all they did—knew exactly what Nooma was doing, and where she was taking her. This other self as well as her present self, really wanted to go up there too. Up to the lookout, or the 'eagle's eyrie'—call it what she would—to where the telescope looked down on Magool Ransome's homestead, Nangardee. Would she, from that distance, see another kind of flashing stone on Imelda's left hand?

In spite of being wholly occupied in the homestead these last weeks, there had been inside Lisa a sort-of waitingness. Something in her had been in a state of suspension.

Occasionally she had thought Tom's nocturnal visits alleviated this feeling of waiting. Sometimes, when Tom had held her hand, just that long, and told her yet again she was a pretty girl, she knew she was waiting for something else. That bright light to appear once again near the crooked bent crag!

But it had never come again.

Now as Nooma beguiled her up between the crags, down through the dips, then up over the top of the west-side gorges, she admitted deep inside herself, she had been waiting for *something more*. One more glimpse of Nangardee. One more visit from Magool Ransome. Just *one* more. That, maybe, would make her heart lie down and be still!

After all, he was—in a way—her patient. She must think of him that way only. It was only reasonable that she should want to know that his eyes continued to be in perfect health.

Even if Imelda were there too, it was better than not seeing him—except through the telescope—ever again.

For the rest of it, there was Tom. Comfortable, strong, sturdy, ten-mile-rider Tom. He was a good worker and a good, if sometimes stubborn, man. A bit like 'Old-fella'. What more could she, an orphan—*the girl whom no one came for*—ask? Besides Pardalote was Tom's home too. A sort-of security . . . was second-best better than no-best?

Lisa, Tom and Pardalote! Was this what 'Old-fella' was up to? Someone to carry on—one day.

'This fella horse belonga Tom,' Nooma was saying. Her finger was tracing a tiny groove at the side of a hoof-mark, half-way up the hill. The right foreleg shoe had a wear mark on it.

'This one other horse belonga Boss Missus,' Nooma went on. Lisa stooped by the girl and looked down at the marks.

'But that one hasn't a wear mark? Or a nail missing? It's perfect,' she said.

Nooma laughed, her beautiful teeth flashing and her eyes lit up like dark opals.

'Tha's ri,' she said. 'Boss Missus horse altogether got good shoes, eh? No other horse ride alla-same this way long-time ago.'

Lisa laughed too. How very simple! She hadn't seen the obvious. Perhaps all the other marks and tracks and sounds, even directions of birds flying, were as simple as these horse tracks in their messages to the bush girl.

They reached the boulder-strewn base of the gorge. Nooma swooped on a mark on the ground.

'This fella big lizard. Alla-same goanna. This fella make big mark down middle, tha' goanna's tail.'

'Of course!' Having been told, Lisa could see the obvious tell-tale marks.

They went on up the cliff face, scrambling between clumps of scraggy jutting bush, and in between clefts of fallen and disintegrating rocks. All the time Nooma showed Lisa something new.

'Parrots get big fright one day maybe two week long-time,' she said pointing to grey specks, almost like dead grubs.

'How do you know they had a fright?'

Nooma laughed gleefully.

'Alla-time *plenty-fella* grey spots ebrywhere. Parrots get

fright they drop them fella spots alla-time. No can stop. You see?'

Lisa saw. 'Poor little parrots,' she thought.

While Nooma tracked this and that, she was quietly edging Lisa up the gorge face.

'No one-fella walk-over here this place longa-time,' Nooma said cheerfully at one stage as they explored a small side track unknown to Lisa.

'How do you know that?' Lisa asked. 'Foot marks wouldn't show on that mat of dead leaves.'

Nooma laughed, really enjoying herself.

'Not look for foot-mark,' she explained. 'If foot-mark there, alla-same tell you what name this fella. No foot-mark so—little bit broken grass here and maybe little broken twig tell you someone come some-time. Dead ants too. When you see dead ants maybe you look quick for foot-mark tell you what name this fella come tread on ants. To-day, no ants dead. No fella come.'

'Oh!' Lisa said, deflated.

'You pretty good alla-same, Lisa. You learn plenty fast. Maybe you make pretty good bush girl like Nooma eh?'

14

Minutes later the two girls rounded the last remnants of a red granite outcrop, turning left as they did so.

They came out on 'Old-fella's' path—only a few feet from the lookout!

Nooma was watching the other girl slyly, her eyes shining with hidden laughter.

'You brought me here on purpose,' Lisa said accusingly. 'How did you know . . . ? I mean, why *here*? As if this place has anything to do with me!' She broke off. Nooma's eyes were wise. 'Of course you knew,' Lisa finished lamely. 'You bush people always know *everything*—'

The other girl shrugged her shoulders, all innocence now.

'You look in that place,' she said. 'Big glass-eye—tele-

153

scope eh? See plenty long-way, all-down Nangardee. Maybe you see my cousin Jabberdee.'

Nooma edged her way into the lookout. Lisa followed slowly.

'You go look-see,' Nooma advised, nodding her head and still smiling. 'I go find witchety grubs. Maybe fat goanna for dinna too. Maybe li'l lizard.'

Nooma faded away while Lisa still stood in the lookout's opening! searching for her conscience. It was lost.

Something else gone-away.

What am I waiting for? she asked herself. *Why shouldn't I look through the telescope? I've done it before. Why feel guilty now?*

Ah! But one night on the think-bench there had been up here a light brighter than the moon-dimmed stars. She had told herself something then. That had been before Tom had taken her hand—and held it.

Lisa shook her head, shaking away thoughts that mattered too much. She glanced down at the ground. She felt herself go stiff all over. She shut her eyes but when she opened them she knew she had seen right.

There, clear and firm, was the footprint of a man's boot. It had been made recently: since yesterday afternoon anyway.

Nooma's first lesson in tracking had come home to roost. Yesterday a soft inland wind had been blowing and last night there would have been a fine film of dust over the floor. That imprint had been made to-day!

Lisa turned away quickly.

At the opening to the track, she stopped dead on the spot. Two figures were coming towards her from over the ridge above. A man and a woman. Their easy manner seemed to say they had a *right to be there*. On 'Old-fella's' property? Surely that was Pardalote's side of the range!

Lisa stood so still she might have been part of the rockscape. They came on, not thirty yards away now. Magool Ransome and Imelda. Magool was tall, sun-browned, and his unique self. Imelda was as striking-looking as at the times Lisa had seen her before. Even in outback clothes she was groomed. There was something professional looking about her too. Maybe, before she came north, she was someone awfully important in the city!

Imelda saw Lisa too. She turned and said something to Magool who at that moment was concentrating on something on the ground.

She made an almost theatrical gesture to point out Lisa.

Magool looked up quickly. Then together they came on—getting closer and closer as they wound their way round rocks, skirting clumps of prickly bush.

Magool lifted his head again and looked across the short distance to where Lisa stood. He raised his eyebrows almost in a mocking way. Then he smiled—that same inimical smile. Lisa's heart eased back into place with an effort.

His manner seemed to say—'So there you are! I thought I was not going to see you again.' This expression changed to a look of faint amusement, which puzzled Lisa. She had an idea he was thinking of someone very youthful. A small, though perhaps endearing child.

Well, he didn't know her so very well, after all.

On the other hand, she might have dobs of rock dust on her face and so looked funny. Well—the dust could stay! She'd wear it as a badge of pride.

She simply stood and waited.

They were on the path now, right in front of her. They both had a sort-of 'well met on range tops' air about them.

The effect of all this was that Lisa unconsciously put on her 'portrait look' again.

Magool, now he was at a standstill, went about the ritual of cigarette making. As he did so he watched Lisa, and catching that quiet, still look on her face, raised his eyebrows quizzically.

'Well, well!' Imelda was saying. 'Here is Lisa from Pardalote! The girl—'

'—no one came for,' Lisa finished for her. Her face gave nothing away of her thoughts. There was a 'waiting' look in her sea-blue eyes.

Imelda's laugh actually trilled—but not in a bird-like way. 'Why, Magool!' she said at last. 'I believe she is shy, but witty as well. Do you think so?'

'No,' he said briefly, tucking the tobacco strays into the

paper-ends with a match. 'There are occasions when she is quite talkative. And *entertaining*. You'll discover that Imelda—if ever you are a hospital patient.'

He smiled at Lisa over the match while he held it to his cigarette. 'It's not with-it to be shy, is it, Lisa?'

'A minute ago,' she answered, ever so quietly, 'you were talking *of* me as if in my absence.'

'Were we? I apologise.'

'Oh *Jim*! Look!' Imelda interrupted. She had spotted the opening into the lookout. 'Whatever is it? Two boulders, giant-high. Hiding what? I simply *must* investigate.'

She stepped gingerly between the boulders then poked her head out again. 'Jim . . . for goodness sake come and look! What do you think? A telescope! Fixed so it can look down over Nangardee—'

She disappeared into the lookout again, obviously to satisfy her curiosity.

'I apologise,' Magool said to Lisa. 'Are we forgiven?'

'Yes. Of course. I'm sorry I said that to Imelda—'

'She said it originally, so she won't complain, I'm sure of that. Imelda has quite a sense of humour.'

'That's good,' Lisa said simply. Her sea-blue eyes were still pools of thought as she looked at Magool. He put his head slightly on one side and returned her look.

'You are very beguiling—standing there alone on the side of a mountain, Lisa. Like a lost child. Do you feel lost?'

She blinked her eyes, then shook her head as if to bring herself out of some distant place back to here, and to the present again.

'I'm sorry,' she said, returning his smile. 'No I don't feel lost. I was surprised, that's all.'

'To see us? Well, it's not very usual for us to be up here, I admit. I wanted to show Imelda by daylight, an unusual formation a few yards over the ridge.'

'She is very interested in the range?'

Magool laughed . . . 'You bet she is,' he said. 'It's her job to be interested. Anyone in my company has to get that way and stay that way.'

'Stay that way?' Lisa repeated thoughtfully. 'Yes, I

suppose that would be so—' Magool's words—about *staying that way*—implied a kind of permanency. Were they actually and ritually engaged? She must look at Imelda's left hand—when Imelda had finished with 'Old-fella's' property in 'Old-fella's' lookout.

'Lisa,' Magool said, 'I'm glad to see you again. I know your grandfather is well. Jabberdee keeps me informed.' His smile became faintly ironic as he added—'It used to be bed-rails that kept us, you and me, apart. Now it's a chain of mountains—and a lot of prejudice.'

Lisa thought he meant this kindly. Perhaps he was sorry Imelda had all but laughed at her. She ought to *appear* to have a tougher skin.

'I came for a walk with Nooma,' she said, to get on to more practical subjects. 'I'm glad to see you too, Magool. I've been up here before—'

'Yes. I know.' He was watching her as he said this, still smiling in a small, but amused way, as he saw the surprise in her face. Then the unbidden blush.

Imelda had put her head and shoulders out of the lookout again.

'Jim,' she insisted, 'what on earth are you doing out there? Come in here, for goodness sake. It's quite a revelation! This will positively *stun* you.'

'Yes, I'll be there in one minute, Imelda. I want to be sure Lisa takes my good wishes to "Old-fella": Wishes for a speedy return to good health—and all that—'

'Oh well, then. Be quick about it, darling. We haven't that much time, have we?' Imelda said, disappearing again into the lookout.

Funny, Lisa was thinking, *I wonder why he didn't show Imelda this place before? He obviously knew about it—*

'Lisa,' Magool said, 'what are you thinking about?'

'I was wondering—'

'Where Nooma had got to? Well, here she comes over the crag behind you. Looks as if she's been on a circular walkabout.'

Lisa turned her head and saw Nooma scrambling over the rocks towards them.

'I see her—' She hesitated, then looked back, straight into his eyes. 'Magool, how did you know I'd been here before? How do you know that telescope is there? It's inside my grandfather's boundary isn't it?'

'If there are such things as boundaries hereabouts, *where Pardalote is concerned*, then I imagine the answer is "yes".' His smile, half ironical, came back. 'I knew you'd been here because, down there at Nangardee, I know when someone is playing with the telescope up here. You see, according to the hour of the day, the sun shines on the glass. The reflection is quite bright. I assumed it would be you. "Old-fella" and Tom were away from the homestead, that first time. There could be no one else—'

Lisa refused to blush again. She had to keep her dignity.

'Of course,' she agreed. 'The reflection would be like a light. Who knows? Someone might be able to send an S.O.S. by it some day—if ever there was the need.'

Magool was not exactly smiling any more. He dropped his match to the ground and put his heel on it. He ground it down quite ruthlessly.

'Who knows?' he said lightly. Then added, coldly serious now, 'I hope you will remember that, Lisa. If ever there *is* an occasion—'

'I'm sure there won't be. But thank you for your neighbourly offer.' She was glad she'd made a point of neighbourliness. Once she'd said it.

Nooma had sidled round a rock and was watching them with a kind-of pleased interest.

'Hallo, Nooma!' Magool said. 'So you've brought Lisa up to the range-top to-day, have you? What tricks are you up to now?'

Nooma turned her head away, pretending shyness. She kicked a toe in the dust. Then she looked up, first at Lisa, then at Magool. Her face creased in a smile. 'I bring Lisa up this one-time maybe see something allasame nice down Nangardee, Boss,' she said cheerfully.

'I see. And not "something alla-same nice" up on top of the range?'

'Oh *no*, Boss. Not me. Not never. That fella Jabberdee, he do that look all-around plenty often. Sometime maybe—'

'Your motives are pure as water from the creek, Nooma,

158

I'm sure of that. Well, if you go down the steep way you'd better take care of Lisa. It's dangerous to those who don't know it. "Old-fella's" past it these days—'

'Don't you worry, Boss. I take plenty good care. 'Sides, I gotta get Lisa down pretty good—'

She let this remark hang in the air as she glanced up sideways at the sky, measuring the sun's position, where it was now in the western arc. She looked childishly innocent. Too much so. 'Tom come-in to-night,' she added. 'Plenty time get Lisa down ar'right. Then mebbe he come-in sundown—'

Her eyes slyly swung back to Magool. His only reply was silence.

Lisa hadn't any idea what this exchange was about. It didn't make sense. What had Tom to do with it all? As far as the hour was concerned, she and Nooma hadn't even had their lunch yet.

She looked from one to the other. Magool's mouth was set and his eyes had a certain frozen punishment in them for Nooma. Nooma, for her part, wore the slow smile born of knowledge that came from days, nights, years, in the wild, lonely, and unknown places of the great Australian bush.

Imelda came once again through the opening between the rocks.

'*Jim, darling!*' she said exasperated. 'You must have had "Old-fella's" entire history by this time: or given it. Do come. I'm dying to show you something in here. There's some of that same crystal formation behind these rocks—'

'Okay Imelda. I'm sorry to keep you waiting. I'm glad I saw you, Lisa—if only for a few minutes on top of this part of the world. My regards to Mrs. Watson. And, of course—Tom.'

'Good-bye, Magool,' Lisa said as she turned away. There was no need for polite good-byes to Imelda because Imelda, a single-minded person, had disappeared once more into 'Old-fella's' lookout.

This invasion of her grandfather's property distressed Lisa, but she could do nothing about it now. Besides, she felt Magool would not be doing anything dishonourable. It wasn't in his make-up. Was it possible they had also found the crystal cave further down? What upset *that* might cause!

Lisa followed Nooma down a lead-off into the gorge. This was the little path she had seen, but not ventured, on her earlier visit. It was as Magool had said—steep, and in places, almost dangerous. It had not been used for such a long time it was overgrown with small straggly bushes, slippery in themselves, and which hid footholds and also handholds on the cliff's side.

Half-way down they found a little cul-de-sac in the form of a loop-way round one enormous boulder that had once graced the mesa-top of the range. Here the two girls sat down to eat a very late lunch. They rested for quite a time while Nooma told Lisa many things about the little insects, tiny lizards, and even bush flies that they saw creeping and flying around them as they sat in the shade of the overhanging rock.

'Nooma?' Lisa asked at length. 'Why did you take me to the lookout at the top of the range? You meant to—didn't you?'

Nooma looked sideways down her nose, then laughed her wonderful flashing laugh. Her large liquid brown eyes were full of mischievous lights.

'Wha' for you come with me up top of gorge, eh, Lisa?' she asked.

It was Lisa's turn to look away. Nooma, like all her people, knew *everything*, what went on in people's hearts too! In her bush-telegraph way she had *known* Magool Ransome was up there. Perhaps Imelda too. She had intended they should meet. But why?

'You lazy-fella, Lisa,' Nooma said, breaking the silence and scrambling to her feet. 'You come-on quick fella. Maybe we go see alla-same *bullai bullai*. He come-in close sundown, by *goondool*.'

'Whatever that may mean, Nooma! Say it in my brand of Australian, please.'

Nooma giggled.

'You fella sometime ask what-name him plenty parrots come in by stringy-bark tree. Little fella finches. Maybe yongana come in to-night. I don't know what-name yongana.'

160

'Is it a bird? Like a parrot?'

'Alla-same cockatoo. This one fella all by 'imself. You see.'

They gathered their belongings and made their way down the path to the foot of the gorge-side.

There amongst the stringy-barks Lisa stood with wrinkled brow, struggling to *remember* something.

What had her mother told her? Suddenly it came to her in a flash.

'*Often at sundown, the birds came into the trees at the foot of the little path up the gorge side. That path leads way-up to the "Sunset Land". I used to go up there to meet your father. The birds watched me go, but one little cockatoo watched most. He was the only one with pink feathers, and green in his comb.*'

Lisa could almost hear her mother's voice. For one minute there was a stinging to her eyes.

As she looked about her her spirits rose again. In the distance the air was filled with tiny birds—midgets in the air. Clouds of them, all winging their way towards her from the south sides of the valley.

Here came hundreds and hundreds of birds. More than she had thought were in the whole world of the north.

They came on in a great cloud, a myriad of tiny coloured finches. They flew straight into the stringy-barks, then set about the noisy twittering business of finding enough perch room for each and all.

Lisa was spell-bound.

She even forgot the waiting, watching, Nooma.

She sat down on a tree trunk and stared and stared. There was such a rainbow of colours as each flight of birds came in, not one flight like another! Red and yellow birds first. Next came the crimson and black: then the grey and white striped ones. They took up every inch of the stringy-bark trees, including the down-trailing branch ends. Some tiny birds were even swinging on the leaf twigs.

Then, barely settled, as if from some order on high, they took off again, covey after covey.

Now, coming across the valley, were yet more birds. These

were larger and even more brilliantly coloured. As they settled where the finches had been a minute before, Lisa saw that these were tiny parrots: parakeets. Again there was a colour-riot amongst the quivering branches and twigs. A flight of red, yellow, and green birds vied for dazzle with crimson, black and gold.

They in their turn had barely settled when, with a whirr of wings and mad with colour, they took off in mass. This time it was to make way for larger parrots. Again there was a riot of even more brilliant colours.

One bird shone out, single and *alone*. It was a shell-pink cockatoo with a rounded head and a grey-blue comb touched with jade green. This jewelled comb was standing upright as its owner took stock of Lisa. It was the most beautiful, lovable bird she had ever seen.

'Lovely cocky!' Lisa said softly. 'Why are you there— all by yourself? Are the parrots taking care of you because you're an orphan too?'

The cocky blinked one eye as he put his head to the side and looked at her.

Suddenly all the combs went up. The parrots turned their heads and looked towards something high in the sky above the hills at the southern end of the valley.

Lisa too looked. It was a big hovering bird. She too felt the same alarm. This was what all the birds had been fleeing from in such brilliant confusion.

'That fella way-up what-name *Woorawa* belonga him,' Nooma said. 'Alla-same *eagle*!'

'A wedge-tailed eagle!' Lisa said, awed. 'A bird of prey! No wonder all the other birds were frightened.'

A shot rang out over the still afternoon air. The hovering bird dropped to the ground like a stone. At once the parrots —and the one shell-pink cockatoo in their midst—took off in a fright. In clouds of colour, screeching on the sun-down world of the valley, they flew off in the wake of the smaller birds.

Lisa watched them go. Alas, there was nothing left now but broken twigs, and the fluttering of tree-debris to the ground.

She watched a last leaf fall, and felt sad. The birds had gone. All of them!

'They-all come back 'nother day,' Nooma said softly, comforting her. 'You see them plenty-fella arri' 'nother time. Maybe sometime soon.'

Lisa believed Nooma and her good spirits came back again. She would see the birds again. This was a roost, or maybe their staging post. The leaf litter and grey spots on the ground told their own story. She would keep a constant watch for them—specially the cockatoo in shell-pink feathers with the colour of jade green in his comb.

Wonderful parrots of Pardalote!

Lisa picked up the Thermos and her shoulder bag. Together she and Nooma headed across the valley for home. Near the stables they parted company, each promising the other they'd go walkabout another day.

'Nex' time you come alla-long other-side see *my* home,' Nooma said.

'I'd love to,' Lisa promised. 'Your mother and your father?'

'That sure thing,' Nooma said. 'My brother and maybe my cousin Jabberdee. How you like see that fella Jabberdee, eh, Lisa?'

'Very much. He could tell me all about Nangardee, couldn't he?'

Nooma only giggled in reply to that. Then ran off.

Lisa crossed the gravel square to the homestead with a light heart. She had had her day out, and it had been a wonderful day—in spite of Miss Imelda Bannister. There had been the flight of the parrots to put a rainbow to her day, and to-night when she was alone in her bed she had many things to think about. Bedtime—not 'Old-fella's' think-bench on the veranda—was her own most private thinking time.

Lastly, Tom would be home, sooner if not later. That meant company: someone to talk to. Tom would tell her about the parrots—where they went to, and where they came from. She had promised herself never to think of that 'third share' again, but perhaps . . . if she asked ever so carefully . . . Tom might tell her a little more about the

163

management of Pardalote. She longed to know everything, because already Pardalote felt like *home*. It *was* home.

The rifle was standing against the veranda wall when Lisa arrived back at the homestead.

She opened the screen door and slipped into the kitchen. It seemed dark in there after the glare of the late afternoon outside. She blinked and shook her head as if to throw away mists.

When the pupils of her eyes adjusted, she could see better. Tom was home already! He was sitting at the table, his legs sprawled out in front of him. The dusty broad-brimmed stetson was taking king-place at the end of the table.

They ought to have a hat rack, she thought.

Tom looked at Lisa over his tea cup, then drew in his legs slowly. He pushed back his chair, and stood up. He was smiling at her in that slow way that sometimes puzzled her. But he was glad to see her—she could sense that. She smiled back gladly.

'Tom,' she said eagerly, crossing the room towards him. 'You shot that eagle didn't you? It might have killed some of the parrots. You saved them.'

'You saw the parrots, did you, Lisa? Quite a sight when they come in like that. One kind after another. Take a wedge-tail or a gun to scatter them off. Remember I warned you about eagles? East-side or west-side of the valley? Man or bird? They're both takers.' He paused as if waiting for her to register some inner meaning to these words, but Lisa only looked puzzled. 'You want a cup of tea?' he asked at length, changing the subject.

'Yes please. Actually I'm dying for one.' She sat down at the table while he went to the stove and brought back the tea-pot.

'Fresh made!' he told her. 'I'll pour it for you. Those cakes are fresh made, that's for sure. Have one.'

'Thank you, Tom. I will. Please tell me. Have you been in long? How is my grandfather?'

'He's back to his old roaring self. Leastwise, he was when I last saw him—belted and spurred, and ready to take off with those two fellas who came in last night. Seems they'd brought Challenger in with them. Sept's gone too, and he'd go nowhere except with "Old-fella".'

Lisa put down the cake she had just taken; and stared at him, incredulous.

'You mean—he's gone *out*? *With those two stockmen*?'

'They aren't stockmen, Lisa.' Tom was sitting down and leaning back easily in his chair; looking faintly superior. 'Those fellas come from back-top of the range. They're two of the lot hacking and digging and shovelling away at rocks up there. That kind buy their change-clothes at station stores anywhere along the track. They kinda like themselves to look like stockmen. They've some fancy name of their own which I've forgotten. They're looking for minerals. What for, I'd never know. This is cattle country. Always has been; always will be.'

Lisa was in a state of near shock. So what Nooma had said about those men was true!

'My grandfather did say they were "his men". Why did he go with them?'

'Because he wanted to. No one ever stopped "Old-fella" doing what he wanted, Lisa. He's good and well now. I saw that with my own eyes, last time I was in. I could see he was rarin' to go. Cunning though. He sent you and my mother off on a walkabout so he could take-off himself without too much arguing.'

Of course! she thought. *Something told me he was up to something. But dressed, and out on the range?*

'Tom, did he leave a message for *me*?' she asked, not wanting to give away her feelings.

'Yes he did,' Tom said laconically. 'Last thing before he took off. Now let's see if I can remember rightly. Crazy sort of message, if you ask me. But then "Old-fella's" been a bit soft in the head ever since he started finding those coloured stones.'

'Tom, dear. *Dear, dear,* Tom,' Lisa implored. '*Please*. What was my grandfather's message? And don't call him "soft in the head". Well, not to me.'

Tom laughed.

'You really care, don't you, Lisa? You know what? Your eyes go the best dark blue ever—when you get all serious like that. Your face kinda reminds me of a picture

I must have seen once. An' I like the way you said "*dear, dear,* Tom". Sounded good.'

'*Tom.* What was my grandfather's message?'

'Okay. Take a pull on your reins, Lisa, while I get it straight. It went something like this . . . Are you listening?'

'I'm listening.'

'Okay, here goes . . . "Tell that granddaughter of mine when she comes in from roaming around with Nooma up the west side, *that a young vixen might have cunning,* but she can't match the old dingo." ' Tom paused watching the effect of these words. 'What do you suppose he meant by that, Lisa? Everyone born north of Twenty-six knows that by yellow-dog's standards, the fox, or his vixen, is a fool. Maybe he knew about a certain predatory bird on top of that valley—eh?'

Lisa's eyes were darker than ever, and her face was quiet-still. She was thinking—*They always talk in terms of animals and birds! All of them! 'Old-fella' was trying to get a message through to me. But what? He even knew where I'd been to-day. Another telescope hidden in the homestead?*

She looked up and caught Tom's eyes searching her face. She shook her head.

'Goodness only knows,' she shook her head. 'Except he was telling me something about that dingo we hear up on the hillside at night. He said nobody can catch that dingo—'

'Maybe he means you can't catch "Old-fella" in the trap of your charms Lisa,' Tom said. 'Have you been trying?'

'Yes,' she admitted ruefully. 'I wanted him to like me. But I don't exactly have *charms*—'

Tom stood up again, and kicked his chair back from behind him.

'Maybe yes and maybe no—for "Old-fella",' he said, taking her hand and drawing her up towards him. 'But for me? Well, that's different. I've got a suggestion. I can't take you to the muster like I promised, after all. They've got the first mob of cattle moving out to the road-head already. The fastest job we ever did. A record! You know why, Lisa?'

She shook her head.

'I got good and tired of riding ten miles in and ten miles out again every time I wanted to see a girl. "Old-fella" said he'd be gone a week or two—but I've to go for stores soon. How about coming with me in the truck to Wyndham? There's no one to say Yea or Nay to you. It's okay with my mother. Actually she's wanted it all along —for *your* sake—that is. Thought you ought to see something of the country up hereabouts. It's quite a trip if you want to see the real wild country. Coming?'

Lisa had no idea why she nodded her head, but nod it she did. It was something to do with her feelings: and not quite caring where she went, or why—at this moment.

She must have failed with her grandfather. Like Magool Ransome, he too was a gone-away man. Both of them! He had left a harsh message—implying *she'd* been scheming. Like the dingo, he was not to be caught.

Tom was looking into Lisa's eyes and she looked back without seeing his face, or realising he was still holding her hand. She saw nothing but her own dark thoughts.

Perhaps she *had* been up to something! She had come north to find a home, and to find out what that mystery 'third share' in her mother's Will meant. Of course, of course! Spelled out that way it looked like '*seeking to get*'. 'Old-fella' had seen it and now was going to deal with it in some 'cunning' way of his own. Mrs. Watson had read it that way too! No wonder she had been unwelcoming!

'*Lisa*!' Tom said, shaking her hand as if to wake her up. 'What were you thinking? You'd like to take that trip wouldn't you? There's fun we could have in the cattle port. Bells on her toes and a ring on her finger—' he said meaningly. 'You understand me, Lisa? You'd like that?'

'Yes,' she said, mesmerised by her own dark thoughts: by Tom's eyes too. Trilby to his Svengali. She hadn't the faintest idea . . . nor did she quite care . . . what she was saying.

'Old-fella' went away without saying good-bye. So did Magool. Even my mother didn't say good-bye when she died. Everyone all my life will do this to me. All of them—always gone-away.

She looked into Tom's face and saw only his solid worth as 'Old-fella's' overseer. The best cattleman in the north.

167

Lisa, Tom and Pardalote! The necessary trinity! Could that be it?

Tom's hand held tight, and was firm. Something to lean on.

'Yes,' she said again. 'I would like to come with you Tom. Very much. I would like to see the wild country—'

'Bells on your toes and a ring on your finger?'

Her smile was a little wintry.

'Yes . . . Bells on my toes and rings on my fingers —wherever you got that nursery rhyme, Tom.'

Tom judged this was not the best moment to start the kissing game. His ear had caught the plural to the word 'ring'. He half guessed Lisa had not really understood what he meant.

But Wyndham was a long way off, and there was plenty of time. Once there—well, there was nowhere for a girl like Lisa to go—except straight into his arms.

'Sit down and I'll pour you another cup of tea, Lisa,' he said with a grin. 'That one on the table must be cold. Then I'll have to leave you. I have to see my mother in the office. About business. When "Old-fella's" away my mother and I run the business side of Pardalote. We have to list the stores, for a start-off—'

'Thank you,' Lisa said, and sat down. She let Tom make her fresh tea and bring it to her. He made her a sandwich too—as she didn't seem to have any taste for the new-made cakes.

She had had a long day and was tired: and now Tom was actually waiting on her. It was good to be waited-on for a change. Specially when she was so tired. She needed someone—badly—

He was very kind.

15

Within two days, without delay for second thoughts, Lisa and Tom Watson left Pardalote on the overland trip to Wyndham.

They had had little more than a few words together

since the decision-making after Lisa's walkabout with Nooma. There had been much for Tom to do. The truck had not been used for some time and he had to put in time servicing it: also checking the tyres and engine —late at night. Finally, he had to load-in and check their own equipment for a long overland run. It would take at least two days to reach the northern town.

'Could turn out longer—' Tom had said vaguely.

'You've taken the truck out in worse condition,' Mrs. Watson said anxiously when she took Tom some hot supper while he was still at work.

'We've more than a hundred and fifty miles to go—over rough country—before we even reach the road-head,' Tom said. He was tired, so was irritable. 'This time I have a girl with me. You don't want a long-time breakdown do you? We've got to get there, and what's to be done when we get there has to oe done quickly.' He paused to wipe his brow. 'Like I said, you have to treat some people like cattle. Muster 'em in at *pace*. That way they don't have time to stampede.'

'You know cattle all right, Tom. But do you know girls? Specially one like Lisa?'

'Leave it to me, Mother, will you? Any rate the idea was yours first. Not mine. That boost talk I had to come an' get round midnight when Lisa'd gone to bed and supposed me half-way back to the muster! No more of that. Right.'

His mother nodded slowly.

'I admit I liked the idea,' Tom added. 'Suits me *and Pardalote*, right down to the ground.'

'Well, fix the truck as you go, Tom. McPhee's arranged the time and place once you get to Wyndham. That old pedal radio of his has turned out really useful. I spent a whole day getting to the outcamp and back just on the hope he'd agree. A good job "Old-fella" gave me that day-off. Lisa too.'

'I thought "Old-fella" had sent you—like he sent Lisa —out—for a change of air. What was *he* up to?'

'He was looking very knowing the night before. You know his way, Tom. As it turned out he was expecting those two men in and wanted to make-off himself. He thought there'd be less chance of ructions if Lisa and I were out. That's about it, I'm sure.'

'Cunning though. Always was,' Tom said thoughtfully, as he tightened the grip on the truck's engine block.

'All the same Tom, I'm thinking about when he comes back. What then?'

'Not to worry, for Heaven's sake. "Old-fella" 'll never be mad at you—if that's what's under your skin. He needs you, and if he didn't know it before, he knows it now. Ever since he had that dizzy turn up by the Number Four bore. He'll pretend different, but he'll go nuts if you're not around.'

'Yes. I've worked that out myself. But don't forget—'

'Forget nothing,' Tom said exasperated, and tightening a belt on his gear. 'Look, I've never known you worry before. He needs us both. I'm the best cattleman in the north and "Old-fella" even goes so far as to say so. Me tied into Pardalote with Lisa will make it even more secure for him. Don't you see that? The Lindsay blood goes on. The best housekeeper and the best cattleman in the north thrown in. Great jumping kangaroos—*he's on toast!* And he'll know it. I guess *that's* what he's up to, if you ask me!'

'Yes, I see that,' Mrs. Watson said, her face lighting up a little. 'It's best for all. Except he has to go at it the round-about way.'

'So you think it's best for all, do you? Then you might try liking Lisa. *And showing it more.* I know you've been giving it a go lately. As long as she's happy about that side of things—'

'Yes, I will, Tom. Besides—'

'Well, what now? Besides what?'

'I've spent half my lifetime looking after "Old-fella". I'm used to him. I'm fond of him too. I wouldn't have anything happen to him. Even when he blusters and bellows. I . . .'

'You've learned not to *hear* that side of him, any more than I do. Time's not far off when I'll do the blustering and bellowing. Sorry to say it again if it riles you, but —*he's getting old*—'

'I think that's what he's afraid of—'

'I wish he'd be afraid of meddling with minerals, rocks, crystals, and such like. And leave Pardalote to cattle. Getting soft in the head about those things. And don't say me *not* on that! Now will you leave me alone, Mother. I have to get this raking truck ready; and a few hours sleep thrown-in for luck.'

Lisa, doing as she was told automatically, packed her bag and was ready to go first thing the next morning. Half of her was looking forward to making this trip across the far north. She kept telling herself it was a wonderful piece of luck to have the opportunity to do it. Her other half was dulled by a strange lassitude.

She was tired of thinking about people like Magool and Imelda, and 'Old-fella'—*all gone-away people*.

She had made all the mistakes herself, of course. She had made mistakes with her grandfather, that was certain. She had tried to tease him the way she had sometimes teased Magool Ransome in the hospital—just talking back the way he had talked to her. It hadn't paid off. Not with Magool Ransome nor with her grandfather. Why hadn't she learned?

Well . . . there was Tom! *He* hadn't gone away! Safe, secure Tom, who did not think she made mistakes! He even thought she was pretty; and said so, which was more important.

She was tired of thinking it out over and over again.

She would pack her bag and go. A trip across the back country to Wyndham would do her good. That was it! She needed a tonic! The long, long way to the far cattle town would be just that. She would be cheerful for Tom's sake. *As from now.*

Mrs. Watson saw them off from the side of the gravel square at sun-up next morning. For the first time Lisa saw Mrs. Watson really smiling in a willing and *pleased* way. This was unexpected because Lisa had been afraid Mrs. Watson would not approve of her going off with Tom. She was so relieved by this apparent 'willingness', she waved happily back. She actually felt happier too. If everybody in the world went round smiling, why what a different world it would be!

She must remember to do a bit more smiling herself!

They drove down the valley. Not once did Lisa look up to the west-side range. She didn't look for the stringy-barks;

171

nor hope for a sight of the brilliant coloured birds in flight. It was the wrong time of the day for birds, anyway. Even the wounded one in her heart.

At the far end of the valley Tom turned the truck north-west; still following the fold between the ancient red granite ranges.

They passed a large acreage of high green grass. It was yellowing a little in the coming of the Dry.

'What is that, Tom?' Lisa asked surprised.

'Sorghum,' he said briefly. 'Another of "Old-fella's" crank ideas. Grain-feed.'

'Does he sell it? Does it bring more money into Par-dalote?'

'Nope. He sends it to this high-falutin' place called "*Northern Cereal Research Project*". That's his way of keeping on the right side of the government—so they don't get sticky about any "pastoral" lease. It's good for tickling "Old-fella's" vanity too. That's all!'

'But you're the overseer. Shouldn't you be interested, Tom?'

'I run cattle, Lisa. I don't hold with growing things like crops up in these latitudes. "Old-fella" has Nooma's brother and father on that lot. They can have it, as far as I'm concerned. That *beryl* and mineral, and such stuff, too. All eyewash! Look to the west, Lisa. See those smokes over there. That's Nooma's relatives talking.'

'What are they saying?'

'I can't read smoke signals, but I guess they're letting the rest of their mob outback know that we're on our way. You and I, Lisa.' Under his breath he said—*I hope they keep their news for aborigines only, for the next two days.*

'I thought it was the didgeridoo that sent special *sounds*,' Lisa said.

'That too, come night time. For a hundred miles around they'll know just where we are as we hit the tracks. Most of them are on walkabout, thank goodness. Out of cir-culation. Some initiation ceremony, I expect.'

Lisa watched the smokes. One thing they would never be able to tell one another!

'Now you hold on,' Tom advised a few minutes later. 'It's rough hereabouts.'

Lisa gripped the door handle.

172

With a fast turn of the wheel Tom pulled the truck round at a right angle. Five minutes later they were on a cattle pad, wider than the track they had been on, but also rough. The cattle had passed through here in the last few days. Lisa could see the fresh spoors on the ground. Remembering Nooma's instruction, she looked for the bent and broken bush stems that were not yet dried-out.

They were travelling through a low valley into heavier tree-country presently. Lisa could identify the konkerberry shrubs and the ironwoods. The grass was deep.

'What is this grass called, Tom?'

'Blue grass,' he said. 'There's some that calls it "bundle-bundle". That name came from the aborigines, I expect. See that dust-haze farther up the valley?'

'Yes. It's the cattle, isn't it? Oh, I do want to see them close up.'

'Can't do, I'm afraid. I came this way to see if the drovers had them in a travelling mob. They're on the move all right. That's all I wanted to know. I'll leave them be —for the first time in my life.'

'Why?'

'I have a date in Wyndham. Have to keep it. Cattle only move six or seven miles a day—hereabouts.'

Lisa said 'Oh!' and wondered what the date could be that it had so *promptly* to be kept. Tom mostly took his *own* time about things.

Half an hour later Tom swerved the truck into the pindan, and it was very rough going through the low denser scrub after that. There was little sign of a track.

Lisa, clinging with both hands to the door handle, wondered how Tom found his way. He knew it, she supposed, like 'Old-fella' had known the way into Pardalote from the south side.

Late in the afternoon they were in a deep depression and passed through groves of tropical vegetation. There were, here and there, huge bottle-shaped baobab trees, palms, and rich-looking acacias.

'It's like coming into a different world,' Lisa said, wondering.

They spent that night under the stars. Lisa didn't have

time to enjoy the magic beauty of the skies because the roughness of the drive through the almost untracked bushland had shaken every bone in her body. Three minutes after she had crawled into her sleeping bag by the camp fire, she had fallen into a deep and dreamless sleep. She hadn't even noticed Tom—who had been sitting smoking a cigarette near her—take himself and his own sleeping bag off to a tree a few yards away. Nor had she noticed that his temper—a little earlier—wasn't as good as usual. She had thought he was dead tired, as she was. That was all. She had been asleep when he had proffered a reluctant 'good night'.

The next morning they were packed and aboard the truck soon after sunrise.

Tom said he wasn't sure whether they'd make Wyndham to-night or not.

'Should do,' he said. 'It's faster going over this bit, but you never can tell, can you? The tank gets a bit near the boil on the long stretches. Maybe we'll stop over another night. One thing, you won't be so tired after that black-out sleep of yours last night. Will you?'

'No, I'm sure I won't. I feel wonderful this morning. My black-out, Tom, was nine straight hours of beautiful slumber: not even a dream. But what about your important date?'

He glanced sideways at her.

'I guess it can wait another twenty-four hours. What do *you* say, Lisa? How about it?'

'If you say so, Tom,' she agreed. She had no idea of any deeper meaning that might be in Tom's words. She had put her trust in him. She was busy watching a brown ball of dust racing along—way out to the west. It was moving in a line nearly parallel to their own. She watched it for a few minutes, then turned to look past Tom to the east.

There the great wasteland over which they were travelling was broken by red buttresses of giant rock-arms that reached out on to the thirsty plain. These buttresses were out-runners from a line of pinnacle-topped, desolate, iron-stone ranges blackly guarding some fearful no-man's land beyond. Above the strange and grotesque pinnacles, eagles hovered. In the foreground a tribe of kangaroos was scatter-

174

ing across the plain as if in fear. Overhead the sky was colourless with the heat.

Lisa turned back to the west again. The rust-ball, with its trailing tail of red haze was converging on them.

'Tom, what is that over there?' she asked. 'Not a willi willi? It doesn't spiral. It runs along like a brown cloud on the ground.'

'Someone in a car of sorts,' he said, not looking up from the track he was travelling. 'I saw it ten minutes ago. Someone making for the road-head I guess. He's coming in off a cross-country pad.'

Tom had to keep his mind on steering the truck between high mounds of spinifex grass, and across dried-out creek beds. Lisa watched the growing dust-ball with interest. It was heading north, yet was converging nearer all the time.

'They'd see us, wouldn't they?' she asked. 'Could it be someone who wants help? Or has lost his way?'

'Well, his car goes all right.' Tom glanced up, then fixed his attention on his own track again. 'If he wants us he'll meet up soon enough. Let him come.'

A few minutes later Lisa was sure the oncoming car intended to cut their track. She thought it would be wonderful to meet some other living persons out here in this empty wilderness!

There was pindan ahead of them now. But to the northeast, bare denuded mesa-hills sprawled across a cracked and thirsty distance that simply had *no limits*.

The strange car had swung round behind them now. Tom did not even glance in the rear-vision mirror. He was wholly occupied in keeping away from the dried-out ruts that criss-crossed the near stretch of country like spider webs.

A few minutes later the rear car, in a spurt of dust and flying ironstone, swung out from behind, and overtook them. *Fifty yards on it stopped; at right angles right across their own track.*

Tom, swearing under his breath, braked to a stop, hard-up by the car's side-panel. The dust was a blinding cloud that meant nobody could see anybody for quite one minute.

A man hefted himself out of the car's drive seat. He was shrouded in the fine smoking red dust his own vehicle had thrown up. Yet there was something vaguely familiar about the almost menacing ease with which he moved. He was tall, and wore a cattleman's broad-brimmed hat. He slammed his car door behind him.

Tom sat quite still, both hands on the steering wheel; and waited. In the vacuum of dusty time, Lisa could see the stranger wore outback khaki shirt and trousers. Again there was something familiar about the measured walk as he came towards them. Even through the dust veil he moved without haste, yet with purpose.

He stopped—right in front of the truck. He stood with his legs slightly apart, his thumbs tucked in his trouser belt.

Lisa's heart seemed to stop dead. Then race.

It was Magool Ransome!

Nobody said anything for thirty long seconds.

Then Magool moved round to the passenger side of the truck and opened the door.

'Get out, Lisa,' he said, his voice peremptory. 'You're coming with me.'

Lisa's heart raced again, then stopped dead all over again. Or so she thought. The silence of the empty land settled around them, as did the dust cloud too. Gradually she came to life, and blinked her eyes. She didn't know whether this moment was magical. Or only a crazy dust-clouded dream.

Magool looked past her.

'Right, Tom,' he said flatly. 'I'll take over from here!'

Tom's hands closed on the steering wheel. He stared through half-closed eyes at the other man. Magool's eyes stayed the way they'd been since he had come through the dust haze—cold, hard. That was all.

Lisa still could think of nothing to say. In an unreal way she felt *saved*: from herself mostly. But in a heavenly way.

The silence was brittle.

'Your little game is up, Tom,' Magool said at length. His voice could have cut diamonds. 'Put Lisa's luggage out on

176

the ground, then keep heading north. You've a date to keep in Wyndham, I understand. Keep it with someone else. Lisa is coming with me.'

His hand was still on the door-handle, but Lisa did not move. She was out of her surprise trance, and was troubled now. She owed *something* to Tom.

'You're the one who had better shoot through, Ransome,' Tom said, his voice truculent. 'This is no business of yours. Pardalote's affairs are none of Nangardee's.'

'No? You'd better ask "Old-fella" about that.'

Tom jerked up his head as if something had hit him.

'You're telling me . . . ?'

'As I said. *"Old-fella" sent me.*'

Lisa closed her eyes. Then opened them, and looked at Magool.

'You mean . . . ?'

'That's right, Lisa,' he said gently. 'Your grandfather sent me.'

'Oh!' An expression of incredulity passed over her face.

'I'm not likely to believe that.' Tom was both contemptuous and sceptical. 'He would have come himself. He's well enough to drive a car. What rights would he give *you*—a Ransome from Nangardee?'

'He conceded me my own rights. Those of Trustee for certain property. I'm here by provision of the Trustee's Act as well as at "Old-fella's" request. Find out for yourself in Wyndham, Tom. Mattinson is temporarily the magistrate there. You know the property of which I am speaking.' This was a statement, not a question.

His eyes came back to Lisa. His voice changed again.

'Are you coming, Lisa?' he said quietly.

She was still dreaming. Or maybe like they said of 'Old-fella', she had gone a bit soft in the head. Also she was aware of a guilt feeling towards Tom. She had trusted him —in her own way.

Magool read all this in her face.

'*Out*, Lisa,' he said peremptorily. He leaned forward and lifted her—almost roughly—from the truck. She looked back at Tom, wanting to say something kind. When she saw the unmasked expression in his face, she remained silent.

He didn't really care a fig about me!

Strangely, that hurt. Yet she herself was relieved—she'd played false too!

Tom leaned into the cabin behind them, hefted out Lisa's travelling bag, and dropped it on the dusty ground beside the truck. It could have been a worthless thing. He looked straight ahead, and started up the engine. He let out the clutch, and moved the gears. The truck rumbled forward. He neither looked at Lisa, nor said 'good-bye'.

In a few seconds, clothed in his own haze of red dust, he too was gone away.

This time Lisa was glad . . . relieved.

It had all happened so quickly. A genie had snapped a finger: a rainbow had thrown itself across the sky: then covered itself with clouds.

On the right side of safety she was in Magool Ransome's care.

He had come for her!

Dear guardian angel above—what does it all mean?

16

Magool put Lisa's bag in the boot of his car, then held open the passenger door.

'Coming?' he said again. His voice was so different now. Patient, and kind-of gentle. Lisa was startled by the change. She stood looking at him: fixed in her own wonder. Tom's truck thundered away in the distance, dusting up the whole continent as it went. The two of them, Magool and Lisa, were alone in no-man's land, the dust swirling around them, but their eyes somehow still managing to see each other through it.

Lisa, trance-like, stepped into his car. Magool closed the door behind her, then put his head in the window. His face was so near hers she had to blink to hide the fact her eyes were misting over.

He reached in his pocket and drew out a tiny leaf-like jewelled thing, and held it through the window.

178

'To "teacher" with love,' he said softly. 'A peace offering! Will you take it?'

It was a pardalote's feather as worn by the birds that had flown through the stringy-barks. It was downy-soft and very beautiful.

Magool was smiling at her now—*in a very teasing way*. She ventured a half smile herself as she took the feather from him. How could she explain to him this relieved, saved feeling that possessed her?

He put his hand under her chin, tilted it just that much, and kissed her. Like his pardalote's gift it was a feather-weight touch of his lips on hers.

'Also to "teacher"! One kiss, with my love!' He looked quizzically right into her eyes. 'Do you trust me, Lisa?'

She nodded. She could not tell him, *for Tom's sake*—about being saved. *From her own foolishness*, of course.

Magool went round the car, eased himself into the drive-seat, slammed the door, and put his hand on the starter key. Then he let his hand drop. He looked down at Lisa where she sat turning and twisting the feather in her fingers so that the light caught it and shone-up the colours till they looked like the sunset. *Magool comes from the 'Sunset Land' too*, she was thinking. *The place over the range . . . Where my mother went . . .*

'I'm glad you like the feather, Lisa.'

'It's beautiful. How did you know I would love it?'

'I thought you would: and Nooma advised me you would like it best of all gifts. I've thought about you, Lisa. That's a way of getting to know what you might like, isn't it?'

'Thank you for the feather, Magool.' Then drawing in a breath for courage she added almost in a whisper—'And thank you for the kiss too.'

'Maybe we can do that again another day. *I* liked the kiss too.' He really started up the engine this time: and swung the car round.

After a while Lisa said—'Why did you come for me, Magool?'

'Shall I tell you as we go along? We've a lot of distance to cover.'

'Why did my grandfather send you? *Why* am I in your
179

car—because you're "trustee for property"; or something?'

'Hold on tight, Lisa, we've rough country to cover till we get to the track.'

'I'm holding on.'

'Good. Now keep quiet and listen, like a good child. I'm the one with the chalk and blackboard now. In places where there's only one man to a hundred miles, there has to be an honorary magistrate—just in case, as it were. A Justice of the Peace. You understand that? Hereabouts, that's me.'

'I see. Mr. James Magool Ransome J.P.?'

'Right. Now in *your* case the Public Trustee, down in the State's capital, is inquiring into certain property rights for you under your mother's Will. He won't come up here personally and look into your interests. So he sends up north and puts the job on the local J.P. Once again, that's me.'

'I see. And the local J.P.—that's you—didn't think it was in my property's interest—for me to go to Wyndham with Tom?'

'No darn fear he didn't. It was not in your *personal* interest either. Tom had plans to walk off with you, Lisa. Matrimony, in other words. The law calls it "being placed under duress". That would give Tom a *moral lieu* over you. After all, you are due—when the business is finally settled —to own as much of the right to Pardalote as "Old-fella" does . . .'

'*Please*. Am I allowed to interrupt?'

'Go ahead, but don't do it too often. I want to make a water-hole over there for late lunch. Nooma loaded down the back seat with the kind of goodies she feels worthy of you.'

'*Nooma*?' Lisa was still bewildered. 'She told you about the feather too.'

'Yes, infant. Nooma has been to-ing and fro-ing between Pardalote and Nangardee with detailed reports of the goings-on over there in your valley. Likewise her brother has been keeping "Old-fella" informed out on Knob Hill at the Number 4 bore. Jabberdee—their cousin—has kept me briefed. They're all one tribe, you know.'

'*So*—' Lisa said slowly. 'I've been living in a sort-of spy nest? Why should Nooma, her brother, *and relatives*, be involved with me?'

'This whole weather-worn spinifex-splashed, range-rutted area is their *tribal hunting ground*. That's why. It's theirs from time immemorial. They have a vested interest in seeing all are happy; and that all goes well with the white inhabitants thereon. You don't blame them do you? They like to exercise their over-lordship—in their own way, some of the time! See those smokes over on the horizon, Lisa?'

'Yes.'

'They're telling "Old-fella" we're coming.'

'I don't understand. Why my grandfather? He went away—'

'Are you telling this story, or am I?'

'You are,' Lisa said, deflated.

'Okay. Don't interrupt unless you positively have to. Right?'

'Right.'

'Tom the overseer put it about—as soon as he had wind of *your* mother's death—that "Old-fella" was not only old, but could be getting soft in the head. Tom knew very well "Old-fella" didn't have formal "*grazing* rights" to Pardalote. No Lindsay ever thought it worth while to take them up. After all—the land was empty. They were here. No one told them to go. Not once in generations. But Tom, *having worked the area* for many years, would have a claim to the rights. That claim would need bolstering, of course.'

'I liked Tom . . .' Lisa said loyally.

'Good for you! He's one of the best cattlemen in the north. I'd advise you to keep him on as overseer.'

'*Me*? Magool, how did *you* know about my mother's death?'

'The Public Trustee. He's a fellow insatiable for information. But he gives out too. When it's necessary, that is. You're wondering how your mother could leave you a third in Pardalote—if there were no legal grazing rights?'

'Yes.'

'Hold on tight while I cross this creek bed.'

They went over the dried-out rut with a series of bumps. Lisa did as she was told and held on to the door handle.

'To continue—' Magool went on. '*Pardalote*, for the last three years, has been the registered name of a *mineral exploration lease. Not* a grazing area. Hence some con-

181

fusion. The area of the *mineral* lease covers Pardalote, Nangardee and a whole lot more territory besides. Your mother held one third share in that—*the mineral exploration rights*. She left that share to you.'

Lisa was still puzzled: and troubled. 'You said I owned as much as "Old-fella",' she said uneasily. 'That makes only two thirds. Who owns the other third?'

'I do.'

'You *mean* . . . ?' Lisa gasped. 'You mean *you* and *I* are *partners*? With my grandfather too?' She put her hand to her head as if, at any moment, it might ache.

'I do.'

'But you must have known that—when you were a patient at Finch's Creek?' Lisa was so bewildered she didn't know whether they were coming or going. She didn't believe she was hearing right.

'I did know. But then I looked like being your trustee— oh, on behalf of the Public Trustee, of course! I was bursting with curiosity when I heard those sweet dulcet tones coming from a sometimes emphatic girl sitting by my bedside feeding me, or reading me the Day's Digest.'

'And you didn't tell me?' Lisa asked accusingly. Then added sadly. 'You even went away without saying good-bye to me.'

'I was officially acting as your trustee, Lisa. Official honour was at stake. A Trustee cannot take benefit. I thought I'd better run for it before I found myself with a painful heart problem. I sent for one of my geologists to come and fetch me. *Pronto*.'

Lisa didn't quite understand the 'painful heart problem' bit, unless he meant he was in lonely need for Miss Dazzling Bannister's company.

'Imelda?' she asked, astonished. 'A geologist?'

'Yes. Bannister and Company. Consultant geologists. Imelda is one of the best—bossy and dictatorial—but she knows her job. Better than some men. That's why she caught up with me at Pardalote homestead when "Old-fella" was brought in. She had a new "Find" to report.'

'She's *beautiful* too . . .' Lisa said slowly: very slowly, not quite taking in the meaning of all this.

Magool laughed.

'No woman is all beautiful, Lisa, who has as relentless
182

and single-minded an ambition as Imelda has. And who is always *right*. Leastways not to a man. It all adds up to making a darn good geologist, who has to manage teams. A man's wretched ego demands that he be leaned upon a *little*—once in a while. Of course I admire her immensely. We're good friends. That's all.'

'Oh . . . !'

'Why that long drawn out"Oh"?'

'I was jealous of her,' Lisa said, quite simply.

Magool's foot went down hard on the brake.

'What did you say, Lisa?' he asked, his hands frozen on the steering wheel as if they too were listening. He looked straight in front of him, half closing his eyes, as if the sun's rays were too bright for him to cope with just now.

'I was jealous of her. She came for you and took you away. I was foolish, I know, but I sort-of thought of you as belonging to me: that is, while you were blindfolded. Nurses get that way about their patients, you know. Sort-of possessive, I'm afraid.'

'I didn't know.'

'Then,' Lisa added, 'at the lookout *she* was the possessive one. That was her *right*. I minded terribly that you went without saying good-bye—' She hesitated, then finished with a rush. 'Now I've told you, you had better drive on, please. My grandfather will be waiting for us.'

'He can wait!' Magool said flatly; yet not unkindly. 'He left you waiting at Finch's Creek. That was because he knew I was being driven-in to the hospital. He worked it out that both of us cooling our heels there might reap rewards. For "Old-fella" and Pardalote too. A wily fellow, is "Old-fella". Has the cunning of the dingo.'

Grandfather's boast of cunning! Lisa thought. *His little game—of chess: human beings for pawns!*

'You were angry?' she asked, oh so carefully!

'No, I was amused. He had come round from hereditary antagonism to swapping concessions with the Ransomes the first day Tom Watson put it in his head that *when he became really old* he would be entirely dependent on his overseer. "Old-fella" had to do a simple sum, whether he liked it or not. He needed someone he could claim as belonging, to claim successfully those long neglected grazing rights. Otherwise they would lapse. Anyone could apply

183

for them then. Mostly Tom Watson. So he buried the hatchet. He would come in with me on the Pardalote-Nangardee *mineral* rights. He made concessions of area and I allowed the Nangardee name to be left out. We met each other half-way.'

Those mysterious concessions! Lisa thought.

'And he brought my mother in too?' she asked aloud.

'No. I brought her in.'

'*You* did? But I don't understand—'

'I could see for myself he would need, some day soon, someone to look after his interests for him. Someone who cared. It had to be his daughter. Your mother! Time had caught up with "Old-fella", Lisa. Neither of us knew it would *not* be his daughter, but his daughter's daughter who would be the one to come north.' Magool paused, then added gently—'Nangardee owed your mother something, Lisa. It was my father's jackeroo she married: and with my father's connivance. Because of that she lost her inheritance. I felt honour bound—'

'*Honour bound!*' Lisa repeated softly. After a little while she asked—'My mother knew? About the mineral lease?'

'Yes. But she was afraid nothing might come of it. The minerals had yet to be found in *commercial quantity*. I think that is why she didn't tell you or her lawyer, Lisa. So you wouldn't be disappointed if nothing came of it.'

There was a long silence as they sat there in the blinding light of the midday sun.

Lisa was moved by his generosity. She was sad for her own past mistakes. For her lost mother too. She was glad Magool had made peace with her grandfather and sealed up the rift between the two families.

'Right inside me, I really knew it!' she said aloud. 'There was *something*—'

'Knew what, Lisa?'

'That you are kind and generous. You only pretended to be a difficult patient at Finch's Creek, didn't you? It gave the nurses something to talk about. It was all done to fool us into spoiling you, because you knew we enjoyed spoiling you—' She paused, then went on. 'You have done something for "Old-fella", to help him in his old age. But he still isn't sure, is he? He had to keep a telescope trained on what you were doing down in the Nangardee valley. I love him, Magool. In spite of his "wily-ness" he is lovable. Mrs. Watson feels that too, or she wouldn't be devoted. But I know he enjoyed *confusing* people. It was a game with him. Like chess. That way he wasn't lonely. He deliberately pretended to make it hard for me to meet you again—'

The tautness in Magool Ransome eased away as she spoke. He smiled wryly.

'When it comes to "Old-fella",' he said, 'Not even he can live down a lifetime's suspicion—three generations of suspicion—in a few months, Lisa. None of us could do that easily. I understand "Old-fella". He enjoyed his little game. He has been a great pioneer of this country.'

'He was able to potter amongst the beryl crystals in the cave on top of the range too!' Lisa said. 'He loves his prize gem-stone. It's very big; the most beautiful blue. A lovely name too—*beryl*.'

Magool's smile broadened. He looked at Lisa and his white teeth lit the dark burned-brown of his face. Her heart turned over.

'That blue stone he carries round with him? *Beryl*!' he said, 'Beryl be damned! It's amethyst, Lisa, but none of the geologists has the heart to tell him. It would kill him.'

'Then what—?'

'Amethyst is found in clumps of crystal in odd places on the ground. It's not that rare nor that precious. Neither is *beryl*—except when green in its most precious form—*emerald*. Let the old man have his dreams, Lisa. It's silver, lead, copper and even nickel we're exploring in those hills. "Old-fella" thinks they're so much rubbish. In the raw state they're not vitreous blues—they're not beautiful, and they don't shine. That's why.'

He turned the starter key once again. The engine roared, then purred.

'I'm sorry my grandfather embarrassed you by leaving me at Finch's Creek,' Lisa said regretfully. 'I had no idea—'

His face suddenly looked withdrawn, and this made her sorrier than ever.

'"Old-fella" didn't embarrass me, Lisa,' Magool said

almost roughly. 'He gave me the best eight days of my life. That's the way it was. Shall we get going?'

The engine was turning over but the car wheels did not move. His hand was on the gear-stick but he did not move that either. He looked at her instead. First there was rue, then tenderness, in his eyes.

'You have a dear voice, Lisa,' he said quietly. 'Sweet and gentle. You looked so lovely, and so vulnerable, with that quiet face of yours, with its hint of sadness and innocence in it.' He sat looking into her face now, as if absorbing every line and curve—to keep for all time.

'Oh yes!' he went on wryly. 'I often took a squint under the bandages, when my ears told me you were looking somewhere else as you talked.'

Lisa sat upright with a jerk.

'But your wounded eyes?' she cried aghast. 'You could have . . .'

'My eyes be damned! It was my heart I was worrying about. Nobody gave me medicine for *that* complaint. Not even a needle once in a while—'

Her eyes were suddenly lost in his.

'You mean . . . ?'

'I fell in love with a dear little girl—one straight off a mail truck. A rattle of flying flintstones outside, and bang went my heart—cracked from stock-rail to tank-stand! It was as simple as that. I love you, Lisa. My dear, gentle, Lisa. Very, very much.' His face was serious, almost sombre. 'But you see, a trustee is in a position of trust. *His motives must be beyond reproach.* So, my darling Lisa . . .'

'Please Magool—' Lisa interrupted pleading, running her words madly together. 'Please, please Magool! Give all that trustee business to the magistrate in Wyndham. You said there was one there—to Tom. It's *my heart* I'm worrying about, not any property. My heart hurts all over. Nobody ever told me what medicine to take for that. Only you . . .'

'*Only me?*'

For one spell-binding moment they sat there, lost in what they could read, each in the other's face.

His hands came off the steering wheel, and he held them

towards her. She leaned forward: and his arms went round her.

'Lisa, Lisa? Are you sure?'

'So sure!' She dropped her forehead on his shoulder. She felt his cheek resting on her hair. Then his lips. He put his hand under her chin and tilted it upwards. He kissed her mouth: not feather-light this time.

Lisa's eyes were shut so tight she was seeing stars. *He loved her!*

Could it possibly be true!

'At least we know one thing "Old-fella" will be glad about,' Magool said after a very long time. 'He meant it to happen, the old schemer. His chess-board must be looking very pretty right now. Pardalote and Nangardee safely sealed—for ever! But with *love*. I wonder if he bargained on that?'

'Yes. I can see it all now. He left me at Finch's Creek —just in case. His friend Jimmy Come-up would know everything as all the aborigines do. Jimmy would have read hearts, and told my grandfather. Then ...'

'Then what, Lisa?'

No. She couldn't tell him that little bit about 'contrary women' doing the opposite to what they were told. Not yet. Nor how she went up the west-side gorge against her grandfather's apparent, but not *real* wishes. She would tell him later. Much later. Now was too precious for such a silly little confession. He might laugh at her. 'Old-fella' had held out the west-side, and its way to Nangardee, as a mysterious and enticing adventure, simply by veiling it as an all-but-forbidden place. He knew she would want to see the way her mother had gone from Pardalote to Nangardee. Where her father had come to the range-top too. His 'cunning' gave that special allure. An incentive to adventure. Dear, dear, game-playing grandfather!

'What is it, Lisa?' Magool prompted gently.

'Just that one day I really will learn chess. Then I'll play a game with my grandfather. *Then ...*'

'Why—Lisa—you sound quite fiery.'

'Not really!' she said more quietly. 'I love my grandfather. He's unique, isn't he? I don't think, after all, I would want to beat him at any game. Magool—let's go and tell him the news? *Please?*'

'My darling Lisa! Nooma, Jabberdee—the whole darn tribe—will have told him everything—just as Jimmy Come-up did at Finch's Creek. Look over to the west, Lisa. The smokes are talking again. The go-betweens will be running, and telling. "Old-fella" will be sitting back chuckling —waiting to tell us—*that he knew all the time.*'

He started up the engine once again. The car rolled forward into the great sea of dust and spinifex; south-west this time, edging towards 'Old-fella's' camp, and after that, to the 'Sunset Land'.

Lisa put her head on Magool's shoulder. Once she lifted it to ask a troubled question.

'Magool? What will happen to Tom and Mrs. Watson?'

'Nothing,' he said with a grin. 'Tom will go on being the best cattleman in the north: and "Old-fella's" overseer. Mrs. Watson will go on being the devoted housekeeper, and continue to look after "Old-fella" and the homestead. It's their home. He knows that. None of the three of them knows any other way of life, and each of them needs the others. My darling gentle kind Lisa will marry me—and make Nangardee happy ever after?'

'Yes, Magool.'

'Jim-for-short.'

'Jim-for-love!'

One lone shell-pink cockatoo with a jade-green colour in his comb, fluttered from the group of mulgas and flew away—soaring high and far into the southern sky. Lisa, watching it, thought it had flown back to tell the other birds of Pardalote that, like itself, one more lost-one was found.

They live so long, these cockatoos! she thought. *Almost a hundred years: some of them.*

Maybe this beautiful pink and jade bird had lived long enough to see yet another man from Nangardee take yet another girl from Pardalote—for his wife.